STEPHEN STROMP

WHERE THE CATS WILL NOT FOLLOW

STEPHENSTROMP.COM

W.O.P. Press

In memory of Thomas

THE TRICK

I found myself lost in an apple orchard at dusk. It was so foggy, I couldn't make out the trees. I could only see the ends of their twisted, pointy branches. Behind the cloak of fog, I could hear scurrying and hushed chatter. I knew it was the monsters. They were waiting patiently in the mist for the right moment to attack and devour me.

I stepped forward blindly, hugging myself, waiting for the inevitable to happen—when suddenly, down the center of the path, the fog parted. Through the tunnel of swirling fog, Everett appeared, riding a bike. As he pedaled toward me, it looked as if he had just broken free from a smoldering fire. Behind the bike, he pulled a makeshift rickshaw. It looked like something he had made himself. Nothing more than a large wicker basket on wheels.

When he reached me, he climbed off the bike and gently lowered the kickstand before steadying the frame in the loose gravel. I couldn't help but find the juxtaposition humorous: our ominous surroundings and him casually riding a bike through them. Moreover, taking the time to assure he had parked it properly.

"You know, they won't get you if they think you're already dead," he reminded me.

"I know," I replied. But I always forgot.

He pulled a sheet out of the basket and motioned for me to climb inside. So I did. He draped the sheet over my body. Since it was too small to conceal me completely, I hung over the edge with my arms stretched low and my head limp, trying my best to look like a corpse. As he began to pedal, I heard the grunts and whispers of the monsters slinking out from the trees and spilling onto the path. They crept behind us curiously, cautiously. Close enough to grab my dangling arms. Close enough to pull me deep into the murky night. Yet they did not.

Everett pedaled through the orchard. He pedaled until the fog lifted. He pedaled until dawn. The trick worked. Of course it did.

WHERE THE CATS WILL NOT FOLLOW

PART I
CABIN ON ANOTHER PLANET

1
HERO iN RESTRAiNTS

My feet poking outside the covers made me feel even more vulnerable. Yet I didn't dare reach for the blanket. Not that my stillness mattered all that much. I knew that what hid in the corners could smell me. Could see in the darkness. Could hear my heartbeat. To them, the simple functioning of my organs—my heart beating, my lungs rising and falling—must've sounded like thundering convulsions.

I scanned the room, lit dimly by the moon. The pale light allowed me to view the sinister faces hidden in the pattern of the faux wood paneling. Some had sloped, vacant eyes. Others had twisted, melted skin. And then there were the ones with sharp teeth and thick horns protruding from the sides of their heads. But the cheap paneling wasn't the cause of my fear. It was the thought that these macabre portraits were merely impressions of what had escaped the wall, what had materialized into flesh and become whole. They could've been anywhere. The fields. The woods. Even within the swelling shadows. Watching. Waiting for the perfect moment to pull me off the bed and swallow me whole.

If only I could've gathered the nerve to leap out from the covers, maybe I could've been saved by the light. Maybe by my flipping on the switch, the brightness would've killed the shadows and disinfected the entire room of evil. But there I lay, worrying that my movements would only entice an attack, fearing that perhaps the switch *was* already on and that the light had been sucked away, overpowered by the darkness.

I desperately wanted to call out to Everett across the hall. He wouldn't have been afraid. He would've protected me. But I couldn't call out to him. My voice wouldn't allow it. If I shouted his name, I just knew it would've come out a whisper. If I screamed, it would've come out a muted shriek. And I knew if I had tried and my voice had failed to reach his ears, it would've been worse than movement. It would've compelled them to instantly rush upon me. No, paralyzed silence was my best hope for survival.

Yet the longer I remained still, the more I became a ball of unreleasable energy. My neck ached. My legs boiled under the covers. And in the center of my stomach sprouted the most unbearable itch. I clenched my hands into tight fists, fighting against the temptation to scratch. But my concentration only made it more intense. No longer able to withstand the agony, cautiously I inched my hand beneath the covers. My movements were so slow, so careful, that the blanket barely moved. When I at last reached my stomach, I dug my nails into my skin with fervor. I had my relief. But what was more, I had moved—and hadn't been attacked.

Released from my immobile prison, I looked down to see the hair on my chest—and a spark of awareness came over me. It was a peculiar sensation, realizing that although I was in my parents' house, in the small twin bed of my childhood, I was in my adult twenty-six-year-old body. I was not the child I had once been, sleeping in that room, living in that house. Why then was I stuck, helpless, with Everett being the only one who could save me?

Brashly, I flung the covers to the floor. Warm air rushed over my legs and torso. In a flash, I scooted to the end of the bed, stood upon my electrified legs, and grabbed the doorknob. Yet before I left, I took one final look at the room behind me. It was then I realized my self-assuredness was premature. No matter what age my body was, I was still as vulnerable as a child. The shadows had grown into a single mass enveloping half the room. Darkness as black as oil oozed over the edge of the bed and inched near my feet. I hurriedly slipped through the door and pulled it tight behind me.

In the hall, I stood before Everett's door. I gently placed my hand on it, and it creaked open slightly. I pulled away without looking inside, not wanting to know. Frightened he wouldn't be there. Frightened to confirm I was alone.

I headed down the open stairway. A low wind must've picked up because the enormous blue spruces relentlessly scraped against the side of the house. They scratched not with violence, but with the slow persistence of a pendulum swinging without a force to stop it. Yet the more I listened, the less it sounded like pine needles at all. It was more like pointy fingernails poking through the window screens and tapping on the panes. So polite they were, as if asking permission to be let in. As I crept across the living room, a low growl overlapped with the taps that I hoped were nothing more than sudden gusts of air forced between the needles.

As I entered the dining room, I pleaded under my breath for the noises to stop. The pines pressed against the row of windows overlooking the table. Outside, the night was still. There was barely a breeze. No leaves dashed through the yard. And the pines—stood motionless. Yet *something* was ripping through the screens and incessantly tapping on the windows. And *something* outside was growling. The long row of windows was designed to let in light. Yet it was darkness that wanted to be let in that night. I rushed down the line, slapping shut the slats and latching every wooden blind. My stirring activity caused whatever was outside to become even more insistent. Tap! Tap! Tap!

Dizzy with terror, I tugged on the front door and then the side door by the basement steps to ensure they were secure. But the thought of checking the sliding glass door in the sunroom made me the most uneasy. If I was in front of the wall of glass, they would see me. And clearly, I would see them. Yet as I took one timid step into the room, I could only see my reflection in the glass. There was nothing but blackness on the other side. The stars that had shown themselves on so many nights had been snuffed out by the thick Michigan clouds.

Before I could test the lock, the sound of stairs creaking held me back. Our house was built over a hundred years before, and you could always hear when a person made their way down the stairs, even from the other end of the house. My mind raced, thinking of places to hide. But hiding would've been futile. What had escaped from my bedroom walls already knew all the hiding places. It dwelled in the hiding places. So I stood right where I was, deciding to finally face what pursued me. And into the sunroom, with his hands kept coolly in the pockets of his jeans, stepped—Everett. Everett, whose imposing stature alone could scare away demons. Everett, my protector.

"You're home!" I shouted. It wasn't a surprise that in his presence I could actually speak.

He smirked at me looking so frantic in my underwear. "What're you doing up?" he asked.

"You know," I replied gravely. I knew he did. He lowered his eyebrows, seemingly disappointed I wasn't keeping up my half of the charade. "I wasn't sure you'd be here."

"I just came down for a drink." He continued to play along with it all yet at the same time threw me a quick wink.

I was just glad he was there. I wanted him close until it was over, until the terrible night ended. I pushed on his broad shoulders like a needy child, insisting he be the one to check the door. It wasn't like him to turn down a challenge. But Everett wouldn't budge. And that's when I remembered. It wasn't as if he didn't want to help. He couldn't. Wasn't allowed. So instead, in a reversal of roles, he gently grabbed *my* shoulders and positioned me in front of him, at arm's length, facing the glass door. I looked upon my reflection and took a deep, uneasy breath. "Remember the cats," he whispered.

For him to bring up the cats, he understood my degree of fear. They were the furthest thing from my mind that night. But because of Everett, I *did* think of them. I thought of them circling me like they were performing a ritualistic dance. Momentarily, I was transported to the wonderful scene. The sun was a soft yellow, making the coats of the felines shimmer. I held my hand out to touch them. Their fur was soft. Such large cats. Healthy and muscular. They were perfect. I feared they'd be scared away. Yet no careless child stomped through the field. Not even a distant gunshot was heard. I smiled. On a night I never thought I would've been able to, I smiled.

Everett released me. Alone, I stepped forward, imagining the cats circling my body like a shield. While their faces remained hidden, as I approached the door, I could see their hands crowding the window. Their wet fingertips squeaked across the glass. Pressing. Sliding. Smearing. Their fingers were green, moldy green with black fingertips. The tips didn't appear to be nails but rather bones, sharpened to a point, poking through the ends of their fingers. The reflection of my face warped and twisted as the glass strained from the pressure.

They were under the powerful floodlights that had allowed us to play outside at night when we were children. And light, I knew, they were not fond of. I flipped the switch beside the door and was elated to see that even against the oppressing darkness surrounding the house, the bulbs actually worked. Glorious light burst upon them. It shot over the patio and stretched into the garden. At last, the monsters were exposed.

It was the horned ones, at least a dozen of them. They were no more than four feet tall. The skin on the rest of their body was as moldy green as the skin of their fingers. And just like their impressions on the wall, bulky black horns protruded from the sides of their heads in the shape of shark fins turned sideways. Their red pupils had difficulty adjusting to the light, yet they dared stay beneath it. In fact, they seemed to relish the exposure no matter how painful it was. They opened their oversize jaws and bared their long, sharp teeth. They smashed their faces against the window, smearing it with their juices.

In the reflection, I could see Everett behind me. He looked on with his arms folded across his chest. Saddened. Powerless. They saw him too, and his presence made them furious. They rammed their horns against the glass. It shook and began to splinter.

I rushed to the dining room, petrified. In a final, desperate panic, I grabbed the edge of the table. As I managed to topple it over, the vase that sat upon it, filled with freshly cut lilac blossoms, rolled to the floor. The lavender blooms were crushed as I dragged the table into the sunroom. Their sweet scent permeated the air. I frantically propped the table on its side and shoved it against the door. The monsters crowded near me, licking the other side of the cracking glass. As soon as I had the table in position, the door finally gave way, showering me with broken glass. I stumbled backward. The monsters chewed on the shards, letting the broken pieces slice their lips and tongues. They grinned with delight as their teeth dripped green blood.

Drained, defeated, and as if a magnet had pinned me there, I surrendered by lying on the dining room floor. I looked up to see Everett towering over me. I couldn't see his face at first, just the bristles on his neck and chin. When he finally brought himself to look upon me, I saw tears welling in his eyes. One slid down his cheek. I closed my eyes and waited for it to land on my face, but I didn't feel it. Perhaps he had caught it? Everett was the one who watched them shred the table. He was the one who saw their small haunting bodies creep into the house and crowd around me.

I felt their bony fingers all over my body. On my chest and in my mouth. I felt their hot breath on my stomach. They liked my stomach most. They went for it first. It was like being tickled too hard when they tore into it. They used their pointy fingers to take the pieces they wanted and crammed their heads in to slurp up the rest. It didn't hurt so bad. I wanted to tell Everett that it hardly hurt at all. I wanted to tell him there was pleasure in being devoured by these demons. Pleasure in finally submitting and being released from their torture. It might have made him feel better. But they were crawling all over my body, and I couldn't communicate. I could only smell the powerful lilacs.

2
EiGHT MiNUTES

I woke to the overwhelming scent of lilacs. I could hear birds. Bugs humming. I didn't open my eyes. I didn't want to confirm any assumptions that I had about my surroundings. I liked not knowing where I was. I could be anywhere I wanted as long as I didn't open my eyes. Once I opened them, wherever I was couldn't be changed, even if I decided to close them again. I imagined I was in my own bed. I imagined the familiar surroundings of my small apartment: my Siamese fighting fish in his bowl upon the dresser, my ivy plant cascading down the stand in the corner. I even began hearing the morning traffic not too far away on Holland Avenue becoming heavier and heavier the longer I procrastinated.

Yet as I attempted to trick my brain into believing this scenario, I couldn't help but sense the musty smell of the room. I couldn't ignore the rays of morning sun striking me when my apartment had no window facing east. And the aching in my wrists called attention to the fact that my hands were locked in place over my head. But most of all, his presence kept me from escaping the room. I knew that he was there. I sensed his slight movements beside the bed. He'd been waiting. If I opened my eyes, I knew I'd have to face him, disappoint him. Bits of my bedroom disintegrated with each floorboard creak and breath I heard him breathe. Slowly I was dragged away, flooded instead with fragments of how I had arrived in that foreign bed.

I recalled lying in the fetal position, my head resting on his leg or perhaps a bunched-up coat. My consciousness was hazy at best. The constant whirring of the vibrating engine held me under its spell, although the occasional bumps caused my eyes to slip open. It was in those moments that I realized how stiff my muscles were. How dizzy I was. My head pounded with painful rhythms that seemed connected to the beating of my heart. I caught glimpses of his black dress shoe on the gas pedal. But I could only hold my eyes open a few moments at a time before the droning engine would call me back.

I wondered how he got me from the truck to the bed. I was too heavy for him to carry, and I was sure he was alone. Perhaps I was dragged. I adjusted my legs under the scratchy blanket. If only I had the nerve to peel back the disgusting covering, at least the dry breeze could've reached my legs. My hair stuck to my face. The pillow was soaked in my sweat. There was a kink in my neck. I jerked my tingling arms forward only to be reminded that my wrists were affixed to the bedpost.

The power of the physical world was just too great. I was no longer able to drift. My surroundings, though my mind still hadn't a picture of them, were winning. He had to suspect by then, anyhow, that I was truly awake. I feared that he'd call my bluff and shake me into joining him in cruel reality. So before I would let that happen, I opened my eyes, barely a squint. Immediately, a painful blaze of light exploded before me. All I could see were millions of dust particles dancing in the air, illuminated by the morning sun. Slowly I forced open my eyes the rest of the way, focusing on the figure bathed in light. Sunlight struck his blond hair, making it glow. I had caught my first glimpse. There was no turning back.

Phillip sat on an old wooden stool a few feet from the side of the bed. He had changed out of his work clothes and wore a short-sleeved button-down shirt with cargo pants. I looked into his tired blue eyes and remembered asking him once if he wore contacts that made his eyes that blue. "I don't wear colored contacts! My eyes are *always* this blue!" he snapped. He made it sound so imperative that I understood that fact. He followed his statement with such a serious stare that only when his lips began to curl did I realize he had been using a mock offended tone. Laughing, he then revealed he did in fact wear contacts, but they were clear.

For a moment, I imagined it was Everett on that stool. It wasn't hard to do. I'd often find Everett waiting bedside for me to wake. He'd spend entire nights watching me sleep, wondering, I imagined, like Phillip, which world I was in. Even though they didn't look all that much alike, Phillip could've more easily passed for Everett's brother than me. I was like a poor reproduction. A photocopy of a photocopy. Everett had deep brown hair that lightened in summer months. I had black hair, and my eyebrows were dark and thick. Everett was muscular and agile. I grew up tall but had little muscle tone. I was hopelessly clumsy, always tripping and banging into things. He had a smooth way of talking that was calm yet direct. I had to constantly remind myself to keep my mouth shut to avoid something ridiculous flying out. The contrasts were endless really.

Thinking of Everett, I was still hiding, in a way, from Phillip. It took his voice to make me focus. "Good morning." He looked exhausted but somehow forced a measure of cheerfulness in his greeting. It was apparent he stayed up all night anticipating the moment I'd wake. He leaned forward, eager to hear what I had discovered for him. I didn't want to open my mouth. Didn't want to admit I had failed him. Instead, I began to rationalize, to defend myself in my mind. *I had no need to feel ashamed! He was the one who dragged me, literally, to wherever we were! I was the victim!* Yet as much as I tried convincing myself, I didn't *feel* like Phillip's victim — even with my hands tied to the bed.

I kicked off the covers. The air was stale, but at least my skin could breathe. To give relief to my back, I managed to stand up on my knees. I swiveled toward the headboard. My wrists, tied to the wooden dowels, had turned a reddish purple. "You were jerking like crazy." He shrugged. He grabbed a pocketknife off the nightstand and sliced the rope. Freed, I swung my legs over the side of the bed and let the warm breeze blow against my face and dry my hair.

"Where are we?" He moved to the door without giving an answer. "I'm not going to run, Phillip." I looked to the view out the window. "How *could* I run?" I said quietly. We were in the middle of what appeared to be an endless field. Bugs hovered above the dewy ground. Queen Anne's lace and milkweed swayed in the breeze, intermixed with other weeds and tall grasses. The lilacs that must've grown nearby all but overpowered the faint fragrance of pine trees. "We're up north, aren't we? Still in Michigan, right?" I scooted to the end of the bed. "Whose cabin is this?"

Leaning against the door, he set his eyes on mine. I tingled with apprehension. I knew the moment I dreaded had come. He didn't bring me there to discuss the wilderness. I was well aware of his purpose. "Did you see her?" he asked flatly.

"No." I was stunned by his bluntness and stunned by my own blunt reply. His eyes fell to the floor, saddened. So callous I had been. I wondered sometimes why I was even given a mouth. He placed his hand over his eyes for a moment and then wiped his forehead. The natural fairness of his skin accentuated the redness of his face. The way his eyes shot daggers at me, I didn't suppose he was red from the heat. I wanted to shrink into myself. I attempted to disappear by lowering my shoulders and taking short, unnoticeable breaths.

"Then as far as you're concerned, we're nowhere." He brought his face to mine. "Nowhere!" He charged to the window and pulled down the shade. The tattered thing leaked light through its many holes. Tiny circles and gashes of light freckled the aged floral carpeting. "We're not in Michigan! We're not in America! We're not even on this planet until—" He stopped short, finishing only with deep breaths.

His tone made me sick to my stomach. "It was just one night," I said timidly. "I can try again." He stood silent, staring at the sparks of light on the floor. I escaped the room as fast as I could by hastily thinking about the sun. I learned once that it took eight minutes for its light to reach the earth. I thought of how in another eight minutes, the awful floral pattern would be supplied with fresh light generated millions of miles away. "Eight minutes," I said in a whisper.

He charged toward me and clamped his hand on my shoulder. His grip was so tight, I thought he'd strike me. I looked to his feet and braced myself for him to do his damage. That's when I noticed he was wearing sandals. I let out a short laugh as I was brought back to the time he had driven the two of us to Lanford Community College and had worn sandals. I had never seen him in sandals before. And before I had a chance to censor myself, I found myself saying, "No one wants to see your feet." The truth was I didn't find his feet repulsive. In fact, I was never all that comfortable showing my own feet. It always made me feel a bit too exposed.

But Phillip knew better than to be offended. His lips curled downward. They did that when he found something humorous. "Sorrrry," he apologized sarcastically, followed by one of his stuttered laughs. "Don't worry. After today, you'll never have to see my feet again," he promised.

So as I stared down at his open toes, I blurted, "No one wants to see your feet." I was so sure his lips would curl downward and I'd hear his signature laugh. Yet the look I received was void of emotion. Before I could say another word, he released his grasp on my shoulder. "Phillip—" He left the room, slamming the door behind him.

I stood from the bed. Dizzy. My head pounding. I staggered to the dresser and held its edge to keep my balance. Dust clung to my wet fingertips, leaving an imprint. I held my other hand firmly to my tingling stomach, trying to quiet the distant sensation of it being torn open by black fingertips. I stared at the doorknob, wondering if it was locked, if I truly was his prisoner. I didn't attempt to turn it. I didn't want to know. I didn't much care if I *was* his prisoner, I supposed. Strange, I felt entirely safe in that foreign room. I found there could be safety and relief in submitting yourself to the whims of another, letting them think for you and determine your actions. Maybe he *had* taken me to another planet. He was right. It no longer mattered. I sat on his stool and gazed at the tiny bed. I imagined him watching over me the entire night. How uncomfortable it must've been. As I looked about the rustic room, I thought of how it had come to be, how gentle Phillip had been driven to such a thing.

3
PHiLLiP'S REQUEST

I received his desperate call at 2:00 a.m. I knew it was 2:00 a.m. because the voice on the line said, "It's 2:00 a.m. It's been five days, and it's 2:00 a.m. on the fifth day."

"Who is this?" I asked the question but immediately knew it was Phillip. I hadn't heard from him in over five years. Yet even in his frenzy, I identified him by his first word spoken, by his light yet masculine voice.

"I've already called the police. Please don't tell me to call the police. Why is everyone still telling me that like I haven't already? Like I'm some dumb asshole? I left the light on. The light over the driveway. I always leave it on for when she comes back."

I forced back a yawn. How could I listen to his delirium and still be tired? "Comes back from where? What are you talking about?"

"Jogging. She jogs at nighttime in the summer. It's better to jog at night. You're not supposed to jog in the heat of the day. The light, it's on now. She's not home. It's been on for five nights. And she's still not home."

Confident Phillip was unraveling. He sounded confused. Frightened. Agitated. I figured the caliber of confusion coming from him was reserved for someone like me. Not rational Phillip. Not the young man who was disciplined enough to achieve perfect attendance in high school, never missed a class in college, and received his degree in accounting in just three years. It was frightening to think that his sanity, of all people's, could be so easily shredded. "Are you drunk?" I wondered.

"No. I'm high." As soon as he mentioned it, I began picking up on his nervous drags. "I haven't smoked pot since college," he revealed. "Remember when I asked if you wanted a smoke, and you said Everett wouldn't let you?"

"I remember."

"You always did what he said. Listened to him, didn't you? When I first met you, I thought he was your mom." Instead of a laugh, he let out staggered puffs of air from his nostrils. "Well, I should've too. Listened to Everett, I mean."

"So why are you smoking then?"

"I didn't believe him," he continued, missing my point as I missed his. "She went for a jog. And now no one knows where the hell she is. I've called all her friends. I've asked all the neighbors. She's not at her parents'. I've driven all over this goddamned city."

"I haven't seen her either," I offered.

He took another drag. "Listen, Ayden, I have to find her."

"You will," I said automatically.

"Will you help me?" he asked. "I know you can help."

I wanted to help Phillip. It was the least I could do after all he had done for me. He was the one who had pushed me into shallow water when I was in too deep. He was the one who had sparked the changes in my life that had finally given me a sense of normalcy. "Of course I'll help."

"OK. I'm coming over," he declared.

"Wait . . ." But it was too late. The line was dead. He had never been to my apartment and hadn't asked for directions. On top of that, he probably shouldn't have been driving in his frantic state. But it was Phillip. He'd find his way.

No longer tired, I rushed to the closet. I chose a light-brown polo shirt accented with thin black stripes across the chest and put on my best pair of jeans. I attempted to look at my apartment as if I were seeing it for the first time, as if I were Phillip. Would he be pleased by my accomplishments? That I had my own place? That I had finally become an adult with adult responsibilities? I paced with an energy that was fueled partly by nerves and partly by excitement. I aligned the candle and coasters on the end table so they perfectly met its border. I straightened the pillows on the couch. I moved the dishes from the sink to the dishwasher. I cleaned the specks of toothpaste from the bathroom mirror. I dusted. I thought of vacuuming but figured I wouldn't have time.

In only about a half hour after he hung up the phone, I heard the knock at the door. I opened it with an anxious grin. There he stood, now a successful accountant in a crew cut wearing a white dress shirt with pin-striped pants—smoking pot like a high school stoner. I felt shy, as if we were meeting for the first time. "Phillip the CPA and his doobie," I finally blurted as a joke.

"Hey." He flicked the short joint onto the cement and snuffed it out with his shoe. When his blue yet bloodshot eyes met mine, his lips curled upward for a moment before quickly relaxing to make a perfect line across his face. I had never known Phillip to be other than clean-shaven, but that night blond stubble grew from his chin. It was a humid August night. A drizzling mist caused his clothes to cling to his skin and his face appear to perspire. He rubbed his neck, where a tie surely had been knotted earlier. He pulled his shoulders close to his ears and shuddered as if it were cold. He looked past me and into the apartment.

I opened the door wide and stepped aside. "Come on in," I offered. "I've got air-conditioning." I rolled my eyes at myself as I shut the door behind him. He stepped past me without comment and made a direct path for the couch. He sat with his eyes to the floor. "I've lived here for about a year," I said as I stood before him. "The rent is kind of expensive. But I think it's worth it since the washer and dryer are included. Only bad thing is I can't have pets.

Well, besides my fish. But I really want a cat. Maybe someday. Maybe a black cat. I heard people don't like to adopt black cats because of superstition. So it would be good to give a black cat a home. Don't you think?"

His head remained low. He looked as if he was concentrating on something far away. I could see it in the narrowing of his eyebrows, in the bunching of lines on his forehead. I eased myself into the overstuffed chair next to him. "I picked out the furniture myself. It was pretty easy. Remember my favorite color is green? Anyway, I picked out the first green set I saw. The saleslady called it 'hunter green.'" He said nothing. Did not even allow his eyes to scan the room. "Do you want something to drink?"

"No," he said solemnly, finally lifting his head. "Have you seen her?" It was clear he only wanted to continue the conversation he had begun on the phone.

"No. I already told you—"

"No. In your dreams," he clarified.

"Oh." My heart picked up its pace.

"I know you can help me because"—he inhaled deeply—"because I know now that Everett was telling the truth. He was right all along."

"No." My voice cracked. "Everett *never* told the truth." I tried to keep my breathing steady as the years I thought I had been so successful at burying began to instantly brew toward the surface. *What was Phillip doing to me?* "It was *you* who told me the truth. Not Everett. I listened to you. I even went to that psychiatrist because of you. And finally, it all made sense. Finally, because of you, there was logic to it all."

"Logic? Some things cannot be explained logically." He began to talk with more concentration, making sure his voice was heard through the curtain of marijuana. "Look, I'm not saying Everett was the best brother in the world. God knows he wasn't. God knows he forced you into dangerous situations. I know what harm he caused. I know how bad he messed you up. All I'm saying is, he was right about one thing: you have a skill that no one else on this earth could possibly possess."

I protested by emphatically shaking my head. I was horrified by what he was asking of me—and by his not entirely convincing change in theory about the past. He wanted me to use a gift he was suddenly so sure I possessed, a gift that he himself had helped convince me wasn't real.

He persisted. "Even if you don't believe me, don't you think it's worth a revisit? It's worth a try at least, isn't it?" His chin sank to his chest.

It was clear to me at that moment that Phillip was simply lying to himself. He was desperate, grasping for what he believed was his last hope. Naturally, I felt sorrow for him. He had literally lost her. Yet at the same time, thoughts of the Phillip I had known from years before flooded my mind. I wouldn't have questioned that Phillip. I had trusted him always, even before Everett told me I should've. I trusted him like I had once trusted Everett. How could I have protested anything he had to say? That's what made it all the more confusing—and frightening. "I don't even remember her," I said. "I don't even remember what she looks like. Why don't we go to the police station in the morning and—"

"I told you not to talk to me about the police! It's been five days, and they haven't found her. They don't even have a lead. Do you think I want to wait until they find her dead? Dumped in some ditch? By the time they find her, it'll be too late."

"I don't even remember her name."

"Ginger." He said her name as if the sound of those two syllables put together momentarily healed him. *Ginger.* I did remember her. I remembered her chestnut hair that framed her face in loose curls. I remembered her olive skin and the fluffy white sweater she wore that fall years ago. I remembered beautiful Ginger. How Phillip loved her brown eyes.

He leaned in closer. "Aren't you tired?" he asked.

"Tired! After what you've just told me? How could I possibly be tired? I'm more awake now than ever."

He checked his watch. "But it's so late."

"What am I supposed to say? You helped me see the world for what it is." I looked about my apartment. "*This* is reality. This life I have now is reality." I reached over and grabbed the edge of the couch. "Don't take it away from me. You exposed Everett. You killed his myth. Please, don't bring it back to life."

He reached in his pocket and produced a photograph of Ginger. He held it before my face. There she was. While not in the white sweater I often visualized her wearing, it was Ginger, her brown eyes staring back at me. "What I am experiencing now is not reality. Her being gone is as far from reality as my mind can leap. Logic no longer applies. Logic is for police who do nothing but question me of her whereabouts, wasting time while she is somewhere frightened. Hurt. God knows what. So I say it's time for bed."

"Yes," I answered to her photograph with barely a whisper. I was nowhere near tired, however. And as I stood, I was the one who began to shudder as if it were cold. Phillip had spoken, and I had no choice but to do as he requested. I slowly shuffled into the bedroom, my legs weak, as Phillip followed. I undressed slowly, methodically folding my jeans and polo shirt. As I eased under the covers, Phillip knelt beside the bed and handed me the picture of Ginger. I held it in front of me for a moment before placing it facedown on my chest.

"Help me," he requested hauntingly.

Phillip watched over me, a transformed Phillip, one who had lost his reason and was begging me to do the same. I closed my eyes, attempting to force myself to sleep, attempting to concentrate on Ginger. Yet instead, I found myself struggling with thoughts—of Everett. I saw his face. Clearly, as if he were looking directly at mine. I was confused by his smile. My childhood instinct told me to be comforted by it. But my adult reason made me cautious, afraid.

Frustrated, I opened my eyes. "Even if you're right, it's been so long. Dreams don't tell me anything anymore. I haven't had one lousy dream that has led me to anything special. I can't even find the socks that go missing in the laundry." I turned to him. "I'm sorry Ginger is gone. I am. I just don't think this is the way to find her."

I should've felt satisfied with my honesty, yet I turned away from him with an incredible feeling of guilt. Phillip said nothing of my rejection, and the silence was agonizing. I hated silence. It could've meant anything. I studied the white swirls of paint on the ceiling, hoping that if I concentrated on them intently enough, I'd be transported out of the room and away from the awkwardness.

His response was more direct than words. In my peripheral vision, I noticed him digging in his pocket. Then, without warning, his half-closed hand slammed into my face like a brick. Before I knew what was happening, he pried open my mouth and jammed in two fingers. Out of instinct, I clamped my jaws shut. He bellowed in agony, but I wouldn't release my grip. I felt his bones grind between my clenched teeth as he pulled with all his might. My front teeth ached as they ripped open his flesh. His blood pooled on my tongue. "Goddamn it!" he shouted before delivering a swift punch to my gut. As I grimaced from the blow, he was able to free his fingers. Immediately, he slapped his bloody hand over my mouth. And with his other hand, he pinched shut my nose.

It was then I could taste it. Among his blood was the bitterness of small pills he had managed to cram into my mouth. Mixed with his blood and my saliva, the pills quickly began to dissolve. He sat on top of me, his face red with anger. "Swallow!" he demanded. Squirming, convulsing for air, I had no choice but to swallow, to let the bloody mixture slide down my throat. To telegraph to him that I in fact swallowed, I overexaggerated the movement of my throat. Satisfied, he finally released me. I gasped for air as he grabbed my polo shirt and used it to wrap his bleeding fingers. "Motherfucker!" he shouted in pain.

"What'd you do that for!" I yelled as I leapt to my feet. He looked surprised I was so angry. I sprinted out of the room and down the hall. Just as I locked the bathroom door behind me, he began tugging on the cheap plastic knob. I flipped up the lid and knelt over the toilet. I eyed my index finger a moment before plunging it deep into the back of my throat. I gagged. My eyes filled with tears. But nothing. I tried once more, gagged again, but was unable to bring anything up.

"Open the fucking door!"

I stood at the sink and ran cold water. I splashed it on my face. I cupped my hands and took a drink. I looked in the mirror, trying to convince myself that the pills, whatever they were, would have no effect. But something strange began to happen. I struggled with the meaning of time. Moments seemed to stand still yet go by at warp speed. I had difficulty grasping how long I was shut in the small bathroom. I couldn't focus. Couldn't think. Each bang on the door, each tug on the knob sounded farther and farther away. "I just wanted you to sleep," I heard a distant voice warble.

One thing was clear. They weren't sleeping pills. Whatever he had forced me to swallow were much stronger. In my swirling haze, I decided I needed to defend myself. So I opened the medicine cabinet and rummaged for a weapon. But my vision was like a camera continuously zooming in and out at breakneck speed. I knocked a box of Q-tips on its side. As the swabs spilled out, I couldn't take my eyes off them, tumbling in slow motion, hitting the tile like miniature, fuzzy drumsticks.

I managed to grab hold of a can of air freshener. I aimed it at the door, waiting for the moment he'd break in. I hoped I had the nozzle pointed in the right direction. A wave of relaxation crawled up my legs, loosening my muscles. Before I knew it, I was on my knees. It took all my strength to hold my arms in front of me until they too were taken over. Slowly, they lowered out of their firing position. My eyelids were heavy. I blinked slowly. I felt like liquid as my body oozed to the floor. The cold, hard tile felt soothing against my hot skin. Then it was gone. I had been lifted from it. I had entered another world.

My feet poking outside the covers made me feel even more vulnerable. Yet I didn't dare reach for the blanket. Not that my stillness mattered all that much. I knew that what hid in the corners could smell me. Could see in the darkness. Could hear my heartbeat . . .

4
LiLACS

I pulled open the top drawer of the old pine dresser. Dust rolled out and added itself to the rest of the dust swirling about. The drawer was empty. I pulled open the second drawer and, to my surprise, found several of my own shirts. They had been folded and placed in two piles. I opened the third drawer and found a selection of my cargo shorts and underwear. In the bottom drawer were two pairs of my jeans. I slipped on my most comfortable shorts and grabbed my green T-shirt. *What kidnapper would think of packing clothes?* Phillip wasn't a kidnapper. He was my friend. I grasped the knob confidently and swung open the door. As a dry breeze rushed into the room, the tattered shade blew out of control. Of course he hadn't locked me in.

My eyes explored the old cabin as my lungs filled with the less stale air of the larger space. There wasn't much to the place. There were two bedrooms, with a small bathroom in between. At the center was a living space furnished with mismatched chairs and a couch huddled around an old television. The kitchen was separated from the dining area by an open counter and low-hanging cupboards. On the table was a plate of scrambled eggs and a bowl of soggy cereal.

I opened the screen door. The humming bugs were even louder out in the open. The large porch I found myself on looked like it had been recently added, awkwardly affixed to the aging cabin. I stepped up to the railing. The view was panoramic. The sky was magnificent. It was the softest shade of blue. Endless. The few far-off clouds glowed, backed by the shimmer of the early-afternoon sun. The sky met the forest in the distance. And between it and the cabin was nothing but a vast field. Shadows of trees loomed over the overgrown yard, so I knew another forest must've butted up to the back of the cabin. Leading up to the gravel driveway was a thin two-track that mimicked a road. I had a good idea that if no one was to drive on it in a season or two, the weeds could easily erase it.

Phillip had traded his sandals for sneakers and was digging near the front of the cabin. He had already dug two holes, each about two feet in diameter. I clenched the railing, waiting for him to notice me. Afraid I'd continue to go unnoticed, I finally hollered, "Thanks for breakfast!"

He stopped digging, held his shovel at arm's length, and faced me. "It's gone bad by now."

"That's OK. I'm not really hungry. Must be the heat."

"You've found your clothes. I guess I forgot to grab you some socks." I looked to my bare feet. "You can use mine. Your shoes are by the door."

"Thanks. So what're you digging for?"

He nodded toward the bundle of uprooted bushes. "I found these lilacs growing in the field on the other side of the pines." The blossoms were closed and drooping, yet their fragrance remained powerful. "I'm going to plant them along the front of the cabin. They're Ginger's favorite."

He threw down the shovel and traded it for a bottle of water. He took a long drink and gestured the bottle toward me. I gladly took it, letting the water refresh my parched mouth and throat. Even though it was lukewarm, I didn't want to put it down. I finished all but the last of it. He sat on the steps. I followed his lead and sat next to him. "My parents gave me this place when they moved out of state," he said. "I hadn't been here in years. Only started coming up this spring. I put this porch on. Strengthened the foundation a bit." He looked to the lilacs. "We were going to spend our summer vacations here. Would've made a great spot for our honeymoon too."

I was puzzled. "I figured you were already married."

"No. Every time we planned it, something got in the way. We bought a house. Her father died. We helped my parents move to Virginia. I switched firms. It just kept getting put off."

"But you've been together for so long. I just assumed—"

"I know. After a while, it felt like we *were* married. It was my fault. I just thought of marriage as a formality. But we should've done it. I should've married her years ago. I'd marry her right now. Today. Right here, if I could." He lifted his gaze to the forest in the distance. "God, I miss her. You know what I miss most about her?"

"Her fluffy white sweater?" I let the air out of my lungs, embarrassed that I had said it aloud. "Sorry."

Befuddled, he brought his eyebrows together for a moment before continuing, "I miss sleeping with her. Not just the sex. Holding her. Just sleeping with her and holding her. Keeping her safe. I wake up at night forgetting she's gone, and then—" He closed his eyes, picturing her, I assumed.

"I dreamt of monsters last night," I revealed. "And of Everett. I hadn't dreamt of either since I saw that psychiatrist."

He wiped the sweat from his forehead. "That's not so surprising. You're just getting started. I asked you to concentrate on finding Ginger, and in the past, you've associated your—talent— with Everett, with his sick games and tricks. Now that you're trying to use it on your own, it makes sense that you've kept those associations."

"I guess," I answered reluctantly. "But I've got to know. Why do you believe Everett now? Why after all these years?"

"Because," he paused with a long exhale before admitting, "I've tried everything else." His eyes flooded, but he did not allow any tears to spill over.

"I'm sorry, Phillip." Truly, I was.

We looked to the horizon, to the sun dangling over the top of the forest. He took a few deep breaths, calming and composing himself. The somberness of the situation turned strangely serene with the help of the continuous hum of nearby cicadas. "I'll find her," I said. I knew I was making a promise that in all probability I wouldn't be able to keep, but I needed to offer him something. I would've done anything for Phillip.

"How'd we end up here?" he asked, still gazing into the distance.

"What do you mean?"

"How did we end up at this age? At this cabin? Where did this all start?"

I realized Phillip's questions were rhetorical. I knew a person wasn't supposed to answer a question that was rhetorical. But I also was never one to know the right moments to speak or not to speak. "I found myself standing in a forest," I began.

PART II
THE ADVENTURES OF
EVERETT AND AYDEN

5
THE METAL FOREST

I found myself standing in a forest. Though my surroundings were somehow strangely familiar, it was clear I never could've stood in the forest before. One distinction made it glaringly obvious: The trees were not of wood and pulp. Instead, the trees in this forest were made of—metal. Shiny silver metal. Some of the polished trunks were massive, while others were no more than thin metal rods jutting from the forest floor. Stark, leafless branches reached in all directions, their ends coming to sharp points. Connected to the larger branches stretched a network of smaller branches that further segmented until they were nothing more than wiry wisps. As I looked into the distance, the forest became a crisscrossing mesh of metal.

And then there was the moon! It hung just above the tree line, so low and so close that it filled the sky. It glowed dimly from within, barely providing enough light for the trees to produce shadows, yet enough to allow me to study its colossal magnificence. I couldn't have gotten a better view of its surface had I been peering at it through the world's most powerful telescope. If I would've climbed the tallest of the metal trees, I could've touched it, felt its dust and gray craters with my fingertips. The near collision of these celestial bodies seemed strangely natural in this most unnatural of forests.

Draped over the backside of the moon was an equally colossal black curtain. It stretched to the edges of the forest, where it dropped behind the farthest trees. The dense fabric created a sky of deep black and blotted out whatever lay beyond it in the distance. It gave the impression that the forest was planted in an infinite field of darkness. Yet my very detection of the curtain told me that there were in fact boundaries—and that I was boxed inside the fantastic place. I could see no spot where the curtain parted, but excess fabric pooled where the black night met the floor—of ice.

Except where punctured by the tree trunks, the entire forest floor was a clear, smooth, and solid sheet of ice. Its transparency allowed me to view below the surface. Although the icescape was frozen solid, it evoked a sensation of movement in its depths. I was entranced by the web of metal roots that twisted and overlapped until they were obscured by distance. After nearly losing myself in the marvelous chaos below, I brought my bare feet above the surface into focus. I hadn't realized how cold they were until I saw my flesh pressed to the ice. I moved one foot on top of the other, but that did little to help. Despite my frozen feet, the cold was tolerable, even while just in my sweatpants and thin undershirt.

There I stood, lost in uneasy wonderment, perplexed, like some amnesia victim wondering where I was and how I got there. A light breeze blew so gently it didn't even move my hair. The metal trees glistened under the dim moon, striking in their sterility. The place was haunting. Yet it was also familiar. It was a place that, somehow, I felt I knew quite well—perhaps in another time or dimension. But standing there, at that moment, it was a place I couldn't wholly comprehend. I knew there had to be a reason, a purpose for me being in that forest. Only I couldn't remember what it was. The idea was unrecognizable yet faintly there, like an elusive word on the tip of one's tongue. Faint, like the first of the metal clicks I heard.

It sounded like a faraway pebble had dropped on a sheet of metal. I strained to listen. There it was again. And again a few moments later. Soon, the clicks multiplied and began coming in waves. As the waves came closer, I realized that the forest was waking up—and moving in my direction. Trees joined the waves by shifting their branches in unison. And by the end of the wave, each metal branch pointed in the same direction. Their militaristic movements echoed throughout the forest like an amplified snare drum. And just as the silence would return, they'd shift again, simultaneously stretching in a new direction with a thunderous clack. They'd shift. Then pose. Shift. Then pose. Each time, more trees joined in, set off by neighboring trees. Unable to escape it, I found myself caught in the middle as the branches surrounding me became possessed by the contagious ritual. The animation of the trees rolled on until the entire forest joined the mechanical, synchronized dance.

Trees danced dangerously all around me. Dodging the sharp ends of the reaching branches, I managed to make it to a small clearing where no trees poked through the ice. There, I was safe from the violent limbs. But it was also there, beneath the ice, that I found something strangely out of place. Something opposite of pristine, manufactured metal. It was something—organic. At first, it looked like a log composed of actual wood. But as I peered closer, I knew the texture was too smooth to be bark. My eyes followed the curious thing until I slowly slid backward to reveal a pair of eyes gazing hauntingly into mine.

Her hair stood on end, floating in delicate, frozen waves. It was clear she had tried, without victory, to free herself from her frozen prison. Her open mouth was pressed against the surface, locked in an eternal scream. Her hands were palms-up, her fingers fixed in a clawing position. Her torso was mangled, caught in a snare of silver roots. And her legs disappeared into the obscurity of ice and overlapping metal. Frozen in terror, she was nonetheless strangely beautiful.

Suddenly, a light began to glow from beneath her. The golden light grew in size and intensity, as if her soul had awoken and was attempting to melt the ice with its radiance. I inched away uneasily from her frozen tomb and realized that, although she was certainly the most striking, she was not alone. Across the surface of the forest floor, more lights began to glow from beneath the ice like warm beacons, revealing that the forest held dozens captive.

The trees continued aggressively posing their branches, uncaring of the illuminated corpses below. I dashed across the ice, searching for a spot where I wouldn't be impaled by a limb or forced to stand atop a frozen figure. Yet this proved impossible. Every spot I leapt to that was safe from shifting branches, I'd find a frozen face beneath my feet. At least unlike the frozen beauty in the clearing, the others seemed to have been resting peacefully in their ice chambers. Arms folded. Eyes closed. Serene expressions.

In the midst of my panicked scramble, my eye caught an anomaly near the base of one of the largest trees. Affixed to its lower trunk was a smooth, flat outcrop of metal. Unlike the long-reaching, sharply pointed branches, this stub of a branch refused, or was unable, to sway. Like running an obstacle course, I ducked and sidestepped the striking limbs as I made my way to the tree. I hoisted myself up on the metal pedestal and clutched the massive, rattling trunk to keep balanced. My shadow wobbled as it loomed over the dark ice, which reflected the all-encompassing moon. The moment I stepped from the ice, the lights below dimmed until they no longer lit the bodies. That is, except for the lone light that continued to radiate beneath the captivating woman in the clearing. Despite the distance, suspended a few feet off the ground, I was still able to make out the shape of her twisted body, her hands clawing for the surface.

I heard a light hiss overhead. "What now?" I moaned as I looked skyward to the tree towering over me. A branch at the very top had punctured the moon with one of its violent strikes. Thick, sparkling spirals poured out from the gash. The peculiar snow began to cascade through the trees. The sparkles delicately brushed the metal, producing the light shhhhhhhh sound. As it came closer to the ground, it began to cover my hair. I then realized that what fell from inside the moon was not snow at all, but millions of swirls of silver glitter.

I bowed my head to prevent the specks of glitter from falling in my eyes. Glitter danced all around me. It fell throughout the forest, dusting the ice. Fascinated, I hopped off the metal platform and shuffled my feet. Glitter collected between my cold toes. Cheerfully distracted, I quickly forgot about the frozen bodies beneath. I playfully cupped my hands and lifted them toward the sky. When they began to overflow, I dumped the glitter and watched it swirl through the air and add to the sparkling piles that had begun to accumulate.

The light dusting that had begun only moments before had quickly evolved into a full-scale glitter downpour. The trail I made had already been erased by fresh glitter. And by the next time I heard the ricochet of the metal branches, I found myself lost in a glitter blizzard. Glitter stuck to my hands. It stuck to my hair and eyelashes. It pasted itself to my skin. I shielded my eyes with my forearm as I stumbled about blindly.

Abruptly, I felt a cold jolt in my back, followed by a stinging pain. I reached behind me to find I had finally been pierced by a metal branch. I stood paralyzed for a moment, skewered in place. I feared that I'd soon be tossed across the forest with the next shimmy of the blade. So before I let that happen, I thrust forward, successfully dislodging from the tip. I collapsed to the ground and felt for the wound, but glitter had already begun caking into it.

I crawled along the forest floor, attempting to find my way back to safety, back to the tree with the pedestal. But I could barely keep my eyes open. Soon I was forced to shut them altogether. I hopelessly felt my way across the ice. Coats of glitter covered my skin until I myself was as silvery as the trees. And like them, I eventually became immobile, frozen to the landscape like their metal trunks.

Stranded in the middle of the metal forest with the moon bleeding glitter, I could've easily been overcome. But at that moment, more than ever, I knew I needed to concentrate. I began by reaching in my mind for what was most familiar. I thought of forests with leaves. Green leaves. And bark. Bark that peeled off trunks when weathered. I thought of a breeze rustling branches high above treetops, causing them to sway gently in the wind. And I thought—of Everett. Of course! I *did* have a purpose in that forest. I had been given a mission.

By then, the glitter was up to my elbows. But my renewed clarity energized me. I clawed the glitter from my eyes and forced them open. I dove into drifts of the thick stuff. On my hands and knees, I felt along the ice, searching. I swept methodically, back and forth across the surface, standing every so often for gasps of glitter-free air. I could cover the whole forest in sections, I reasoned, and eventually I'd find what Everett had sent me to find.

My search, however, was prematurely halted when my hands suddenly became wet. I stood cautiously and brought them to my face. Water ran from my palms, bringing trails of loose glitter down my wrists. My sweatpants were soaked. A puddle of water sloshed beneath my numb feet. All became still. The trees had stopped posing. The glitter had stopped falling. I too stood completely still, bracing myself as if nearing the crest of a hill on a roller coaster. I took only a few light, terrified breaths. And then, the surface of the forest left me. As easily as I had been standing on ice, I was in the next instant underwater. My legs were suddenly tangled in metal roots and the limbs of the dead, freed from their frozen prisons, while my head bobbed among the mass of floating, shimmering glitter.

With glitter no longer being dumped from the sky, I realized I wasn't very far from the tree with the jutting platform. I swam toward it, grimacing as my legs were cut by sharp metal and felt by dead hands. I used the metal ridge to hoist my torso above the floating glitter. Yet the piece of metal I so desperately clutched began to bend under my weight. It drooped toward the water as if it were slowly turning to liquid. In a desperate move, I let go and swiftly wrapped my arms around the massive trunk. I hugged it as tight as I could. But unable to fully reach around its girth, my arms trembled, and I began to slide. As my chest slid past the weakened outcrop, it finally tore away from the tree and plopped into the water.

I struggled to keep my head above the glitter. And as if my situation wasn't grim enough, small pieces of metal began pouring out of the freshly torn hole. The flat, round pieces bounced off my head and then plunked into the water. I soon realized they were coins. Hundreds of them sprayed over me as if I were trapped beneath a giant slot machine. They pelted me with such intensity, I was forced to give in. Finally, I released my weak grip. I slipped through the layer of glitter and under the water, where the plinks and plunks of coins dropping all around me became the only sound.

I allowed the overwhelming feeling of weakness to subdue me. I welcomed it actually. In that moment, I only wanted to fall. I only wanted to drop farther and descend gently into the abyss, like the coins passing me by. I closed my eyes and imagined I was one of them, slipping past the dead bodies and jagged strips and twists of metal. The deeper I sank, the more I relaxed. My breathing was steady. I could breathe under this water! I continued my descent without opening my eyes. I didn't want to see the chaos above. Instead, I concentrated on my breathing and allowed myself to drift for miles.

6
THE ORGANIC FOREST

Slowly I opened my eyes. There was Everett like I knew he would be, sitting at the foot of my bed. He saw my eyelids lift and immediately flashed his smile. I was just thirteen then. He was fifteen. He had set up a weight room in the basement and already had a solid build for his age. "My feet are freezing," I said. I leaned back on my elbows to see my bare feet sticking out from under the covers.

"Oh yeah?" Everett leaned forward and sandwiched my foot in his armpit. "Is this better?" he joked.

"Gross," I said with a laugh, yanking my feet away from him.

Instantly he turned deadly serious. "Did you find it?" he asked. I couldn't contain my smile. Everett slowly shook his head, impressed. "I knew you would."

"It took me most of the night. And it wasn't easy. But I think so."

"Let's go!" He bolted for the door, eager to see if I had in fact completed his mission. But a gnawing feeling of unease soured my excitement. I remained on the bed, my hands clamped on to my frozen feet. "What is it?" He turned back and sat next to me. "What else did you see?"

Everett had always been curious about my dreams. He'd listen to me recount the bizarre and fantastic situations I'd find myself in. He liked hearing all the strange details. In one dream, I found myself floating outside the second story of our house. I was unable to lower myself safely to the ground, so there I hovered, desperately moving from window to window, pounding furiously for someone to let me in. About a week later, we were at the store, and Mom had locked her keys in the car. Embarrassingly, she was forced to ask the manager for help. The resourceful man eventually unlocked the door by removing his shoelace, tying it into a lasso, and slipping it through the crack in the window to grab and pull up the knob.

I didn't connect the dots. But Everett was convinced I had predicted it—that me attempting to get into the house through the windows symbolized us attempting to get into the locked car. "You were just a bit off. That's all," he said. "That's the way it works with futures. Dreams are tricky. So details are important. Even if they don't seem important at the time, you've got to pay attention. You've got to remember the details." He'd keep track of it all to see if any meaning could be later extracted. He told me my dreams weren't ever going to be crystal clear because I'd never know exactly what to concentrate on, and the dream could easily lead me astray.

But Everett had an idea, a way around having to wait for an event to happen before sifting through details. What if I *did* know what to concentrate on? What if I were to focus on the *present* rather than picking up ambiguous clues to a murky future? And that's how he came up with the idea of giving me a task to complete. He figured if I was given a mission to concentrate on, my dreams would be more specific, and their accuracy would improve. According to Everett, having a target, a focus, would make it easier to glean useful information. Even so, spending the night in the metal forest didn't seem easy.

"I was in the woods," I reported. "But the trees were metal. The moon was as big as the earth. And the ground was made of ice. Under the ice were people. Dead people. Frozen dead people. It started snowing. Only the snow wasn't real snow. It was glitter. And it dumped all over me."

"Slow down," he pleaded, trying to record his mental notes.

"Then the ice melted. I had to swim with the bodies. And you weren't there at all!" I scolded.

"I was busy in my own dreams," he countered with a wink. "Nothing can hurt you in your dreams, you know."

"I know," I said solemnly. "But this woman—"

Everett stopped me from going any further by bringing his finger to his lips. Sure enough, the stairs were creaking. The one rule he had was that we didn't share my dreams with anybody. I liked being in an exclusive club with Everett, us having secrets no one else knew about or could participate in. It felt like Everett and me against the world. A moment later, Mom darted her head into the room. "You boys coming down for breakfast?"

It was Sunday. On Sundays, she'd always make a big breakfast since it was the only day we'd all be together. Dad was a truck driver. He'd be gone most of the week, hauling all kinds of tobacco products through parts of Michigan, Illinois, Ohio, and Indiana. Mom was a secretary on the cardiology floor at the hospital. She worked second shift. So most days after school, it was just Everett and me.

We scarfed down Mom's thick pancakes as fast as we could before taking off through the field of tall grass and weeds behind our house. Many years before, cows grazed there. Later, corn, cabbage, and alfalfa grew on the spot. Mr. Peterson, an old farmer, used to own much of the land surrounding our house. When he retired, his children weren't interested in inheriting his farming business, so he sold most of it off piece by piece to those in the neighborhood. My parents snatched up the acre and a half directly behind our house. The only land Mr. Peterson kept for himself was the small strip of forest that lay between our field and his farmhouse.

Our neighbor Mr. Newberry decided to try his hand at farming field corn with the land he acquired. His cornfields grew on either side of our field and along Mr. Peterson's woods. In the middle of the largest cornfield sat a rusted pile of old farm machinery that had originally belonged to Mr. Peterson. It was apparently too burdensome to move, so Mr. Newberry simply planted around the old plows and tractors heaped on top of each other. Everett and I would climb on the equipment. When we were younger, I'd sit on the seat of one of the upright tractors, bouncing up and down, pretending I was driving. Sometimes we'd lie on our stomachs on top of old cushions beneath the rubble and imagine we were in the cockpit of a spaceship, flying high above the cornfield, shooting laser beams at targets below.

The morning sun made the tall weeds glow with a golden hue. We made our way along the thin dirt trail we had made with our bikes. "Let's race!" Everett announced.

"You'll just beat me."

"Maybe. Maybe not. Let's find out." With that, he took off sprinting through the field. I ran after him, quickly falling behind. It looked as if the tall stalks had swallowed him as he cut into the cornfield. I could see the yellow tassels swaying ahead of me as he ran for the woods. I leapt into the corn after him. It was darker in the cornfield, where the morning sun couldn't easily penetrate the dark-green plants. The dewy leaves slapped my face as I dashed through the thick maze. My face was red-hot, but the air was cool. Stalks rustled in the distance. "C'mon!" he called. I ran faster, panting, following his voice and the rattling stalks.

When I could no longer hear him in front of me, I slowed my pace—and eventually stopped, bent over with my hands on my knees to collect my breath. Clearly, he had made it to the woods. There was no use trying to catch up. In the middle of the cornfield, the only sounds were the pounding of my heart and the tops of the stalks gently caressing in the breeze. In the distance, in every direction, was a collage of green leaves and stalks. I looked up to the striking blue sky. Inside the cornfield was a different world. If I had a ladder, I could've brought the outside world into perspective. I had a pretty good idea where I was in relation to the house, our field, and the woods. But still, there was an unsettling feeling not being able to truly confirm my bearings.

I squeezed through a thick cluster of stalks. My pant leg became caught in the tight mesh. As I untangled myself, I caught a flash of white streak by. Realizing I must've caught a glimpse of Everett's T-shirt, I quickly pulled myself out of the tangle and began running again. When I figured I had run far enough to be parallel with the woods, I cut back to the edge of the cornfield. It wasn't long before I came to the narrow strip of no-man's-land that divided the woods from the corn. I stood outside the edge of the forest for a moment before exchanging one world for the next. Wild grapevines draped over the trees like a curtain keeping the forest secure. I knew Everett would be in there, waiting.

The small forest was old. Not many young trees had a chance to take root. The few saplings would eventually die because the tall, mature trees blocked the sunlight. Because of this, there was also little foliage. Yet in the spring, bellflower and nightshade grew along with other wildflowers. And in the summer, the forest floor was carpeted in large patches of mayapple.

Even if not as fantastical as the forest of my dream, to me, it was the most whimsical place on earth. Ever since we were children, we had made it our playground of make-believe. We had constructed countless forts out of dead trees. We'd play war. We'd pretend we were vampires, our lair hidden beneath a hollowed mound. When the forest would flood in the springtime, we'd imagine the stagnant water filled with mosquito larvae was liquid acid, powerful enough to strip the skin from our bones should we fall in. We'd make a game out of finding ways from one end of the woods to the other without touching the water. This involved balancing ourselves across a network of fallen tree trunks that connected sporadic mounds of dry land. But on that day, we were no longer playing pretend. Our mission was real.

I peeled back the thick layer of grape leaves and stepped inside. I scanned for Everett while at the same time comparing the organic forest to the forest of metal and ice. I was surprised how accurate the reproduction in my dream was. Sure, the floor of the organic forest had random mounds and slight hills, whereas the floor of the metal forest was a smooth sheet of ice. But much like reality, the metal forest was virtually barren except for the silver trees. And to the best of my recollection, each organic tree seemed to have an uncanny metallic counterpart, similar in position, height, and girth.

Suspiciously, Everett was nowhere in sight. Alone, I passed the remnants of our most ambitious fort. We had built it on top of one of the largest mounds. With the forest a virtual lake in the spring, we had our very own island. It had been several seasons since we last worked on it. Although it had mostly deteriorated, its skeleton, made up of short logs and sticks, was still intact.

I was drawn to the small clearing, where in my dream I had seen the frozen woman. The ground in this spot was remarkably clear. No mayapple grew. The forest floor was virtually exposed, covered only by a thin layer of scattered twigs. I pressed the tip of my shoe into the clearing and kicked up a layer of dirt. I couldn't help but imagine her just below the surface. Her eyes pleading for her release. Her gaping mouth. Her clawing hands.

A rush of movement from the edge of the forest startled me. Branches bowed and swayed as Everett burst inside. "Man, you're fast!" he said as he hurried toward me, effortlessly leaping over a downed tree trunk. "You take a shortcut?" I smirked, knowing full well he had hidden in the corn until I had made it inside the woods. "So what's this?" he asked.

"It's where one of the bodies was. A woman. Her eyes looked right into mine. She was afraid. She was fighting, screaming when it happened."

"When *what* happened?"

"When she was killed, I guess."

Everett knelt beside me and patted the earth. "Well, she's not here now. Don't let it bother you."

"There were many others," I muttered, "trapped under the ice."

"Remember, it's different this time. We have focus. So let's focus." He spun me away from the patch. "Now, where are those coins?"

"Over there," I pointed.

Several years before, old Mr. Peterson had hired Everett to cut down the thicket taking over the outside of his dilapidated barn. Everett spent nearly a week in the hot sun cutting through the growth with a rusted scythe he had found and yanking down the creeping ivy. When he finished, he was invited inside the old farmhouse. On the counter sat several pickle jars filled with coins. Everett waited patiently as Mr. Peterson counted out quarters and dimes before begrudgingly sliding three dollars worth across the counter as payment. Everett fumed for days, swearing he'd never work for the old man again. "I'd make more money picking up pop cans along the highway!"

Not long after, Everett was working on adding a bridge to our main fort when he spotted Mr. Peterson tromping through the woods. We knew the old man didn't take kindly to trespassers. In fact, our parents had warned us not to even play in his woods. But Everett wasn't easily dissuaded, even after we were chased off on a few occasions. Everett crouched in the fort, peering through the camouflage as Mr. Peterson passed by muttering to himself. He strained to see what the old man was up to and noticed he was clutching one of his pickle jars. But when he passed by the fort again on his way out of the woods, he no longer carried the jar.

Together, we searched in hollow logs and in foxholes. We even dug shallow holes in the area Everett thought he saw Mr. Peterson last holding it. But the jar remained elusive. Eventually, we gave up. That is, until Everett charged me with the task of locating the infamous hidden pickle jar filled with coins.

"That tree," I said, motioning to the one with the thick trunk a few yards ahead. As we rounded the tree, I immediately noticed a piece of an old stump crammed into a large opening a few feet up its trunk. The broken stump created an unnatural protrusion. It looked as if it had been carved in the shape of a teardrop to fit perfectly snug in the crevice.

"I can't believe it. This old beech tree? We must've passed it a thousand times!" moaned Everett. He used his jackknife to scrape away the dried mud and clay that cemented the broken stump to the tree. He then yanked as hard as he could, falling backward as it dislodged. Unfazed, he thrust his arm deep into the opening. "I feel something!" he announced. When his arm reappeared, he presented to me like a magician what he had found. It sat in the palm of his hand beneath a tattered cloth. I was just as amazed as he was when he pinched the top of the cloth and pulled it away to dramatically reveal—a pickle jar filled with silver coins.

"Holy shit! You did it!" He placed the jar in my hands. "Feel how heavy it is." While I held the jar, he opened the lid and dug out a handful of coins. He let them slip through his fingers and fall back into the jar. "Wow. All silver dollars." Everett beamed with excitement and pride as he firmly patted my shoulder. "It's amazing. *You* are amazing."

He shoved the stump back into the tree's opening, and we scurried across the woods with our stolen loot. We took it to our field, where we sat in one of the patches of weeds matted by the deer that liked to lie there. The matted patches were like small islands in a sea of tall weeds. Sitting inside allowed us to disappear. Everett sat on a rotting log with a patch of wild daisies growing behind it, and I sat with my legs folded in the middle of the soft bedding. Everett took off his T-shirt and on it emptied the coins.

"What're you going to do with the money?" I wondered.

"Count it."

"OK." I grinned. "*Then* what're you going to do with it?"

"It's not mine to do anything with."

"Then why'd you take it in the first place?"

He ignored me and began dividing the coins into separate piles. I eyed the silver coins reflecting the morning sun. There was a bust of a woman on one side and an eagle spreading its wings on the other. When he seemed satisfied, he counted his piles. "Hundred and fifty-six dollars," he declared.

"Wow. Doesn't look like that much."

"And they're worth a lot more than a dollar apiece by now, I bet. Most of these are from the early 1900s." He scooped up the piles and dropped the coins back into the jar. "I'm not going to take the money," he reiterated. "And we're not giving it back to Mr. Peterson either. That old man probably forgot where he hid the jar anyhow. These coins—are yours."

"But you're the one who saw him hide the jar," I protested.

"Yeah. But without you, we never would've found it."

I didn't argue with Everett a moment longer. If he said the coins were mine, then they were mine. "But I don't know what to do with them."

"Whatever you want," he said. "Get a moped or something." He laughed to himself, imagining me on a moped, I supposed.

Embarrassed by his praise, I held my gaze to the ground. I followed a black ant weaving in and out of the tapestry of matted weeds. Everett shook his shirt clean and pulled it back over his head. "So what'll it be? What do you want to try for today?" he asked, sporting his devilish grin. "How about some bees? Or a grasshopper? Blackbirds? A rabbit?"

Having lost track of the ant, I rested back on the mesh of weeds. They created a firm, comfortable bed. I closed my eyes. "Not sure," I replied. I listened to the wind rustle the nearby corn and swoosh through the surrounding weeds. I used the wind. Let my mind drift with it. I rode it. Let it swoop me up and carry me above the fields and woods. I swirled weightless in the air just above the tallest trees.

"What do you see?" asked Everett.

"Just us. In the field."

"What do you *want* to see?"

I thought for a moment. "Cats," I replied.

"*Cats?*"

"Yeah. Like those cats in Mr. Peterson's barn. They never let me get close enough to pet them."

"Cats. OK."

I thought of the feral cats that were abundant in the neighborhood, the ones that used the barns and woodsheds for shelter. I pictured them: black, gray, orange, tiger-striped, tortoiseshell, playing in the abandoned barn down the road, cleaning and sunning themselves in the grass. I imagined those same cats marching through our field, batting at the swaying weeds, tumbling playfully as they approached our hideout.

My eyelids fluttered as I heard dried weeds crackling behind me. It could've been Everett. Or an intruder wandering into our island in the weeds. Somehow, the noise added weight to my floating spirit, and I promptly plummeted from the sky. After abruptly coalescing with my body, my eyes sprang open. I took a deep breath as I sat up, woozy from my rapid descent. It took a moment for my vision to become clear. And when I was sure what I was seeing was in fact there, I whispered excitedly, "Beside you!"

On the log next to Everett sat a large, black cat. Its glossy coat shone in the sun as it casually cleaned itself. It seemed oblivious to Everett sitting right beside it, his arm brushing against its fur. The cat stopped bathing for a moment to glance in my direction with its piercing green eyes. It then leapt off the log and strolled toward me, its tail bobbing in a friendly greeting. To my surprise, another cat hopped on the log, taking its place. This cat was also large and sleek, yet its coat was a smoky-gray. As the first cat circled behind me, the second cat bounded my way. I was delighted when a third cat appeared. It was a mix of caramel browns and yellows. I stood slowly as it jumped down to join the others. One by one, more cats leapt on to and then over the log. There were six in all by the time they stopped appearing.

With their tails pointing straight in the air, they encapsulated me, and I became the center point of their entrancing, moving circle. The circle paused when the orange-and-white-striped cat stopped to rub against my pant leg and again when I bent down to scratch the gray cat's chin. The happy cat reacted by standing on its hind legs and stretching its front legs up my shins. I ran my hand down its coat from its ears to the tip of its long tail. I could feel its strong muscles beneath its fur. Its rib cage vibrated with a powerful purr.

"Where do they come from?" I asked. I stepped out of the circle, toward Everett, and the circle came undone. Methodically, the cats formed a single-file line behind me. I jumped onto the log, and the black cat leapt on to the log after me. Everett stood out of the way as I spread my arms for balance and stepped across the length of the log. I looked behind me to see the cats following my lead. I smiled at Everett. He smiled back, keeping his hands coolly in his pockets even as he watched in astonishment. Pure happiness washed over me. I began to laugh uncontrollably. I jumped from the log and marched into the tall weeds, laughing, the cats following not far behind.

"I don't know where they come from," he replied. "But I know they're here because of you."

7
THE DiG

Too shy to make eye contact, I looked to his corduroys and button-down red-and-white-checkered shirt as he stepped in the garage. Everett pulled three shovels off their hooks and handed one to Phillip and one to me. "Hello," I finally managed, momentarily catching a glimpse of his blue eyes before promptly letting my gaze fall again.

"Phillip's gonna help us dig—even though he's dressed like a little boy on his way to church," Everett quipped. Phillip *did* seem a bit overdressed for the occasion. Everett and I were typically in jeans and T-shirts whether we planned on getting covered in dirt or not.

"I take it I should've dressed like you? In a wifebeater looking like I just strolled in from the trailer park?" Phillip shot back. I laughed cautiously.

Everett had warned me Phillip was going to help. He said we'd need the extra muscle. He assured me that Phillip wouldn't tell anyone what we were up to. It was rare for Everett to bring a friend home from school, so I knew Phillip had to be all right. If Everett could trust him, then so could I. Still, even though I liked Phillip immediately, I worried about myself. I didn't have any friends. Just

Everett. I just knew I was bound to say—or do—something embarrassing in Phillip's presence. Something uncool. Something I'd regret. And that fear made me petrified to be around him.

"So, fellas, if you found money in a tree, what's with the shovels? Why are we digging instead of looking in trees?" Phillip rightfully asked as we trekked to the woods.

"How many trees do you know with convenient money-hiding holes?" Everett countered. "Besides, maybe it's not money we'll find. Maybe we'll find—something else."

The truth was Everett had thought some more about my dream. Although my purpose was to locate the hidden jar of coins, he realized he had been too quick to dismiss the peripheral information. Everett was passionate about my dreams. He insisted we must learn to trust them. Unravel them. Investigate every possible meaning. Could there have been meaning behind the trees of metal? The snow made of glitter? Why were there bodies beneath the ice? And what was the significance of the woman with the frozen scream? His plan was to conduct a digging expedition. Neither of us expected the dig to yield much. But maybe, just maybe, it'd reveal some clues.

"Exactly what *else* could we possibly find in the woods behind your house that would be so exciting?" asked Phillip in a sarcastic tone.

"Bodies," I answered.

Phillip let out a short laugh. "*Bodies*, huh? You didn't say anything about *bodies*, Everett."

Everett tossed a glare my way, and I immediately felt the shock of his scold. It caused my face to flush. I knew my sin. Clearly I had spoken without thinking first. Everett covered for me by forcing out a boisterous laugh. He then said, "Who knows what else crazy Mr. Peterson hid out there? Maybe we *will* find bodies."

"Or the old man's porno stash," joked Phillip.

After entering directly from the back of our field, the three of us stood on the inside edge scanning the dark forest. "Where at?" asked Everett.

"All over," I replied. Everett stared at me intently while gripping his shovel. He leaned forward, wildly blinking his eyes in an overt gesture of impatience. "What?" I wondered before finally realizing I wasn't exactly being helpful. "Oh. Right." I took a moment to think about how the bodies in the metal forest might correspond to the layout of the organic forest. "How about someone digs over there?" I instructed, pointing to the small mound behind the beech tree where we had found the coins.

"Um. Wait a minute," Phillip interrupted. "How do you already know where to dig? Do you stalk this guy daily or what?" Everett took off for the mound without bothering to help me come up with an answer. Alone with Phillip, I stared awkwardly at his shoes, too afraid to open my mouth. "Well, OK then," he said, puzzled by my muteness. "You seem to be the captain of this expedition. And since you're the captain, where would you like me to dig, sir?"

I fought back a full-blown smile and instead merely smirked at his silliness. I stepped a few feet up the nearby ridge and pointed in the direction of our old fort. "Over there," I finally said.

"Yes, sir!" he replied, giving me a salute.

While Phillip headed uphill, I dragged my shovel behind me as I made my way to the same patch I had been drawn to the day before. I gripped the handle and took a deep breath. I began by carefully removing the topsoil around the outer edges before digging out the center.

While I worked, I could see Phillip on top of the hill out of the corner of my eye. When I stopped to catch my breath, I turned to look at him directly. His blond hair was in his eyes. Sweat made it stick to his forehead. He pulled a tuft of it behind his ear. Like Everett, he was strong and unafraid of hard work. I could hear his light grunts as he forced his shovel into the tough ground. "It's nothing but clay up here!" he yelled to me. Embarrassed that he only called out because he had noticed me watching him, I swiftly turned away, pretending his voice hadn't carried to me.

Everett blew my cover when he shouted from his much farther distance, "Same over here!"

Keeping my back to Phillip, I let the forest's solitude soothe my mind as I worked. I thought of its animals: the rabbits in the bushes, the owls watching from high in the trees, the foxes darting in and out of their holes, and the deer stepping up to one of the ponds for a drink. And then I thought of the bones of small animals that littered the ground below the tree where the hawk had her nest, the rotting logs that would eventually turn to soil and be reabsorbed by the earth, the sprouting mushrooms fueled by all the decay— and of the woman I dug for who lay trapped underground.

"Ayden!" Phillip whispered down the hill. "Be quiet!"

At first, I feared that I had been thinking aloud and that he was requesting my silence. Yet as I turned to face him, I found myself locking eyes with a deer that stood between us. It was a doe with a flawless tan coat. Her right ear twisted to focus on Everett's shovel slicing into the earth in the distance, while her left ear homed in on the subtle movements Phillip was trying so hard not to make behind her. Her large, black eyes stared into mine. When I looked into her eyes, I felt a connection. It was as if she wasn't an animal at all, but a human in an animal's body—or as if I were a deer in a human's body. She was a part of the nature that surrounded us. And being in the forest I knew so intimately, I was a part of it as well. I gently set down my shovel and stepped forward.

"What're you doing!" Phillip whispered.

I reached out my hand and took another step forward. And the doe too stepped forward. "It's OK," I assured her. Slowly we closed the gap between us. Up close, I examined her dark hooves and the patches of white that painted her neck and belly. I lightly placed the back of my hand to the stiff hairs of her neck. I stroked her softly as I continued looking into her eyes. She was the part of nature that was innocent. Pure. The essence of goodness.

Phillip, no longer able to keep his volume at a whisper, slipped out a "Holy shit!" in amazement. Spooked by his outburst, she perked up her head and backed away from me.

"What is it!" Everett yelled. He burst through the branches, crunching twigs as he rushed toward us. "What'd you find!" The startled doe crouched on her hind legs and sprang into the air. She leapt past me and darted through the woods. I spun to see her white tail bobbing between the trees. Phillip and I watched as she disappeared into the field.

"Did you see that!" Phillip called to Everett, nearing us. Phillip climbed down the hill, and the three of us met in the middle of our dig sites. "A deer came out of nowhere, walked right up to Ayden — and then he petted the damn thing. It didn't even flinch!"

Everett looked to me with a stone face. "Is this true?" he asked. I gave him a half smile and a shrug. He closed his eyes and wiped the sweat from his forehead. "It wasn't a wild deer," he sighed.

"What do you mean it wasn't wild? It came right from the trees," said Phillip.

"There's a deer farm over on Lincoln Avenue," he explained. "They're tame. We used to ride our bikes over there and feed them all the time. One must've gotten loose is all."

I could see the exhilaration drain from Phillip's face. "We *did* used to ride our bikes there," I confirmed, although I was certain the deer farm had closed years before.

"Forget about that," said Everett. "While you two were busy playing with farm animals, *I* actually found something." Phillip and I followed Everett back to his site. Behind the beech tree, a pile of dirt mixed with chunks of heavy clay sat beside a pit several feet deep and several feet wide. "There." Everett pointed. At the bottom of his pit was a yellowish-brown object jutting from the clay. "I didn't want to bust it so I stopped digging."

Phillip got on his knees and peered into the pit for a closer look. I laughed to myself seeing that his *church-boy* corduroys were covered in dirt up to his shins. "That's a root," he announced.

"No," Everett contested. "That's what I thought at first too. And then I thought it was an old beer bottle. But it's not. Feel it." Phillip jumped into the pit and felt the object for himself. Not satisfied, he began removing the surrounding clay. Everett took out his switchblade and joined Phillip. As Phillip used his fingers, Everett used his knife to scrape away the heavy clay. After a few minutes, Everett held up the dislodged thing for us to see. It looked like some kind of thick seashell. One end was curved, with a thick outer rim, while the other end was jagged.

"Is it bone?" I asked.

Everett nodded. "It looks human."

"Now let's not get delusional," warned Phillip as he raised himself out of the pit. "It's *not* a human bone. It couldn't be. Not out in the woods."

"Why couldn't it be?" questioned Everett.

"Because—I'm sure it's an animal bone. I'm sure these woods, just like every other woods in the world, is loaded with animal bones. This is where animals live. And this is where they die." He pointed toward the field behind our house. "And didn't you say there used to be a cow pasture over there? Some sick old cow probably came a-wandering into these woods, sat her fat ass down, and died right here. What we are looking at is a cow bone, gentlemen," Phillip argued.

"It's *not* a cow bone," Everett insisted as he examined it carefully. "It looks like a piece of a hip bone to me—a human hip bone."

"Oh? Now it's a hip bone? OK, Mr. Anatomy, whose hip bone do you think it is?" Phillip asked.

"Mr. Peterson's a murderer," I declared softly.

"Now slow down, Sherlock," advised Phillip. Yet despite his skepticism, I could see something change in him. It was a twinge of fear. I knew how he felt. I felt it too. It meant my dream was a reality. It meant the woods was in fact littered with dozens of dead bodies.

"We need to keep digging in the other spots to find out if there's more," suggested Everett. "Phillip, how far down did you get?"

"Few feet."

"Ayden, grab your shovel," he ordered. "With the three of us digging, we'll get deeper faster."

Although the clay became thicker the deeper we dug, we quickly widened and deepened Phillip's pit. We dug until the hole was up to our knees, until it was roughly the same depth as Everett's. We dug until I heard Everett yell, "Stop!"

And there it was. We found ourselves looking upon another bone protruding from the earth. The piece of rounded bone was the same yellowish-brown as the bone in Everett's pit. As Everett and Phillip again scraped away the thick clay, I watched the bone slowly emerge from obscurity and into frightening recognition. First, two sunken holes directly apart from each other appeared, followed by a third, slender hole centered beneath them. The rounded portion that had been jutting through the clay became the forehead. And when they uncovered the upper jaw, there was no mistaking that what stared back at me were the empty eye sockets of a human skull. Each time I blinked, the vision of the skull was transposed with visions of the frozen faces in my dream.

Phillip scrambled out of the pit in a panic. "OK. I see what's going on now," he said, his arm trembling as he pointed at me. "You told us where to dig. And we just *happened* to find bones in those spots. Obviously, this joke's on me," he concluded. "Right?"

Everett let out a sigh. "He was *guessing* when he told us where to dig."

"It didn't seem like he was guessing."

"Well, he was," Everett vowed. "I was just letting him pick the spots for shits and giggles. So either he got lucky. Or, for all we know, there are skeletons buried under every square inch of these woods, and it wouldn't have mattered where we dug."

As they argued, I climbed out of the grave and peered down the hill. Though an ambitious start given the size of the area I was attempting to excavate, I had barely uncovered a foot. We had found bones. The people in my dream were real. Surely she'd be there. She *had* to be. Her light was the brightest of them all.

"Why don't you let him speak?" Phillip demanded.

"Fine. Ayden, tell Phillip you didn't know about the bones. That we didn't plant them."

But I wasn't even registering their dispute. I had already started down the hill, dragging my shovel behind me as I headed for the clearing.

"Ayden!" snapped Everett.

I turned back. "We have to dig for her," I said apologetically.

He was startled for a moment by my open reference to the dream. Yet instead of becoming angry, he simply nodded in acknowledgment and grabbed his shovel. At that point, with the discovery of human remains, he no doubt found whatever caused me to be so emphatic worth exploring. Phillip followed reluctantly. "This is batshit," he muttered.

We dug with ferocity. Even Phillip, questioning our truthfulness, did not let that compromise his contribution. With each shovelful, I could feel us getting closer to the frozen woman. I knew she was there just waiting to be freed. I pictured her beautiful hair flowing round her head as if it were her aura.

"Easy now," advised Everett as the pit became knee-deep. We removed chunks of clay in individual portions, careful not to damage any bone that might've been just beneath. We dug that way for what seemed like an hour, until the edge of the pit nearly met our hips. We were exhausted, but Everett could tell by my relentlessness that it was important we continue.

Phillip, however, failed to see the point. He slowed his efforts until he finally pitched his shovel aboveground and rested against the dirt wall. "There's nothing here," he moaned, wiping the back of his soiled arm across his forehead.

"Please," I begged. "Just a little deeper."

But after some time, even Everett laid down his shovel. He placed his hand on my shoulder. "We've been digging for almost an hour." He then leaned in and whispered, "Maybe she's in another spot."

"But she was right here!" Frustrated, I hurled my shovel out of the pit. Where could she have been? If my dream had been right about the other bodies, why wasn't she there?

Yet I didn't have long to contemplate how the frozen woman had evaded me. Suddenly, we heard footsteps. Fierce and deliberate, they crashed through the woods and charged toward us. We cowered in the pit, peering over its edge. "Who the hell is in my woods!" a hoarse voice bellowed. Intent on pursuing his trespassers, he marched straight past the grave holding the unearthed skull. The old man stomped his way down the hill, trampling the mayapple in his path. He wore a camouflage jacket and orange hunting cap. His face sagged with age, but he remained a strong, powerful man.

"That's Mr. Peterson," I whispered to Phillip.

"The murderer," added Everett before defiantly climbing out of the pit to face him. "We found your bodies, you murderer!" he shouted at the old man. "You're gonna die in prison!"

Our hiding spot divulged, Phillip and I reluctantly scurried from the pit. "Shut the fuck up," Phillip whispered tersely to Everett. "Let's just get the hell out of here."

It wasn't until we stood aboveground that I noticed Mr. Peterson held a shotgun at his side. "You fuckers better get the hell off my land!" he roared, raising the gun. With its barrel aimed directly at us, Everett and I took Phillip's advice—and ran. The three of us tore out of the woods, leaving our shovels behind. "That's it! Run! Goddamned pieces of shit! Get the hell outta here!" he croaked.

With my heart leaping out of my chest, we escaped the trees and ran through the field. My legs were rubber by the time we reached the house. Dirt shook from our shoes and clothes as we rushed down the basement steps in a stampede. Everett shut the door to his weight room behind us. Still panting, he picked up the phone. "I'm calling the police," he announced.

Phillip looked as if he was going to protest but did not. He instead collapsed on our old foldout couch. I sat next to him, exhausted and exhilarated at once, listening as Everett described our grim discovery in the woods.

8
LiGHTNiNG BUGS

By uncovering the bones, I imagined we had solved countless murders. But Mom wasn't the least impressed. She made it clear she wasn't thrilled with the idea of our digging holes in the woods, especially when it led to us being chased by a man aiming a shotgun at the back of our heads. So instead of being treated like heroes, we were immediately grounded. And not just a normal grounding—a *confined to our rooms* grounding. Everett was given additional lectures for putting me in danger and for not calling to warn she'd be greeted after work to the scene of Everett, Phillip, and me in the back of a squad car. Everett'd have to endure similar lectures when Dad was home on Sunday.

But by the very next afternoon, I found myself peering over the driveway at a police cruiser and two officers talking to Mom—and Everett. *Of course* Everett was out there. He had a way of defying our parents' orders. He could talk his way out of—or into—just about anything.

I cracked open my window in hopes of hearing why the police had stopped by unannounced, but the wind swept their voices away. Mom looked weary. Her graying, brunette hair was tousled by the wind. She nervously pinched her bottom lip as she listened to the officers. Everett wore his baseball cap. I couldn't see his face. At one point, he looked up to me and flashed a smile. I opened my hand in a still wave. One of the officers noticed Everett's gesture and gazed up to my window. His large, mirrored sunglasses made him look like a humanoid bug. I quickly closed the blinds and retreated to my bed.

After what seemed like an hour, I heard the doors to the police car slam. Not a moment later, Everett bounded into my room. "You're not supposed to be in here," I reminded him.

"Oh. OK. I'll leave," he replied and performed an about-face.

"Get back here," I commanded with a laugh. "So did they arrest Mr. Peterson yet?"

"Mr. Peterson's—not going to be arrested."

"Why not!"

He picked up an arrowhead off my desk that I found while walking the cornfields. I found it just before the planting season, when the ground had been freshly cultivated. I collected several of the carved spears that day. The rest of the collection was in a jar somewhere in the basement.

"It turns out he didn't kill those people."

"Who did then?"

"No one. Well, some could've died in a battle, I guess. But most probably just died of old age. Or got sick maybe. The skeletons we dug up—were Indians."

"*Indians?*"

He handed me the arrowhead. I felt the dulled yet still jagged edges along the sides of the stone before placing the tip of my finger on the point. I imagined an Indian from another time using other rocks as tools to chip and carve the stone into a weapon, making it sharp enough to kill an animal or perhaps a rival from another tribe if necessary.

"The mounds we used to play on—turns out they're actually burial mounds. The police sent some experts into the woods. Even though the bones are probably a couple hundred years old, they're preserved so well because of the ground being mostly clay."

"Are they going to dig for the others?"

"No. They're just going to do some testing to see if they can date the bones and find out what tribe they're from. Right now, they're guessing Ottawa. Or Chippewa. But they don't really know for sure. The police contacted some Native American association that deals with this stuff. And they want the bones left where they are. They don't have much of a say in it, though, because it's private land. But they got Mr. Peterson to agree not to mess with the graves."

"Oh my God. You called him a murderer!"

"Yeah. Tell me about it."

"Are we going to be arrested?"

"No. We're not going to be arrested. And he's not going to press charges for our trespassing—for now at least. But he's made it damn clear we're not to go on his land. Ever again." My heart was broken. Knowing it was Indians buried underground, I could stop obsessing over the frozen woman. But the woods was a part of me. I couldn't imagine never being able to slip through to the other side of the grape leaves again. "We'll go back. We just have to let this blow over," Everett promised, sensing my dismay.

"I don't know what possessed you two to start digging out in those woods. But you've sure caused a lot of trouble for Mr. Peterson," Mom scolded from the doorway. "You know he hates anyone stepping foot on his property. Yet you just had to provoke him. He's an old man, you know. He was questioned by police. And now he has all this ruckus going on in his woods."

"But we thought he was a murderer," I countered.

"Well, you're lucky he's not. I can tell you that." She took notice of the sleeping bag beside my bed that Everett used from time to time so he'd be near me when I woke. She began rolling it up. "I'm covering Gloria's day shift tomorrow. I have to be up early, so I want you two in bed soon." She held the sleeping bag tight under her arm while pointing at Everett. "No sleepovers tonight. Got it?"

"Sure thing, Mom," Everett replied in an extra syrupy voice.

"I've caused so much trouble," I moaned as soon as she was gone.

"She's pissed. But she'll cool down in a couple days," he assured. "She always does."

"I should've known those were Indians buried in the woods. I should've known Mr. Peterson didn't murder anyone."

"Go easy on yourself. How could you have known? You can't expect to decode everything in your dreams. I asked you to focus on finding the coins. And you found them, which proves you're getting more accurate. And . . ." He leaned in close to make sure I was paying attention. "You're also getting stronger. Those bodies you found, I didn't ask you to look for them. But there they were, buried in the woods. Don't you see? It doesn't matter if those skeletons belonged to Indians or if they *were* people Mr. Peterson murdered. The important thing is you saw them in your dream, and they were there for real."

"I guess."

"And there's something else. Do you remember those lightning bugs when we were kids?"

It seemed like such a random thing for him to bring up at that moment. But I nodded, thinking back to Everett and me camping in the backyard. Just before bed, I watched a lone lightning bug flicker its yellowish-green glowing abdomen from across the lawn. As I dozed off, I allowed my mind to replay the blinking light. I focused on it floating its way through a dark night. And as I slipped into a dream, the lone twinkle multiplied into hundreds of flickering lights. I was lost in the calming twinkles when Everett shook me awake. He peeled back the flap of the tent, and I saw a cluster of the same glowing lights that were in my dream. The bugs hovered just outside the entrance of the tent, flashing like Christmas lights in July.

"Well, I've been trying to find a way to go beyond dreams," continued Everett. "And then yesterday and the day before, I've seen you go so far beyond."

"What do you mean?"

"Those lightning bugs were nothing compared to those cats—and that deer."

"But those cats," I protested, stunned, "they were probably just hunting mice in the field. And that deer—it was just an animal in the woods."

"What did you say you wanted to see when you had your eyes closed in the field?"

"Cats."

"And what were you thinking just before you saw that deer?"

I tried to remember my thoughts as I dug in the clearing, just before Phillip alerted me to the presence of the doe. "The forest. The animals," I answered. Everett didn't say another word, allowing me to fully absorb his point.

9
MONSTERS IN THE CORN

It was a warm and windy night. We stood in the side yard boxed in by the enormous blue spruces along the side of the house and those that lined the edge of the property. Everett kept his arms folded as he gazed up to our parents' bedroom window. My attention was instead drawn to the pines behind us, creating an ever-present roar as wind rushed between their needles. In the near darkness, with their limbs bowing and swaying, they resembled an ink drawing that had become animated.

"Light's finally out," Everett reported, calling my attention back to the window. Before I knew it, he darted off into the darkness of the backyard. "C'mon!"

Only the distant light atop Mr. Newberry's pole barn allowed us to see faintly into the summer night. We rushed past the small garden. The tall sunflowers, densely packed sweet corn, and cherry tomato plants thrashed in the wind. The wind felt charged. Electric. As it flowed up and under my T-shirt, causing it to flap against my stomach and chest, it felt as though it were transferring its energy to me. My pupils grew to take in as much of the night as possible. Staring wide-eyed into the infinite darkness with an energy flowing through me that seemed impossible to deplete, I felt like an animal.

I felt compelled to run and leap into the darkness all through the night.

We ran side by side through the field and cut toward the corn. The tall stalks thrashed high over our heads. "What're we doing out here?" I wondered.

"Experimenting," he replied. "Like in the field with the cats."

In my manic state, I offered myself up bravely without hesitation. "What do you want me to do?"

"Just stay close. And stay low," he answered, hunching over as we slipped farther into the corn. "We've got to keep hidden."

"Hidden from who? Mom and Dad don't even know we're out here. And no way Mr. Newberry's out here in the middle of the night."

"Not from *who*. From *what*," he corrected. "We're not hiding from Mom and Dad. Or Mr. Newberry. We're hiding—from monsters." A strong mix of fear—and curiously, excitement— rushed over me. But I was still profoundly confused. "The monsters from your bedroom walls," he clarified.

My heart leapt to my throat as my mind instantly brought forth the mesh of figures he spoke of. Thick horns protruding where ears should've been. Wide grins boasting elongated, sharp teeth. Skulls too stretched to be human, with hollow, unevenly sloped eyes. Unnaturally twisted and melted faces.

These were the imprints etched into the cheap paneling in my room, at least what I saw when looking at the twists and knots of the faux wood. The awful pattern repeated itself throughout the room, multiplying the grotesque monsters thirty or so times. My bed was pushed against the wall. And during the day, when I felt safe, I'd use my finger to trace their shapes. But at night, I'd turn my back to them, praying they'd remain contained inside the two-dimensional pattern. When I was younger, I'd line up what I considered to be my most brave stuffed animals between myself and the wall. They were my soldiers, my protection were the monsters ever to reach for me in the night.

"They're real," declared Everett, his voice low and serious. "And after all this time, they're loose. They've finally escaped your walls. Didn't you see them behind us as we ran? They were hot on our heels. They chased us from the house and through the yard. We've lost them for now. But they could be anywhere. The field. The woods. The cornfield. Do you hear that?" He appeared startled as stalks whipped behind us.

I told myself that Everett was only pretending. That the stalks were only moving because of the wind. Regardless, I stuck close to him. And then I began to wonder. If I allowed myself to believe what Everett was saying was true, then based on their impressions on my wall, the monsters, in their true flesh and at their full statures, would no doubt be terrifying menaces. "Let's go back to the house," I pleaded in a whisper.

He shook his head. "There's no going back. I told you. They're right behind us."

"But Mom and Dad are still at the house. What about them?"

"Eaten by now, I bet."

"Not funny." But Everett's face was grim. He was concentrating, taking in the danger. He fed on it. Finding hidden treasure and watching me play with affectionate cats wasn't enough. He craved something more. Something darker.

"Over there!" He pointed deep into the stalks. I peered down the row. It sounded like a zipper being swiftly pulled up and then down as I caught a flash of something slipping between the leaves. I wasn't sure what it was. All I knew at that point was that I was petrified. A moment later, I saw it again down another row. Leaves curled around it and then released as it streaked by, causing the zipping noise. It was circling us. In front of us one moment. Alongside us the next. As we huddled together, Everett warned, "We'd better get outta here and head for the center of the cornfield."

Before I could ask what was at the center of the cornfield, the grouping of stalks before us peeled apart. The stalks were clenched in tight bunches—by two giant fists. Each finger was the size of a human arm. No flesh covered the enormous hands. Instead, they were raw bone. Although I didn't want to, I couldn't stop myself from gazing upward. I was both terrified and in awe as its colossal skull lowered before us, its exposed prey. Its chin protruded well into its chest. Its jaws, lined with massive teeth, jutted upward in a dramatic slant that gave it a sinister, frozen smile. It did not have eyes, but rather two large, uneven openings, which allowed us to see into the back of its hollow head.

As its massive frame stood, it easily uprooted the cornstalks still in its grip. We were showered with dirt and rocks. The mammoth skeleton creature towered over us as tall as the tallest tree in the woods. I couldn't move. I was transfixed by its bright bones glowing against the black night. It was larger and more terrifying than I could've possibly ever imagined. And just when I thought it couldn't be any more intimidating, it began producing a low moan. I couldn't be sure if its moaning was something it produced consciously, or if it was simply created by the wind rushing through its gaping nasal cavity and vacant eye sockets.

It crossed its heavy arms. When it uncrossed them, stretching its limbs to their full length, it released its grip, and the stalks were flung clear across the cornfield in opposite directions. With its hands free, the creature swung for us. Everett ducked. But I stood in frozen amazement, watching the gigantic hand brushing through the tops of the stalks like a tidal wave careening straight for me. Just before I was about to be obliterated, Everett tackled me from behind. Still on the ground, he repeated his command: "Run for the center of the field!" He motioned for me to follow before launching into a mad sprint.

Intending to launch into my own sprint, I scrambled to my feet—only to find the skeleton's tree-trunk-size legs blocking my path. I attempted to run around it. It swiveled on its hips, its long limbs reaching for me. When I broke out of my semicircle, I ran ahead as fast as I could. But I didn't get far. Its powerful hand clamped on to my shoulders. Its fingers curled over my chest. And my head was wedged between its thumb and forefinger.

I screamed for Everett, who turned back to the terrifying sight of me being dragged backward through the stalks. He ran beside me, furiously attempting to pry off the giant fingers. But it was no use. When the monster finally halted, it lowered its menacing jawbone and began lifting me to its mouth. Everett leapt through the air and grabbed hold of my torso. As we dangled, he used his weight to repeatedly jerk downward. He was able to loosen the monster's grip just enough, and I slipped from its fingers. We crashed to the ground, my cheek planted firmly in the dirt.

By the time we flipped onto our backs, the skeleton was standing over us. It swung its arms high over its head. Like a swinging pirate-ship ride at a carnival, its fists paused a moment at the highest point before plummeting back down with deadly force. As it dropped its fists over us with every intent of pulverizing and pounding our remains deep into the ground, we quickly rolled in separate directions. The massive fists smashed to the earth. The monster struggled to dislodge its fists half-buried in craters created by the forceful impact.

Everett sprang to his feet. Using both hands, he grabbed one of the fists. He appeared to help the skeleton free its limb from the ground. But before the creature could gain control, he yanked with all his strength. The tall monster jerked forward. Everett yanked again. And again. And on the fourth yank, its arm ripped straight out of its shoulder socket. The giant limb collapsed like a falling tree.

The angry skeleton thrust its bulky frame backward, freeing its remaining arm. It then lunged forward and swiped at Everett. But Everett was quick to jump out of its path. The creature's forward move, combined with the loss of its appendage, caused it to become unbalanced. Everett took advantage of its wobbling legs. He pushed the creature—and it toppled over. As it collapsed, several of its ribs cracked. The battered skeleton thrashed in the corn, attempting to stand. But before it could even sit upright, Everett rushed to its skull. He grunted while repeatedly kicking its frozen, sneering face. He kicked until its hollow head cracked to pieces and collapsed into itself. He kicked until the skeleton was nothing more than a feeble pile of bones.

We had vanquished our first monster but had no time to celebrate. Soon, we heard the distinct zipping sound of thick bone curling the corn leaves. All we had to do was look up to confirm the terrible discovery: a second skeleton stalked us from its towering vantage. It wasted no time swinging for our heads. Everett quickly spun and grabbed the dislodged limb behind us. He held it over his head like a massive sword. When the colossal bones collided, the force threw Everett to the ground. Yet his quick thinking saved us from certain double decapitation.

With his new weapon, Everett went on the offensive. He got back to his feet and charged the skeleton, forcing it back a few rows. The skeleton, enraged by Everett's resourcefulness, raised its arms. A burst of strong wind rushed through its hollow head, allowing it to roar into the night. Everett wielded his weapon awkwardly yet managed to block the monster's blows.

"There's a craft in the middle of the cornfield!" he shouted as I cowered behind him.

"A craft?"

"If we can make it, we can use it to fight them. Find it! I'll meet you there! Go!" he instructed as giant bone clashed with giant bone.

I didn't want to leave his side. But reluctantly I did as he said and ran up the slope. I knew when the ground leveled off, I'd be somewhere near the center of the field. I only looked back once. The sight of the giant creature swiping at the severed arm, controlled by an unseen force beneath the stalks, was hauntingly surreal.

10
THE CRAFT

My night vision was at its most keen at that point, leading me through the dark maze of corn. I neared the top of the slope, anxious to begin my search for the mysterious craft Everett spoke of. But as I charged tenaciously through the stalks, I felt as if I had been abruptly punched in the gut. Whatever I had collided with was forceful enough to knock me on my back, and I collapsed into a thick bevy of stalks. Covered in a blanket of the rough leaves, I didn't dare move, unknowing what dark entity had bowled me over and was lurking just on the other side of my thin cover.

Without warning, the stalks nearest my feet were torn away. I peered down the tunnel of overlapping stalks—and a new monster was revealed. Compared to the statuesque skeleton creature, this monster was the size of a three-year-old child. It had stubby, muscular legs. Black horns, wide and thick at the base, curved upward from each side of its head before narrowing to points. It stared directly at me, its wide eyes glowing a dim shade of red. It grinned with a disturbingly large mouth, filled with razor-sharp teeth, that stretched from one side of its face to the other.

I was paralyzed with fear. And it knew this. It savored my undivided attention. My reaction was what it craved as it lifted one of its long, thin fingers, opened its mouth, and stuffed the finger all the way to the back of its throat. It then clamped its jaws. As I squirmed, it slowly dragged its finger through its clenched teeth. I could hear its bones crushing. With its lips curled upward, the monster seemed to relish the pain. It held its unblinking gaze on me as green blood squirted between its teeth and oozed down its chin.

With its mangled finger hanging limp, it boldly stepped up on my legs, balancing itself without breaking its intimidating stare. In excruciatingly slow movements, it began stepping its way up my legs. When it reached my stomach, I took short breaths, trying to sustain its weight with as little motion as possible. And when it reached my chest, it squatted, looking at me as it bared its sadistic smile. Up close, I could see that its flesh was moldy green and that its body was full of scars and bite marks.

It covered its face with the hand it had not desecrated. It then displayed its pointy fingers to me the way a mime might—by slowly unfurling them over its eyes until each digit was subsequently tucked under its chin in a dramatic fashion. It repeated this gesture several times. Its movements were so slow, so delicate, yet held the subliminal threat of it turning ferocious at any moment. I wanted to call out, but fear caused my throat to close up. I could barely breathe as it lowered its face close to mine and opened its drooling mouth.

I suspected a single bite from those jaws could've easily taken off my head. Just as I was about to find out for sure, I felt a tug under my arms. I had been grabbed and suddenly found myself being dragged backward. I looked up to see Everett. He had of course won his duel with the second skeleton creature and had come to rescue me from the horned devil.

The monster lost its balance and fell off my chest. But as Everett heroically attempted to pull me to safety, it quickly latched on to my ankles. When Everett saw the monster clawing its way up my thrashing legs, he dropped my shoulders and kicked the evil thing in the face. It tumbled backward. When it came out of its somersault, it assumed a curious stance: it sat frozen, with its legs folded. It held its hands beside its horns, its fingers clenched in a clawing position—one dangling, wilted finger naturally not cooperating.

Everett bravely approached the creature, which appeared to be in some sort of meditative state. Yet the idea that it focused on peaceful thoughts was highly dubious. Everett raised his foot, intending to stomp its head while he had a clear shot. But the demon simply tilted back its neck and opened its massive jaws. Everett, luckily, was able to retract his leg before its bear-trap-of-a-mouth clamped on to his foot.

As it remained in its strangely serene yet disturbing pose, we very cautiously stepped past the monster. As soon as we put the distance of a few rows between us and it, we took off running up the remainder of the slope. Fearful it had been compelled to follow, I looked over my shoulder. Much to my horror, our situation had become much grimmer. Not just one, but a dozen pairs of red eyes flickered behind us, multiplying as we ran.

Everett stopped abruptly. We had made it to the center of the cornfield. I knew exactly where we were. It was the spot where the pile of old rusted farm machinery sat that we used to play on. Except on that night, as we peeled back the surrounding stalks, the equipment was no longer there. *Something* was, however. It was as if the old tractors and plows had reconfigured and transformed themselves—into some type of futuristic spacecraft. Just like Everett had promised, I found myself standing before a craft that silently hovered a few feet above the ground. About the size of a car, the metallic machine was oval, with a darkened window slanted down its front.

Overlapping growls permeated the surrounding stalks. Red eyes glowed all around us. Slowly, the group of horned monsters emerged. With haunting grins plastered across their faces, they began to encircle us.

Everett placed his hand on the metal craft. Beside it, a numeric keypad lit up. He looked into my eyes and in an encouraging voice said, "You know the code. Punch it in." How could I possibly know the code? But I nodded anyhow and punched in the first set of numbers that popped into my head: 27-16-08. I didn't know where the numbers came from. But they came to me quickly, like I had known them all along. The keypad blinked twice, and after a few seconds, a hatch opened vertically. The monsters stepped closer as Everett and I slipped inside. They were patient, curious about our attempts to elude them. On the inside was a large red button next to the hatch. I immediately slapped it with my palm, and the hatch shut as quickly as it had opened.

We found ourselves in an air lock of sorts, pressed together in the tiny space. Buttons and blinking lights covered the walls. I spotted a keypad similar to the one outside the craft. I punched in the code, and a second, internal hatch opened. I was first to enter the main compartment. The space was cramped. It was like being on the top half of a bunk bed that was too close to the ceiling. I crawled across the floor, made of a white foam material, and lay on my stomach in one of the two grooves. The foam adjusted to comfortably fit my body. Everett slid into his groove next to the hatch. He slapped a second red button, which sealed us into the main compartment.

In front of us was the window, allowing us to see horned monsters continuing to emerge from the corn. As they approached the clearing, they stepped slowly over fallen stalks and clumps of dirt without looking to their feet. It was as if somehow they had memorized, or inherently knew, every inch and subtlety of the land. Some stepped, holding their hands beside their horns in a clawing position like the first horned monster we encountered. Others sat with their pointy fingers folded in front of them. Yet each stared intently, unblinking, at the floating machine.

Beneath the window was a panel slanted toward us. It was full of levers, buttons, and three screens. I touched one of the screens, and it crackled to life. In popped an enhanced image of the cornfield, allowing us to see in the dark. I tapped the other two screens and realized that one gave us the view from behind the craft, while the other two covered the sides.

With the horned monsters gathered in a tight grouping around the craft, three new skeleton creatures lumbered just behind them. I shuddered at the group of sadistic beings. The thick horns. The razor teeth. The colossal hollow skulls with sloped eyes. Everett had been right. The monsters from my wall *had* come to life. They were real. And they had us surrounded.

Ready for the taste of our meat, the horned monsters began dragging their sharp fingertips across the metal, creating wince-inducing screeches. I used the knob below one of the monitors to adjust the camera's angle. Demons clustered outside the hatch. They scratched at it like rabid dogs, determined to get inside.

Everett randomly grabbed a control on his side of the dashboard that looked like a joystick. He yanked it to the left, and the vehicle swung sharply to the left. The monsters nearest the craft were bashed in the head as it rotated. Some dug their claws into the metal and held on, their legs dragging over the trampled stalks. The vehicle stopped abruptly when Everett let up on the control.

The sudden movement invigorated the monsters. Those at the back of the pack began pushing their way forward, smashing the others against the metal. Eager to join in, the skeleton monsters hoisted their long arms over their heads. They took turns hammering the roof with their gigantic fists. The craft rocked. The ceiling began to cave. Between the sharp claws tearing into the metal and the powerful pelts overhead, I feared that the craft would split in two.

Everett tried again to rotate us. But the craft wouldn't budge against the horde of muscular fiends. He furiously flipped switches, turned knobs, and punched buttons. They seemed to have no effect—until he reached a row of small red buttons. When he touched the first one, a beam of white light shot out from beneath the craft. The beam exploded the horned monsters in its path before colliding with the leg of a skeleton, pulverizing it into thousands of tiny fragments. The giant creature teetered backward, then forward. It sounded like a shower of bricks as it collapsed directly onto the craft. It was still for a moment, draped over the roof. I figured it was dead. But then it began to convulse, kicking and pounding, moaning in fury as it tried to dislodge itself. Its knee jerked into the glass, and the window began to splinter.

Everett tried the next red button. I watched on the monitor as the slew of horned monsters surrounding the hatch were blown away. A surviving demon had one of its horns seared off by the laser. It chuckled to itself, amused as it ran its finger along the still-smoldering remnants. It then chewed on the finger, apparently enjoying the charred flavor.

Everett madly punched all four red buttons simultaneously. Powerful beams shot from all sides of the craft. The resulting chaos and bloodshed worked the monsters into a fury of violence. They hurled their bodies at the craft. And as the rapid-fire lasers turned them into bursts of green gristle, more rushed forward to take their place. On one of the screens, I noticed several of the horned monsters had learned to evade the ammunition. Using their sharp fingertips, they climbed their way above the firing lasers. Clinging to the craft, they tilted their heads and used their strong horns to slice into the already weakened hatch. "They're breaking through!" I shouted.

Everett glanced at the monitor, nodded, and then took a chance by slowly pulling one of the levers on the dash. The craft hummed—and began to rise. He pulled back the lever until we rose well above the corn, until the skeletons could barely reach us. Their knuckles clanked ominously yet harmlessly beneath the craft.

Finally, safe from the monsters in the corn, Everett pushed another lever forward, and the craft propelled forward. Using a combination of the levers, he was able to manipulate our thrust and altitude. And he learned he could steer with the joystick he had discovered earlier that made us spin. After a bit of practice, he maneuvered the craft gracefully through the night sky. As we flew above the field, we could see over the woods and the darkened neighborhood. I looked to the roof of our house and wondered what had become of Mom and Dad. Had a skeleton monster punched through the window and snatched them out of bed? Had a group of horned monsters converged upon them in their sleep?

Everett spun us back toward the center of the field. As we passed over the drove of monsters, he tilted the craft on its side, tossing off the cracked skeleton. As it fell, its long arms reached back for the craft. And when it slammed to the ground, it crushed a half dozen horned monsters and pinned others. Everett dropped the craft to a low altitude and swooped over the monsters again. This time, he fired the craft's front laser at one of the skeleton monsters until it exploded into a million bits. We flew through the powdered mist of pulverized bone before returning for another pass.

Next, he went after the heaviest concentration of horned monsters. He relentlessly fired on the beasts, transforming the field into a grotesque eruption of green flesh and innards. The lone skeleton creature raced to the far edge of the field in retreat. The horned monsters, however, enjoyed the carnage. They stood on their dead to get a closer look at the craft passing overhead. Everett too was enjoying himself. His tongue darted from his mouth as he rolled us into sharp turns. He yelped with glee when he landed a direct hit with the lasers.

Despite our victories in the field below, I was startled to realize that three horned monsters had managed to cling to the craft. I could see them on the monitor. Even as their legs dangled in midair, they continued to saw through the metal with their powerful horns. I nudged Everett and pointed to the screen. We watched as one of the demons used its sharp fingers to widen the gashes before finally busting its head inside the hatch. The monster behind it bunted it inside. Both disappeared from the screen as they entered the air lock. As the third monster crammed in its head, its horns became wedged in the tight opening. Stuck, it writhed in frustration.

Everett dipped the machine just below the tops of the stalks and slowed to a crawl. The monsters below gathered excitedly beneath the hovering craft. The sight of the stuck demon's twisting body drove them into a frenzy. They jumped, swiping and grabbing at its legs. We could hear its angry growls on the other side of the metal door as its own kind clawed and pulled. That is, until its neck snapped and its body was torn from its head. The monsters below converged upon its headless torso like a pack of sharks, devouring it with much jubilance. As Everett pulled us up and away, he grinned devilishly at his own ingenuity.

The monsters in the air lock bashed their horns against the internal hatch. I was terrified knowing they were just on the other side of the metal door. It bulged from their ferocious efforts. When the tip of a black horn sliced through, I clamped my hand on Everett's arm. "Do something!" I begged.

Everett pounded back at them. "C'mon!" he taunted. "Come and get us!" Thin, green fingers poked through the perforations in the metal. Grabbing hold, they tugged furiously, uncaring that their flesh was being sliced open.

"They're getting in!" I bellowed, my fright reaching its crescendo.

Everett casually piloted the craft looking straight ahead. It was as if he had little concern about the monsters shredding through the door just beside him. "They're not inside yet," he coolly replied.

Their red eyes glowed through the gashes. They were at the peak of their excitement, smelling us, knowing in just moments they'd be disemboweling and eating us alive. One finally burst through the shredded barrier. Its head crashed into the cockpit mere inches from Everett's face. Its horns were chipped and splintered. Green blood trickled from its dented forehead. It didn't make a sound. It greeted us only with its unbreakable, sinister grin. I broke into a sudden sweat and began to hyperventilate. All I wanted was to turn my back on the monsters the way I could when they were trapped in my wall. But having escaped, they would no longer be so easy to elude.

It stretched its neck forward while unclenching its oversize mandible and displaying its full set of equally oversize sharp teeth. It drooled hungrily, eyeing Everett's smooth neck. He had to have felt its hot and foul breath. Yet Everett paid the monster no mind.

He continued looking to the horizon, where the dark outline of the trees met the night sky. At that moment, he may have seemed careless with our lives. But even amid my panic, I trusted Everett completely.

"Hold on," he finally instructed. But I was already holding on. In fact, my knuckles had turned white from gripping his forearm so intensely. Even so, I squeezed harder. Without another warning, he rapidly jerked one of the levers to its extreme left position. Instantly, the craft tilted on its side. At once, the entrance to the craft faced the ground, becoming the floor. And suddenly, I was on the ceiling. As gravity shifted, we tumbled across the tiny cockpit. Our backs slammed against the metal hatch, smashing apart what was left of it.

"Turn over," he ordered. "I don't like the idea of our backs to those things!" Neither did I. I finally let go of his arm. Together, we rolled over and straddled the opening, with our hands and knees braced on the outer frame. In our precarious positions, we peered between the fragmented metal and into the dim compartment below.

The monsters had fallen against the outer hatch. One had partially broken through next to the still-wedged, decapitated head. It struggled to pull itself back into the air lock. The trouble was, the other monster had fallen onto its horns. The creature was skewered on its back, the thick horns piercing its chest and stomach. The monster beneath thrashed its head, furiously attempting to shake it loose. All the while, the skewered monster eyed us, reaching for us as it was violently tossed about the compartment. We arched our backs to keep its sharp fingertips from slicing into our stomachs.

Past the monsters, through the rips in the craft, I could faintly make out the tops of the cornstalks lightly swaying some one hundred feet below. A breeze swept into the cockpit. It cooled my face and lifted the hair from my forehead. "This is it," Everett declared as if the breeze had sent him a signal.

"This is *what*?" I wondered as we faced the monsters and the dark field below.

Before he had a chance to explain, I felt an intense drop in the pit of my stomach. Gravity shifted again as the craft fell from the sky. We were tossed upward and pinned to the opposite side of the cockpit. The breeze became a strong wind. It burst through the damaged machine, stinging my eyes. It was powerful enough to loosen the severed head, which flew up and out of the air lock. It struck the wall right in front of my face. Its lips were frozen in its disturbing grin as if it enjoyed terrorizing me in death just as much as it had when alive. Its eyes fixed directly on mine, and we became locked in a morbid staring contest. It was probably a good thing I couldn't tear my eyes from it. I didn't want to see the ground coming closer. I didn't want to know when the inevitable crash was going to happen. Yet gazing into the monster's dead eyes couldn't block the sound of the roaring wind or of the howling demons below.

Above it all, I heard Everett's calming voice say, "You're all right."

"*I'm all right,*" I repeated, pinned to the wall, waiting to crash. And then it happened. Darkness followed darkness. The stare between me and the decapitated devil was broken. I looked all around, but all I could see was black.

11
BODY OF DARKNESS

In total darkness, surrounded by crumpled metal, I couldn't tell if I was on the floor, the wall, or the ceiling. "Everett?" I whispered.

"I'm here. I'm going to climb over you. I think there's an opening." I felt his body slide over mine. I lifted my head, and it banged against metal. "Scoot back and follow me." I backed out of the shallow space until I was able to stand on my knees. I felt for Everett and found his shirt. I clutched the fabric and followed it as it floated through a narrow opening. "It's tight," he said. "Be careful of the sharp edges."

We cautiously climbed down from the crippled metal and rounded the ship. The point of impact was the outer hatch. Its buckled metal jutted from the ground. Gaping holes were torn in the hull. The front window was shattered. The craft was once again a pile of useless scrap like the old farm equipment it had been born out of.

Scratching came from inside the wreckage. Ever curious and brave, Everett stepped toward the sound. I followed behind warily, clutching his sleeve. As we approached, a pair of black horns rose through the rubble, swaying unsteadily. It must've smelled us because the demon suddenly sprang from the crevice. It wobbled down the pile of debris, hissing and snarling, violently slashing its claws through the air. It was the demon that had been skewered. When the ship crashed, it must've become dislodged from the horns of the monster beneath. Wounded, it was especially vicious. It neared us, jaws open, drooling green blood.

"Easy now," said Everett as if he were trying to calm a snarling dog. We backed away slowly—and then ran. We ran side by side down separate rows of corn. I could hear the wild and furious monster right behind me. It ripped through the stalks in its way, while its throat produced an ear-piercing howl mixed with a screech.

The last thing I expected—or needed—was a man suddenly stepping into the row before me. But as I ran for my life, that's what happened. It couldn't have been Everett. He was running right beside me. Was it Mr. Newberry? Old man Peterson? As I came closer, I realized it was neither. This man had to be at least eight feet tall. He stood steady as I ran straight for him. With the zealous creature so close to slashing me to pieces, I had no intention of slowing down. So I cut to the next row. But the man sidestepped into the same row, again blocking my path. I glanced over my shoulder to see that the crazed monster had itself switched rows in its pursuit. It had gained ground and began swiping at my legs. I switched rows again. And so too did the mysterious man.

Closing in on him, I saw he had on tall black boots and wore a long dark cloak. I suddenly realized that what stood in my way wasn't a man at all. On my wall, its skin was so faint, so melded with the pattern, that I could barely make it out. Yet the longer I stared at the two darkened knots that were its eyes, the more I could see the face of the most humanlike of the monsters. Its skin was warped, manipulated by the subtle lines in the wood. These lines came to dramatic arches above its eyes, giving it a most sinister appearance. In "person," it looked as though it had been hastily ripped from the paneling. Its skin retained its pattern, grain, and tone. Its melted flesh was twisted into knots. And like its image on the wall, the skin above its dark and vacant eyes stretched upward, creating high peaks that mimicked eyebrows.

With the horned demon at my heels, I had no choice but to collide with the twisted entity. It opened its cloak, holding the edges of the fabric high above its head, exposing the center of its body. Only from what I could tell, it had no body. All I could see between its boots and its twisted face was—emptiness. It wasn't just dark. It was as if its body was composed of—black space. Just as I was about to crash into it, Everett shot into the row. He smashed into my shoulder, and we tumbled to the ground.

The horned monster, however, didn't have a chance to alter its course. Charging forward with its head lowered like a bull, it unwittingly headed straight for the warped fiend, which did not waver. It stood firm, holding open its cloak. And upon contact with its body of darkness, the horned creature—evaporated. It was absorbed. Eaten by the dark body of the cloaked demon. After devouring the horned monster, it lowered its cape and wrapped it tightly around itself. It tilted its head back as its legs quivered. Having digested its meal, the still-hungry beast flung open its cloak once more. It swiveled on its boots and charged after Everett and me.

We scrambled to our feet and slipped down the rows as quietly as possible. We hid in a tight mesh of stalks, scanning for signs of the demented demon: the rustling of leaves, the sight of its flowing cape, the sound of its heavy boots. I stood up on my knees, clutching a sturdy cornstalk. The moist soil dampened my jeans. Everett looked to me with some measure of sympathy. "How you holding up?" he asked.

"Good," I answered bravely. Sure, I was frightened. But with Everett near, fear was different. It was like riding a roller coaster. Everything out of my control. Yet all the while, securely strapped in. Safe. Protected. He took on the real danger so I didn't have to. And with Everett, fear could also be exciting. It certainly excited him. And I had to admit, if I allowed myself to let go of my anxiety just a bit, his excitement was infectious.

"It's almost morning," he said. "It's been a long night. And you did really well." Everett stood and tapped the underside of my arm before casually leaving the cluster.

"It'll hear us!" I whispered.

But Everett wasn't afraid. With no intention of being left alone, I followed him. And after only a few rows, I found myself standing in the driveway. I couldn't believe how close we had been. It was lighter outside the cornfield, the approaching dawn apparent. I gazed up to the second floor. "Do you think Mom and Dad are still alive?" I asked with trepidation.

He smirked. "I'm sure they are," he replied. "And it's Sunday. So we better get back in bed before they find out we were gone."

PART III
IAN STEIN AND
TODD THE TOAD

12
WHAT WOULD EVERETT DO?

Ian Stein was emphatic that his new metallic-red pickup did not get scratched by reckless classmates. So he parked it back by the tennis courts. Crouched in its bed, I had a perfect view of the entire lot. But when everyone began pouring out of the building and racing to their cars, I couldn't pinpoint him in the crowd. There were too many people. It was too chaotic. And the sun reflecting off the band room's windows was blinding. Yet since it was a Friday afternoon, the lot emptied out especially quickly. In just a matter of minutes, only a handful of cars remained. The buses were gone. The mob of vehicles made its way down the rural road. I heard the procession in the distance—the honking horns, the occasional shouts from students hanging out their windows.

Finally, as the last of the cars trickled out of the lot, a tall figure emerged. Even with the glare, I could tell by his broad shoulders and the way his hair shone in the sun that it was Ian. Girls loved his thick, dark hair. Everett had been right when he told me Ian would be one of the last to leave. He knew his last class of the day was weight training. He figured he'd stay late bullshitting with the rest of the guys. Then he'd have to shower. It was a perfect time, Everett reasoned. There would be little chance someone else would see what I was about to do. I watched stealthily as Ian moved from the blinding light and into clear recognition.

I had listened to Everett carefully. I knew the plan. I had gone over it in my head a hundred times. Still, as I saw Ian strut toward his truck with his gym bag slung over his shoulder, a wave of anxiety washed over me. My eyes darted back and forth between Ian and Everett's car parked just a few rows over. I placed my hand over my pocket to check, for the hundredth time, that the key to Everett's car was still there. I then felt for Everett's switchblade in the other pocket. When the moment came, I knew I'd have to act fast. I couldn't screw up. I had to be ready.

Ian was at least halfway across the lot when someone else stepped into the blaze of light. The figure ran stiffly, trying to catch up to Ian. Based on the bulky size and awkwardly rigid posture, I knew it could only be one person: Todd the Toad. When he caught up to Ian, the two stopped and spoke for a moment. Then, together, they made their way toward Ian's truck. *Shit!* I slipped down out of sight. *It was only supposed to be Ian!* Everett didn't say what to do if someone else came to the truck with him. I panicked, not knowing how the hell I could possibly take on both Ian *and* Todd the Toad.

I couldn't make out the words, but I heard Ian's voice. When he finished speaking, I heard Todd's stiff laughter. God, even his laughter was stiff. I heard their footsteps nearing and the twirling of keys. I curled myself into a ball over the uncomfortable corrugated metal, desperately attempting to will myself to disappear. "Thanks for the ride, man," said the Toad right above me. The truck bounced as Ian climbed in and unlocked the passenger door. It bounced again as Todd took his seat.

A lightning bolt of fear struck me as the engine roared to life. My fate was sealed. I was trapped. Showoff Ian revved the engine. When he released the brake, the truck spun out of its parking space. I was thrown across the bed, and my shoulder slammed against its side. The high-pitched screech from the tires echoed throughout the campus. The air filled with choking smoke caused by burned rubber.

But the worst part was when we raced past Everett's car. *No!* The mission had barely begun, and already I was failing. In the middle of the disaster, I told myself to concentrate. I needed to think clearly, quickly. *What would Everett do?* I wasn't sure exactly, although I *was* sure about one thing: he wouldn't have allowed himself to stay trapped in the back of Ian Stein's runaway pickup.

While holding my sure to be black-and-blue shoulder, I managed to balance myself enough to stand up on my knees. Peering through the rear window, I could see Ian's shiny hair up close and the back of Todd the Toad's thick neck. With Ian about to race out of the parking lot, I knew I had only a moment to act. I made a fist and furiously pounded against the glass. "How'd I get myself into this?" I moaned under my breath.

13
MUSK

A few days earlier, I was standing at my locker, twisting the knob, watching the numbers and the tick marks between them spin. The correct sequence was stored somewhere in my brain. But to retrieve it would mean to focus on where I was. I preferred to languish in the haze. By focusing on the spinning knob, I was able to tune out the commotion of the hall—the bustle of classmates, the slamming of locker doors. And once the noises were gone, I fled not only the hall, but the building itself.

It was during that void, in the five minutes between math and English, that I felt the cold splash strike my back. In an instant, I was pulled back from the ether, and the world I had successfully sequestered to black and white was shocked into color once more. The liquid penetrated my sweater. I felt it trickling down until it reached the small of my back.

"Did you forget your combination?" I heard a smarmy voice ask. I clutched the knob and closed my eyes for a moment, hoping he'd just pass by. But I felt another splash of the liquid. I broke out in an instant sweat. The sweat mixed with the liquid, giving me a moist, uncomfortable feel that sparked a tingling chill across my shoulders. Then came the aroma: woodsy and sweet, with a dash of rubbing alcohol. It was an aggressive scent. It could've smelled appealing in small doses, I supposed. But with the amount doused on me, it was a potent bomb.

Feeling queasy enough to vomit, I turned to face him. He held a dark-green plastic bottle of what had to be the cheapest musk cologne on the market. And my back marinated in it. Ian had this look about him. It was something, maybe in his smile, that made it seem as if I could be, or actually was, his friend. So as pathetic as it was, I smiled back at him. I even laughed a little to show that I was in fact in on the joke too. That I could take being pranked. That I was just like one of his groupies—that's what I called them, in my head at least—the nameless and faceless bunch that gravitated to his meanness.

Once more, he shook the bottle in my direction. It was as if the liquid came at me in slow motion as it shot across the hall. It splashed my face and ran down the front of my sweater. I wiped my face, but nothing could be done to quell the overpowering fumes. My eyes watered. My head began to pound. Ian's deceitfully warm smile disappeared as he burst into laughter. The groupies laughed too, making it clear: I was *not* one of them.

I didn't have friends in junior high. I was used to that. Yet a curious thing happened when I started high school: The friends I didn't have, for some reason, became my enemies. Perhaps I was an easy target. I ate lunch by myself. Was too skinny. Too quiet. Too weird. They laughed because they knew they were untouchable. How safe it must've felt to be part of the group—protected, empowered, and all too willing to point, to laugh, to enjoy the benefits of not being me.

While most of the groupies were just a collage of generic faces, one stood out: Ian's head groupie, Todd the Toad. His response to the situation was to pretend to masturbate while dancing a sort of jig around me, his tongue flicking in and out. I had no idea how to interpret this, how it related to Ian splashing me with the cologne, or how anyone could've found it remotely funny. But of course, to the others, this was hilarious.

On the football team, Todd played whatever position heavy guys were supposed to be good at. He had broken his collarbone the previous season. Ever since then, his neck seemed incapable of moving independent of his shoulders. He reminded me of a toad — thick and stiff. So in my head, I referred to him as *Todd the Toad* whenever I was forced to look at him. His eyes darted back and forth as he stared me down. He breathed with exaggerated groans while he continued his perplexing gestures.

I was pissed off. Afraid. But didn't dare lash out. I couldn't even say a word without being demolished one way or the other. I was powerless. So instead, I did the only thing I could: I imagined the heads of everyone surrounding me exploding, their skulls bursting open and chunks of their brains sticking to the wall. Yet no matter how intensely I focused, their heads remained frustratingly intact. My concentration was broken by the Toad, who finally concluded his performance. "What're you lookin' at, faggot?"

Defeated, I turned away from the crowd and faced my locker once more, attempting to leave the scene as quickly as I had been dragged into it. But I wasn't granted relief. I felt breathing on the back of my neck. I turned to see the Toad, who began squealing in my ear like a pig. His torture culminated in a swift shove. My body crashed into the lockers. Scrambling to gain control of my limbs, I imagined I looked like a marionette dancing with tangled strings.

By the time I steadied myself, I felt a presence blanket the hall. It silenced the crowds. It hushed the ambient chatter and laughter. I no longer sensed Ian, Todd, or the groupies over my shoulder. The reprieve allowed me to once again concentrate on the spinning numbers. Slowly, I rotated the knob clockwise, watching the tiny hatch marks pass under the groove. I stopped at twenty-seven. I twisted the dial counterclockwise until I reached sixteen and spun it clockwise again until I reached eight. 27-16-08. I lifted the latch and tugged open the metal door. *Funny how things come to you.* I swapped my math book for my English book. With some hesitation, I slammed shut the locker, wondering if I'd ever get it open again.

I feared that the calming spell would be broken, that as I turned to face the hall, Ian, Todd, and their persecuting crowd would still be leering at me. Yet they had been swapped out—for Everett and Phillip. I was at once relieved—and crushed—to see them. Had they witnessed my humiliation? I forced my spine to straighten, attempting to appear as though I had some semblance of confidence.

"We're mowing the apartments over on Elmridge tonight," said Everett. "We have to be there before four o'clock. So either you can come with us, or you'll have to take the bus."

"I suppose we could still give him a ride even if he didn't want to come. We'd just have to roll him out of the car as we drive by your house," joked Phillip.

"I'll go!" I happily agreed.

"What's that smell?" Phillip asked, crinkling his nose. I clutched the front of my sweater, futilely attempting to cover my stench.

Everett leaned in close for a whiff of his own. I backed against the locker as he inhaled deeply. Then, like some kind of animal that could decode a rival's message via scent, he turned his head and scowled to the corner of the hall where Ian and Todd the Toad stood talking to the Blonde Eagle and Kirsten. The Blonde Eagle was the girlfriend of Todd the Toad. I didn't know her real name, but her feathered hair, so bleached it was actually white, reminded me of white eagle feathers. I knew Ian's girlfriend's name was Kirsten because she was in my English class. I didn't have a nickname for her—not then anyhow.

Somehow, Everett knew what had taken place. He didn't have to see it. And I didn't have to tell him a thing. He placed his hand on my shoulder. "We'll stop this," he promised. "And I have an idea how. We'll meet in the cornfield, tomorrow after school, to talk it over." I was elated. Since school had started, we hadn't been in the cornfield. I was anxious to get back, especially since the corn was nearly ready to be harvested. Yet I was also confused. Why was Everett mentioning a visit to the field in front of Phillip? Except for the dig, Everett hadn't invited Phillip to take part in any of our adventures that summer. "Yeah, Phillip's coming too," Everett affirmed. "Now get to class." He gave me a wink before he and Phillip headed to the corner of the hall.

I slung my bag over my shoulder and took off in the opposite direction. To Ian and Todd, it must've been intimidating: two upper classmen approaching. And Everett had an overpowering presence, a burning intensity, whenever he was focused or angered. I picked up my pace as I heard a rumbling murmur escalate to an uproar. I neared Ms. Davis's classroom with a smirk on my face, knowing Ian and Todd were experiencing Everett's wrath—and eager to learn just what else he had planned.

14
THE MAGNETIC CEILING

Knobby, leafless trees lined both sides of a dirt path leading to a tiny moss-covered cabin. The surrounding field was full of the most beautiful wildflowers: purple, blue, and yellow. I took my time wandering the path, gazing over the field and to the wilderness beyond. I wondered who I'd meet when I'd finally step up on the covered porch and knock on the door . . . Gazing into my locker's dial wasn't my only mode of escape. The painting above the radiator in Ms. Davis's classroom was even easier to dissolve into. And if I cocked my head just right, no one noticed I wasn't really there.

I was inside the painting when Todd the Toad entered. I didn't notice him until he straddled the desk in front of me and greeted me with, "Hey, faggot." My stomach came alive with that familiar sickness. Normally the Toad sat on the other end of the room, leaving me in peaceful isolation with my cabin painting. That day, however, he was feeling particularly vengeful. "You smell real nice," he said as he brought his nose in for a whiff. "Sexy!" On cue came laughter from several groupies, also straddling their desks to participate in their favorite spectator sport. "We did you a favor," he continued. "Now you can smell real good for your brother. Because we all know you two sleep together. Don't ya, buddy?"

I stared forward, unresponsive. I found it revealing how the Toad became more dominant, more vocal, when Ian wasn't around. It said something about their pecking order. There was an insult somewhere in that thought I could've slung back at him. But I couldn't formulate it on the spot. And even if I could've, I wouldn't have dared.

"Your lover didn't appreciate our favor, did he?" he continued. "Your lover likes to throw a hissy fit when we fuck with ya, huh?"

"I guess," I said meekly.

He let out an exaggerated laugh. "Yeah, I knew you two were lovers. It's all right. You can admit it. You two are bed buddies, huh?" Every eye in the classroom was locked on me, anticipating how I'd answer. The sickness in my stomach became a quagmire I couldn't escape by simply gazing out the window or focusing on the painting. "You guys sleep together, right?" he persisted.

My eyes met his darting frog eyes. My face was red-hot. My throat was dry. Finally I decided to just give in. *Just give them what they want.* Maybe then, they'd be satisfied. Maybe then, they'd feel I'd been decimated enough to leave me be. "Yes!" I declared in the clearest voice I could conjure. "We sleep together."

Todd's face lit up with delight. He flashed his horse teeth as he produced the widest grin. He chuckled at first. The chuckle segued into a more sinister laugh, followed by a look of disgust. "Gross!" he shouted and immediately turned away from me. He scooted his desk forward several feet. The groupies did the same, separating themselves from me. Shunning me. Leaving me with my heart in my stomach and my stomach on the floor. Kirsten, sitting near the front of the classroom, turned back and gave me a half smile. I lowered my head.

By the time Ms. Davis entered the classroom, I had my notebook out doodling. With my angst and nervous energy, I dragged the pen forcefully across the paper, nearly ripping a hole. But as my breathing steadied, so did my hand. I began controlling the pen, guiding it so I could draw what was in my mind. I drew what allowed me to escape back to summer; I drew the outline of a horned monster. Strange how an image of evil could bring me more serenity than a classroom. But it felt familiar. And it was hardly frightening at all since Everett and I had defeated the monsters dozens of times before school had started.

Ever since the night they escaped the walls, the monsters had inhabited the woods and the fields. During the day, they'd hide. I didn't know where. Maybe within the stalks? The tall grasses? Underground? But at night, they'd emerge. We'd often sneak downstairs to find a group of horned monsters tapping on the sliding glass door, politely prompting us to engage in battle. Sometimes we'd sneak into the corn at dusk to surprise the skeletons. We'd creep up on them. Trip them. Everett would grab a giant arm and I a giant leg, and we'd tug on their limbs until they'd collapse. Sometimes we'd have to fight our way through a horde of horned monsters to make it to the craft, which waited for us anew each evening. Other times, we'd make it to the craft unimpeded — only to find it surrounded when we got there. Everett would heroically fend off the demons as I unlocked the hatch. Everett had become an expert pilot. And I turned out to be not so bad of a copilot. We only crashed a few more times.

While at night we battled demons, during the day, we were landscapers. Phillip had gotten a job with RJs Landscaping cutting grass for homes and businesses five days a week. He convinced Everett to apply, and he too was hired. Even though I wasn't an official employee, I'd often ride along when they were sent together on a job. They paid me a small cut of their wages for pulling weeds and trimming with the push mower. My favorite job was the cemetery in Ruthsford. It wasn't easy since it sat on a hill and I had to trim around all the headstones. But I loved reading the old inscriptions. And the setting, bordered by a winding river on one end, was peaceful. The spending money was nice. And better yet, I had become almost as comfortable around Phillip as I was with Everett. By the end of August, I considered Phillip *my* friend too.

It had been the best summer of my life. I enjoyed spending time with Everett and Phillip mowing lawns. But when school started that fall, it was the monsters in the corn I missed most of all.

I looked over the scene I had furiously sketched. It was our spacecraft surrounded by monsters. The monsters overlapped into a montage of haunting figures. I began filling the empty space with crude cornstalks. The more I drew, the more I began to smell the sweetness of their dewy leaves. I began to hear them rustle in the breeze. The gentle sound mixed with the low hum of the ship.

I was forced to evacuate the scene, however, when Ms. Davis's shoe came into my peripheral vision, impatiently tapping beside my desk. I looked up to her, embarrassed. She had the textbook open in her palms while curiously examining my ink drawing. The class erupted in laughter. My face became instantly hot. Without saying a word, I pulled out my English book and placed it over the drawing. She spared me further embarrassment by moving on without calling me out. I flipped the book to a random page and pretended to follow along as she spoke of prepositional phrases, topic sentences, and words of transition.

But my mind still craved wandering. With my options limited, I simply focused on the empty desk beside me. Although it was a rather mundane thing to be concentrating on, I allowed my eyes to follow the metal legs down to the small, circular feet keeping the desk sturdy. I then traced the legs back up to the frame that supported its wooden surface. Aside from their wooden tops, the desks were composed entirely of silver metal. We were studying magnets in earth science class. Metal made me think of magnets and how magnets were attracted to metals that contained iron, nickel, or cobalt.

I wondered what would happen if the ceiling in the classroom was a giant magnet. Such a magnet would surely attract the desks' metal frames. If the ceiling was a magnet and if the magnet was suddenly activated, I hypothesized it would cause the desks to instantly flip upside down. I figured this since the metal was beneath their wooden tops. After flipping, the desks would fly, upturned, toward the ceiling. Their metal feet would then fuse powerfully to the magnetic ceiling, forming an unbreakable bond.

If my classmates were in their desks when the flip occurred, it would happen so fast they likely wouldn't fall out. They'd be held to their seats like water held in a bucket when spinning real fast overhead. Centrifugal force. As the desks rotated, their heads would strike the floor before they sailed to the top of the room. There, they'd be suspended upside down, their torsos draped over the back of the wooden desktops. Their bashed heads would drip blood, which would form tiny pools on the floor. Those not knocked unconscious would be screaming, hysterically grasping the metal frames to keep themselves from falling on their heads. Ms. Davis would run out of the room in a panic, shouting for help.

Because he had such a big head, I imagined when Todd the Toad's desk flipped, his skull would crack when it struck the floor. The magnet would struggle to pull his fat body to the ceiling. If he was alive and conscious, his face would be full of terror. He'd scream. He'd cuss. Under his weight, the wooden top would break from the metal. He'd be the first to fall. And there he'd lie in a pool of his own blood.

Captivated by the scenario, I ran it through my head over and over. It was two twenty-five. *What if the magnet activates at two thirty?* The more the thought cycled through my mind, the stranger it seemed that Ms. Davis continued writing on the board, oblivious to what was to occur in just five minutes.

While the rest of the class sat calmly, my leg began to bounce. I couldn't sit still. I needed to get out of my desk before it flipped upside down. I closed my book and shoved it in my bag. My knees were weak as I stood. I kept my eyes to the floor as I quickly made my way to the front of the room. "And to where are you wandering off, Ayden?" Ms. Davis questioned.

I slipped to the other side of the door before poking my head back in. "Sorry," I apologized. "I guess—I'm just—I don't feel very well." I could hear the classroom erupt in giggles as I scurried down the hall—with just two minutes to spare.

I didn't want to hear it when it happened. I left the building and weaved my way through the lot looking for Everett's car. He bought the white Grand Am from a college student a few weeks before school started. He paid for part of it with his lawn-cutting money. The rest came from a loan from Mom and Dad. I slumped into the passenger seat just about the moment the Toad's desk would've been flipping upside down. I pictured him dangling from the ceiling. Blood dripping from the gash in his head. I eyed the doors. Any moment, I just knew a rush of traumatized students would come running out, screaming.

15
THE FiFTEENTH ROW

Startled by the sudden realization there was a stowaway in the bed of his pickup, Ian slammed on the brakes. I braced my arm against the rear window as the truck jerked to a halt. I sprang over the tailgate. They flew out of the cab faster than I had anticipated. "What the fuck were you doing back there!" Ian bellowed as Todd the Toad joined his side. I stood at the tailgate not saying a word, concentrating on what I had to do. "Are you deaf! What were you doing in the back of my truck, fag?"

My silence especially agitated the Toad. He shuffled his feet. His angry energy only caused Ian's anger to escalate. No longer able to hold in their anger, they rushed toward me. After pulling the knife out of my pocket, I fumbled with it for a moment before locating the switch on the handle. Drawing a sudden blank, I couldn't remember which end the blade would pop out of, so I held the knife between my fingers instead of in my palm. When I finally got the blade to appear, I aimed it toward them. I held it low, behind the truck, should anyone near the building happen to be watching. The sight of the blade instantly stopped their advance. Ian even took a step backward and showed me his palms in submission. Even so, he spouted, "You better put that goddamn knife down, or you are fucking dead."

While Ian tried to convince me to surrender, Todd the Toad bent his knees and curled his arms as if he was going to crush me with some wrestling maneuver. "He's not gonna do anything," he assured. "Let's kick his ass."

I answered him by stepping forward and jabbing the blade into the air. Both jolted back. I grinned. They were truly frightened. Finally, I had them in the same position they had me in so many times. They knew, if only for that moment, what it felt like to be weak in the stomach and dry in the mouth. Their eyes widened as I casually closed the gap between us. "Don't run. If you do, I'm close enough right now to get at least one of you." I noticed Ian's hand inching for the truck's door handle. "Don't you dare," I warned. "Or I'll split open the Toad's fat stomach and stab you from behind before you can even turn the key."

Once I got going, I shocked myself with how bold I could be. I pressed the blade against Todd's stomach. He did not call me a faggot. Instead, he nervously let out an extended, stuttered breath. I looked him in the eye. I hadn't ever looked anyone in the eye longer than I had in that moment. But with the blade in my hand, its power on my side, I stared him down. The power I felt must've been similar to the power he usually felt over me. And with that power, I decided to ask him what I wasn't brave enough to ask the prior two days: "Your head — why isn't it split open? How come it's not wrapped in bandages?"

"What the fuck you talkin' about?"

"Your fat head!" I screamed. "Your thick skull should've smashed on the floor in English. You should be in the hospital right now with another broken collarbone." I couldn't understand it. Why did no one speak of the magnetic ceiling incident? The magically flipping desks should've been the talk of the school. But even at knifepoint, the Toad didn't say a word. He only took in short, nasally breaths while staring at the blade against his round stomach. I shook my head, wondering what could've happened.

"Cheap desks," I finally fumed. "I bet that metal doesn't even have any iron, nickel, or cobalt."

The Toad's eyes followed the blade as I transferred it to Ian's stomach. It was my one chance to say anything I wanted to the person who had oppressed me, who had made the mere thought of school a nightmare. Yet as I looked into his green eyes, the best I could come up with was, "I don't think your hair is all that great. So it's shiny. Who cares? It looks full of grease to me." The funny thing was, the way he closed his eyes and tossed back his head, I believed the comment actually stung.

My eye caught a flash of sunlight reflecting off Ian's watch face. Although I was finding satisfaction holding them at knifepoint, it reminded me I must get on with the mission. "What time is it?" I asked in a panic. Ian looked down at the blade and then back to me, only offering his dutiful stare. "What time is it!" I demanded, poking the knife through his tank top. His wrist flew to his face.

"Quarter to four." I was behind schedule. And not only was I late, I had to remember I had Ian *and* Todd the Toad to deal with.

I tightened my grip on the handle as I prepared for what I was there to accomplish. I lifted the knife to my shoulder for momentum before propelling it toward my hip with all the force I could muster. The tip pierced the side of the truck. I held the blade firmly in place for a moment, my eyes locked on to Ian's, before slowly stepping backward. As I dragged the blade along the side of the truck, flakes of red paint cascaded to the blacktop.

Ian watched in horror as the blade produced a deep, uneven gouge. "Fuuuck!" he cried.

"Geez. You're acting like *you'd* rather be getting stabbed," I said with an eye-roll. When I reached the taillights, I rounded the other side—and ran like hell.

I didn't look back as I sprinted for Everett's car. I slid inside and threw the knife in the passenger seat. I locked both doors before digging in my pocket for the key. When I finally had it in my grasp, I frantically started the car and flew out of the parking lot with the gas to the floor. On the short drive that led to the road, I hit the speed bump with full force. I gripped the wheel as I bounced off the seat. My head hit the roof. At the speed I was going, I expected the tires to burst upon impact. Although the engine choked for a moment, the car kept rolling.

Swerving down the road, I checked the rearview mirror. It was completely filled with the reflection of Ian's grille. The sight was terrorizing. But it meant Everett's plan was working. Ian was following. Trying to convince him to meet off school grounds never would've worked. No, he had to be lured. I tilted the mirror upward to see their faces. Gone were the expressions of fear and submission. There was only anger and vengeance.

We sped down the country road with the football field on the left and the cornfield on the right. Ian's front bumper tapped the rear of the Grand Am. I struggled to keep control as the powerful truck barreled down on me. I couldn't risk flying into the cornfield. I didn't even have a driver's license. But Everett had convinced me it was OK to drive without a license in an emergency and that being chased by Ian would constitute an emergency.

In case we were pulled over for reckless driving, Everett had warned me that the knife shouldn't be in the car, especially since it would have metallic-red paint chips stuck to its tip, proving I had been the one who had vandalized Ian's truck. So with Everett's voice telling me what to do, I somehow managed to steer the careening vehicle with my left arm while reaching to the passenger side with my right. My injured shoulder seared in pain with each crank as I rolled down the window. I grabbed the knife and whipped it outside. It sailed through the air and disappeared between the rows of tan corn leaves. Everett had thought of everything.

As we careened onto Henderson Road, I was sure I only had two wheels to the ground. Ian stayed viciously close, barely allowing a gap between us. We raced past the apple orchards and through the industrial area with the cardboard plant and distribution center. Semis pulled in and out of the intersection. We dodged the slow-moving trucks at high speed. The angry truckers honked their horns at our foolish driving. Ian held his fist to his own horn, honking back at them in defiance.

I glanced at the dash as I took the final turn onto our road. It was almost four. I had made good time, was nearly back on schedule. The woods' mature trees towered in the distance behind the sparsely spaced houses. The rest of the land was blanketed by the golden cornfields. Aligned with the cornfield, the horizon was where the sky met the pinnacle of yellow stalks blazing in the afternoon sun.

I ran the car on the dirt shoulder just past our house. Stuck on my bumper, Ian did the same. As he slammed into me, I held my foot on the brake but was propelled forward, toppling several rows of stalks. I burst out under a cloud of dust. Yet instead of running deeper into the corn for cover, as any logical person would've with two large guys after him, I emerged at the side of the road. They tore after me as I desperately searched for the piece of white cloth that had been tied to the fifteenth row from our driveway. I spotted it just before they were to take me down and surely bash my head in. I leapt into the corn down the fifteenth row like a deer, frightened yet agile.

16
THE PiT

The golden leaves were stiff and brittle. I used their crackling rattle to gauge the proximity of my hunters. In contrast to their clodhopping feet, I was svelte, making little noise as I slipped between the leaves. Had we been in the halls or on the street, they no doubt could've tackled me immediately. But we were in the cornfield. *My* cornfield. And I knew just how to maneuver my way through it. I dashed down the row, anticipating its curves. It was a path I would've felt confident sprinting down any given time. Even so, the night before, I had rehearsed racing down the fifteenth row. Even a nimble bobcat wouldn't have been able to catch me.

Despite my prowess in the corn, there was still one big problem. "Two of them!" I shouted when I figured my voice would be in earshot. "There're two!" I warned again with what little breath I had left in my lungs.

I knew I was nearing the final stretch when I spotted the second strip of Everett's old T-shirt tied to one of the stalks. I slowed my pace just a bit, allowing them to close in. I glanced over my shoulder to gauge their distance. Ian wasn't far behind. Red-faced. Eyes locked on me. I didn't see the Toad until I turned to face forward and saw him out of the corner of my eye. He ran beside

Ian, in the thirteenth row. At his size, I didn't think he had it in him, but he kept up with Ian's pace. He took deep breaths as his heavy frame galumphed down the row.

With a final push, I sped toward the finish line. As planned, the moment my shoulder brushed under the white cloth, my feet left the ground. I leapt into the air, trying for as much height and distance as possible. I didn't look below. Instead, I concentrated on staying airborne as long as possible. When gravity finally forced me to the ground, I crashed into several stalks and landed on my stomach. My breath was gone, the wind knocked from me.

Gasping for air, I flipped onto my back—only to find Ian sailing over the top of me! His descent was magnificent. When he landed, his feet planted firmly on either side of my head, kicking dirt in my face. He had jumped! That wasn't part of the plan. He was supposed to fall. But when he saw me jump, he jumped too. He towered over me, leering at me with his red face. I looked up to him, helpless, unable to bring a breath in or let one out. With his hatred of me boiling over, he rolled his hands into tight fists, eager to do what would truly satisfy him.

But Ian forgot we were not at school. We were in the cornfield. And that meant he was on our turf. Everett shot out from the stalks with the speed and precision of a predator. He grabbed Ian by the shoulders. Ian attempted to grab hold of Everett but, startled by the ambush, was quickly overpowered. Everett gave him a strong shove. Ian fell backward—and disappeared beneath the corn.

I dropped my head to the soil and looked to the blue sky as I waited for my lungs to expand. Everett knelt beside me. He tossed aside the stalks that had collapsed over me and wiped the dirt from my face. "Calm down," he said. "Just breathe." He gently rubbed the upper part of my chest with the base of his palm. He stayed next to me until I was able to take in small breaths. Once assured I was OK, he stood next to where Ian had fallen. He rubbed the stubble on his cheek for a moment before turning back to me. I was afraid he'd be displeased about the mission not going as planned, but, slowly, he cracked a smile and nodded.

"The Toad—" I warned, still catching my breath. "Todd's—in the cornfield."

Everett's face instantly transformed back into the wolf that had rushed Ian. "Shit!" Corn leaves crackled behind us. Everett helped me scramble to my feet.

It was only Phillip. He entered the small clearing that had begun to develop from our trampling. His tan sweater and blond hair blended perfectly with the dried leaves. "What happened?" he asked.

"Todd Snelling's out here too. Stand still," he ordered in a whisper. With the air still, even the slightest movements could be detected in a dry cornfield. We listened intently for the leaves to reveal the location of Todd the Toad. Sooner or later, he was bound to make a move. Yet a low gush of wind suddenly rushed through the stalks, masking any anomalies. "Dammit!" snapped Everett. "I'll find him." He turned to Phillip. "Stay here with Ayden."

Phillip and I listened as Everett marched off into the stalks. It sounded as if he ran toward the road, likely figuring the Toad had headed back to Ian's truck. But after a few moments, his movements blended with the rest of the crackling, making it impossible to determine his course.

"So did it work?" Phillip asked.

"Sort of. Except he didn't fall in. Everett had to push him."

Curious, Phillip stepped forward and carefully leaned over the edge of the pit. Camouflaged by the surrounding stalks, the pit was a well-hidden, oval-shaped trap. Not knowing it was there, Ian was sure to fall in as he chased me—or so we thought. Dug several feet wide and more than six feet deep, it was designed to be easy to fall into yet challenging to climb out of. Stuck inside, he'd beg us to pull him out. But to teach him not to mess with me again, we'd place a board over the top, anchored by rocks. We'd leave him out in the corn, where no one could hear his cussing. And after nightfall, when he was good and whipped, we'd pull off the board. Eventually he'd manage to climb out on his own and would have to find his way back through the field in the dark. Sure, it'd only ruin one Friday night out of his life. But it'd scare the hell out of him. And the humiliation would last forever.

"C'mon, help me with the board," I said.

But Phillip didn't move from the side of the pit. I could tell from the bulge on the side of his face that he was clenching his jaw. He spun toward me with his hands trembling and a look of horror in his eyes. "Jesus Christ."

A wave of uneasiness rushed over me. I joined Phillip and peered below. Ian was at the bottom of the pit, on his back, attempting to push himself into a sitting position. He looked discouraged, confused as to why he couldn't easily lift himself from the ground. It must've been shock that caused him not to notice the jagged piece of rusted metal protruding from his chest—or the other pieces impaling his hip and his leg just above the knee. His clothes were soaked in blood. A bit of it trickled from the corner of his mouth.

The bottom of the pit had been laced with an arsenal of sharp, corroded metal. It didn't take long for me to recognize that the metal came from the old discarded farm machinery up the hill. A variety of scrap had been brought from the heap and spiked into the ground. It jutted from the bottom of the pit, creating a deadly booby trap.

Ian looked up to us. He didn't speak. Unable to process what was happening, he only became more frustrated with his inability to stand. The sun was setting earlier each evening. Pink light had already begun to filter through the stalks. Several fragmented rays reached into the pit and over Ian's struggling body. I was overcome with an odd sensation. I felt so—embarrassed for him. Not five minutes before, he was powerful and virile. But at the bottom of the pit, he was helpless. Pitiful. I couldn't stand to look at him any longer. I lifted my gaze to the stalks. The silk protruding from the tips of the ears of corn had turned from a healthy yellow to a coffee-stained brown. Unwrapped from their protective leaves, the exposed kernels had hardened.

I was startled by a sudden grip on my shoulder. Too engrossed in the scene before us, neither Phillip nor I had heard Everett approach from behind. He gently pulled me away from the edge of the pit, swapping places next to Phillip. "I couldn't find the bastard," he reported to Phillip. "But he's still out here somewhere. The truck's still by the road."

Phillip gave Everett the same horrified look he had given me. "What the hell is this!" he erupted.

"I know you're probably freaking out. But right now, we've got to find Todd."

"Where the hell did that shit come from? Last night there was nothing at the bottom of that pit—but dirt!"

"How the fuck should I know?" Everett firmly replied. "That's not important right now. Right now, like I said, it's important we find Todd. We need to make sure he did not leave the cornfield."

"I don't give a shit about Todd! Jesus, Everett. Ian's going to die!" Phillip stumbled from the pit and bent over as if he was going to vomit.

Everett placed his hand on Phillip's back in an attempt to comfort him. "Ian treated Ayden like shit," Everett reminded, looking to me sympathetically. Phillip lifted his head and looked to me as well as I bashfully twisted a dried corn leaf. "So maybe," Everett continued, "this is what he deserves."

Apparently over his nausea, Phillip shot upright. "*This* is what he deserves!" He gestured toward the pit. "For teasing Ayden? For splashing him with cologne?"

Everett shook his head as if he were a teacher disappointed in a pupil. He squatted at the edge of the pit. "Even Kirsten, his own girlfriend, apologized to me for what he did." He sneered at the powerless Ian. "She said how much of an asshole you could be. And you know something? The way she smiled at me, I think she really likes me." Everett stood and spit in the hole. Phillip looked as if he were about to come out of his skin.

"Watch out!" I found myself yelling as Todd the Toad suddenly burst through the stalks.

This time it was Everett who was caught off guard. The Toad had been hiding near the pit in the same tight cluster Everett had hidden within before ambushing Ian. He attacked Everett with a brutal strike across the face. As Everett stumbled from the blow, Todd peered into the pit, confirming what he had surely overheard. "You sick fucks will pay for this!" he croaked. "I'll make sure of it!" He held up his fists, willing to take on whoever dared step forward. He was wild, fueled by his need for retribution. Everett, still recovering, rubbed his jaw before stepping up to Todd's challenge. The Toad did not hesitate to lunge his massive frame at him, and the two were locked in battle. Todd was powerful. He outmatched Everett in size. But Everett was swift and resilient.

Phillip was silent. Clearly distraught. He didn't have faith in Everett like I had. I remembered what it was like the first time Everett took me into the cornfield to meet the monsters. "Don't worry," I assured him as we watched Everett and the Toad swap punches and throw each other into stalks. "Everett knows what he's doing." I had seen him take on much more fearsome adversaries— and win.

Everett's face began to swell. He suffered a deep gash under his eye and one above his lip. "Get Ayden outta here!" he yelled to Phillip. "I don't want him watching this. I'll handle it. Just wait for me in the woods. Go!" he commanded before Todd charged him like a bull.

Phillip pivoted mechanically toward the woods. "C'mon," he murmured.

I followed Phillip toward the trees. After emerging from the corn, we made our way across the narrow strip of high weeds that lay between the cornfield and the woods. As we approached the trees, the smell of suffocating leaves sweetened the air. Their colors painted the outer shell of the woods vibrant shades of reds, oranges, and yellows. Just before entering, we heard a guttural bellow echo in the distance. I turned to the cornfield. Despite Everett's clear instruction, I wanted to know what had happened.

But Phillip wouldn't allow it. He gripped the back of my neck and ushered me into the forest.

17
OWL iN THE TREETOP

Phillip escorted me well into the woods. He stopped when we reached a massive oak that had toppled the previous summer during a violent windstorm. Its roots were exposed, yet it refused to fully surrender. Its leafless branches pressed against the ground, arching like giant fingers keeping the trunk suspended. We boosted ourselves onto the floating trunk, our feet dangling over the forest floor. All around us, multicolored leaves dropped intermittently. They landed with gentle taps as they mixed with the forest's other discarded jewels that lay decomposing.

Phillip eyed the nearby mound that marked one of the Indian graves. "We were only supposed to scare him," he began solemnly. "It was only supposed to be a prank. We weren't supposed to hurt anyone. That wasn't part of the plan."

It was true. We hadn't discussed lining the bottom of the pit with jagged metal. Everett claimed he didn't know how the metal had gotten there. But it had to have been him. I didn't put it there. Phillip certainly hadn't either. "Everett changed the plan. That's all," I offered. "And you heard him; Ian got what he deserved."

"Just because Everett says something doesn't make it true! Or right!" Phillip exploded. I turned from him, feeling as though I had just been scolded. I began peeling bark from the trunk. "Ayden?" he asked, switching his tone to apologetic.

I looked into his blue eyes. "Yeah?"

"Do you think murder is wrong?"

"Yes," I responded without hesitation. I watched a bird fly through the woods and sit on a nearby branch. It rode the bobbing branch for a moment before darting into a cluster of maples. "Last spring, I saw Mrs. Newberry drowning baby blackbirds in a bucket of water. She said they fight with the other birds, so she didn't want them in her yard. Can you believe that? I could never do something like that."

"I'm not talking about birds. I'm talking about murder. I'm talking about killing—a person."

"Oh. Yeah, I think it's wrong." I thought of the satisfaction I felt holding Ian and Todd the Toad at knifepoint. They deserved to feel as vulnerable as they had made me feel. Yet I knew I couldn't have stabbed them. Not really.

"Do you think it's wrong for *Everett* to murder someone?" he asked.

I figured Everett had good reason for whatever he did. I'd seen him kill dozens of demons in the cornfield. Maybe there wasn't much of a difference between them and Ian. I brushed away the loose bits of bark and watched them land on top of the blanket of dead leaves.

Frustrated by my hesitation, Phillip jumped from the trunk. "This is serious!" He grabbed a twig and snapped it in half. "OK. So let's assume it's *not* wrong for Everett to kill someone. That he suffers no consequences. That God himself gives Everett permission to do whatever the hell he wants, murder included. Fine. But where does that leave you?"

I didn't understand. "Everett protects me. He makes sure nothing will happen to me."

He broke the twig in half again. "Did anyone else see you scratch Ian's truck?"

"No. I was real careful about that."

"OK. How fast were you going in Everett's car when they chased you?"

"As fast as I could. They were on my ass the whole way."

"Were any other cars around?"

"A bunch of really pissed-off semi drivers. They were honking like crazy."

"Because, Ayden, Ian Stein is probably going to die. He could be dead already. He's lying in the cornfield beside your house. And you're saying there are truck drivers—and from all the honking, I'm guessing other drivers too—who saw Ian's bright red truck chasing Everett's white Grand Am—with you driving. And right now, that same truck and that same car are parked on your road near your house. Anyone driving by will see them. All this will fit with the story Todd will be more than happy to tell the police—if Everett doesn't kill him too." Phillip flung the broken bits of the twig across the woods. He ran his hand over his face, through his hair, and rubbed the back of his neck. "Oh God. What's happening? I should be in the cornfield stopping him."

"But you're *not* in the cornfield. You're here in the woods. With me." I smiled. "He asked you to wait here with me. And here you are. See. You're trusting Everett too." I reached for his shoulders. I used his sturdy frame to keep balanced as I tucked my knees under my chin. I perched like a bird on the trunk. "It'll be OK. Everett'll take care of everything just like he said he would. Even in my dreams—" I stopped short.

"*Even in your dreams*—what?"

"Even in my dreams, Everett comes to rescue me," I revealed. "The other night, I was lost in an apple orchard. There were monsters in the fog. Everett rode a bike straight into my dream and saved me with one of his tricks."

"He told you that it was him? In your dream?"

I nodded. "He leaves his own dreams to come find me."

"And you believe him?"

"Sure I do. Because he's there. He tells me he'll be there. And he is." Phillip let out a deep sigh and stepped back from me.

Without his shoulders, I dipped forward precariously before grabbing the back of the trunk to regain my balance. He turned from me and faced the collage of mostly bare branches. I couldn't help but feel sorry for him. He was so tormented.

I peered over his shoulder into the same scenery. The way the branches were hooked together, overlapping and intersecting, they resembled a mangled collection of deer antlers. It was beautiful really. It was nature—naked. I became lost in the branches' intricacies, the twisting and winding, until it appeared as if they were actually moving. Soon I began hearing what I saw: the clack of branches gently tapping each other. At first, I thought it was a deer, a buck moving amid the perfect camouflage of faux antlers. Phillip heard it too. He slowly stepped backward and turned to me with a look of paranoia. "What if it's that old guy!" he whispered. "We're not supposed to be out here." He crouched down. "Get down from there!"

Despite Phillip's command, I remained contentedly perched on the floating tree. I was not afraid. In fact, as the figure came forward, it brought with it an overwhelming sense of much needed peace. "It's only nature," I whispered.

The overlapping branches created the illusion of an ever-changing wardrobe. Although the branches clothed her for moments at a time, glimpses of her bare skin could be seen between them. The closer she came, the more the branches gave way, slowly revealing her naked figure. Apart from her pink nipples and dark mound of pubic hair, she was as pale as powder. Her face was the purest white, aside from her cheeks, which were flushed with a pigment of red that complemented the rich leaves that fell around her.

It was as though she carried forward the backdrop of the woods with her as she emerged apart from it. She did not have hair. Instead, thin, intertwining branches sprouted from the top of her head. They extended almost a foot, making her quite statuesque. Her steps were precise, yet she did not look to the ground. She knew by instinct when to step over a log and where the earth was soft enough for her bare, delicate feet. As she stepped into the red light of the setting sun, it filtered through the trees, painting her skin in a kaleidoscope of crimson shapes. The shapes seemed to morph into flames that flickered in slow motion over her body. She sauntered up to Phillip, and he was captured in her glow.

"What the hell?" he uttered under his breath. Her brown eyes locked on him, and he was simply mesmerized by the beautiful creature. They studied each other's peculiarities. She touched his sweater, examining it as if it were the oddest thing on the planet. She ran her hands over his chest and down to his stomach. Upon determining the material was only a covering, she lifted the sweater with much curiosity. When she saw the skin of his torso, her eyes widened in surprise. She ran her hands under his sweater, across his chest, and up to his shoulders. Phillip willingly lifted his arms and pulled the sweater over his head. Static caused his blond hair to mold into several wisps. Following her lead, Phillip ran his hands across the back of her smooth shoulders while she caressed his chest.

Although Phillip may have been thinking it, it was the woman from the trees who softly placed her lips on his. When their lips parted, she took a half step away to further examine the creature she had just kissed. Phillip quickly reclosed the gap. Clearly, for him their brief kiss wasn't enough. She answered his advancement by grasping his shoulders and leaning in to him. She kissed him again, more powerfully. So powerfully he lost his balance and teetered backward. Still locked in their kiss, he took her with him as he fell onto the delicate bed of leaves. With her palms resting on either side of his head, a wave of movement started from the small of her back. It ran up her spine and to her shoulders, causing her back to arch. When the wave reached her neck, her lips finally parted from Phillip's.

She peeled down his khaki pants and underwear and pushed them to his ankles. He pulled her back to him, his strong hands pressing into the delicate skin of her back. He held her in position as he ran his open mouth over her breasts. She sat on top of him with her eyes closed, concentrating on Phillip's movements, absorbing his touch. Their bodies moved in a rhythm only the two of them could follow. Phillip let out subtle moans as they increased their tempo. He gently touched her face, feeling where the roots of her branches protruded from her scalp.

By the way Phillip writhed in pleasure beneath her, I knew he had forgotten all about Ian in the pit. And about Everett's fight with the Toad. He was even unaware of my presence in the tree above. All his fears and frustrations were gone. To him, in those moments, all that existed was the naked tree woman. With her soft skin and hair of dried branches, she alleviated Phillip's angst.

It was OK, what was happening, I reasoned. She came straight from nature. Innocent. Beautiful like a deer. Delicate like the leaves. And I was the owl, the silent bird watching from the treetop. And gentle Phillip, wrapped in her presence, had become infused with nature too. It surrounded us. Was a part of us. Took us over. I dug my fingers beneath the bark and felt the naked layer of moist skin. Orange and red leaves showered their bodies as Phillip neared the peak of his pleasure.

When it was over, he turned his head my way and blinked slowly as if he were awakening from a drug-induced haze. He looked to his hands, his fingers resting between her mesh of branches. I was so sure he had been utterly contented. But the transposing worlds of the tree woman's beauty and the reality he knew hit him like a bucket of ice water. He stared at her as if she were a character in a dream, as if she was suddenly as obscure as his surroundings had been moments earlier. He jerked his hands from her head, digging his elbows into the leaves. The sudden movement caused her eyes to spring open. He slid from under her in a panic.

She knelt before him as he stood exposed. She did not show him her face again. She held her head low as she rose, only allowing him to see the tips of her branches. No longer able to entice him with her beauty, she slowly stepped out of their bed of leaves. It was mournful to watch her turn away from us. She kept her head hung low as she headed back into the collage of trees from which she came. We watched her slow, somber departure—until her body began to mesh with the branches in the distance and the final rays of red light from the nearly sunken sun.

Phillip hurriedly pulled his pants to his hips. With the sun just about set, it was difficult to make him out, standing just feet in front of me, let alone make out a *new* creature that staggered through the woods. It wasn't the delicate tree woman. That was for sure. It stumbled over fallen branches and trampled patches of mayapple. This time, it was I who was tempted to warn we ought to hide. The brash steps could've very likely belonged to Mr. Peterson. Or worse—Todd the Toad. I jumped from the floating tree. "Get down!" I whispered to Phillip. Yet despite the approaching figure, Phillip continued to stare into the distance, attempting to use the faint, diffused light to trace the outline of her image among the shadowed branches. As it turned out, even after his stunned awakening, Phillip was still enamored by the naked tree woman.

"What's going on?" Everett's voice boomed. He came through the darkness to find Phillip, leaves stuck to his clothes and hair, pulling his sweater over his head. Neither of us dared answer. We instead gazed sheepishly to the forest floor.

I could tell by the way Everett spoke that his jaw throbbed, and I had a good idea that at least a couple of his teeth had been knocked loose. He spit. Even in near darkness, I could see blood gushing from his nose, over his lips, and down his chin. His hands too were covered in blood. He wiped them on his jeans, but the caked-on blood had stained his skin. He was completely spent. "What happened?" I asked.

He ignored my question just as we had ignored his. "Go home," he ordered. "Use the side door. Go down to the basement. Wait a half hour. Then, go upstairs. If you see Mom, tell her you've been in the basement since you got home from school. Tell her I'm with Phillip. Tell her we had to clean blades tonight and will be home extra late. OK?"

"Got it," I confirmed.

"Phillip?" Everett called his name, but Phillip still wasn't entirely on the same planet as us. "Phillip!"

"Yeah? What?" he asked, finally snapping to attention.

"I need your help, all right? You're going to help, aren't you?"

If Everett had pressed him earlier, Phillip surely would've protested. Yet after his surreal encounter, he simply looked at Everett in a state of bewilderment and replied, "All right."

That's when I knew everything was going to work out. Everything was going to be OK. I ran to the house like I was told as Phillip followed Everett without question.

18
CLEVER VIGNETTES

My hands were freezing. My index finger ached from holding down the nozzle for so long. I let up and shook the can, listening to the metal ball clanking inside. For the second night in a row, Everett, Phillip, and I worked to transform the white car into a deep shade of blue—by using the cheapest spray paint available.

Everett had parked the Grand Am in the far corner of the field to keep it hidden from the road. It worked, somewhat, on account of the tall weeds, which had turned a crispy brown. But the woods had become a skeleton of itself. The looming winter had taken most of its leaves. As we worked, the occasional car traveling down Johnston Street clear on the other side of the trees could be seen. The camouflage we enjoyed had been lifted, our secret world exposed.

The work was silent. And awkward. Phillip and Everett didn't speak. Judging by the mood, I figured it best to keep my mouth shut as well. So it was with much relief and delight when I noticed a black cat poke its head through the weeds. Easily distracted and unable to resist petting him, I set down my can and followed as he tunneled away from me. He bounded into the cornfield. He didn't startle as I stepped beside him. In fact, he curled around my legs while I rubbed his chin and the top of his head.

Just like the woods, the cornfield too had become a shell of its former self. It was hard to imagine the desolate land was the same that held the maze in which we battled ferocious demons. The corn had been harvested. Every bit of it. Even the stalks. All that remained were their cut bases jutting from the earth. Revealed were the subtle hills and slopes we had dashed up and down during dramatic ambushes and retreats. Since the corn had been cut, I'd walk back and forth over the barren field searching for arrowheads—and for something else. But I never could find the pit. I imagined Everett had gone to great lengths to make it look as though it had never existed.

The disappearance of Ian Stein and Todd the Toad was all anyone at school could talk about. Letters had been sent home asking parents for any information that might lead to their whereabouts. No one knew where they were. Even *I* didn't know where they were. All I knew was what had happened to Ian in the pit. But the pit was no longer there. Ian's truck was gone. And I had no idea what happened to Todd after Phillip and I had entered the woods. Everett didn't volunteer any information. And when I asked, I was told to forget about that day and never speak of it again. It was Everett's way of protecting me, I figured, sheltering me just in case the attention turned our way. It was smart. The less I knew, the safer I'd be. If I was ever asked, I could truly say I didn't know what had become of Ian Stein and Todd Snelling.

And then there was Phillip. It was hard telling exactly what he knew. Ever since that night, he had been stuck in a kind of catatonic state. He barely spoke. Had become withdrawn. He came over when Everett asked him to, yet he wasn't the same. As he spray-painted on autopilot, I wondered just where his mind truly was.

Although Everett wouldn't speak to *me* about Ian and Todd, he eagerly plugged himself into the school's gossip chain. And soon, several theories began to sprout. One rumor had the pair driving to Mexico, with the plan being to purchase cheap drugs to resell at school. There were several variations as to why they hadn't returned. In one of the more upbeat versions, the pair had decided to skip high school altogether and stay in sunny Mexico. In one of the darker versions, they were kidnapped for ransom by a drug dealer, the value of their ransom proving more lucrative than the proposed deal. In a third version, Ian died of an overdose while sampling their would-be product, leaving Todd too ashamed to return and face Ian's family as well as his own.

Another theory had the duo using fake IDs to gain entry to the Horseshoe Bar in Ruthsford. Driving home drunk, they struck a woman alongside the road near the Ruthsford Cemetery. In one account, the woman was thrown down a steep hill, with Ian and Todd carelessly leaving her to die in the ravine. In another version, the woman miraculously survived the hit-and-run and crawled up the steep bank, seeking help at a nearby house. Both stories ended with the two young men so afraid of being identified that they fled town, heading to Canada or possibly California.

Everett lit his little fires and stepped out of the way. He never claimed to be the source. And he didn't fan the flames. He merely sat back and watched his stories circulate and solidify. Others made them real. It worked all too well. Sharla Ross, a sophomore, claimed her cousin was friends with the woman struck on the side of the road. Even the Blonde Eagle latched on to one of the Mexican drug stories, claiming she remembered overhearing the pair's plan of sneaking away to Mexico for an adventure.

Even with the student body occupied with nonsense, Everett wasn't satisfied. He knew police would be interviewing friends of Ian and Todd—as well as their enemies. No one became that popular without having a few enemies. Luckily, I was considered neither a friend nor an enemy of Ian and Todd. Never acting on the terror they had caused me, I was simply a quiet victim. The trouble was, Everett and Phillip *had* acted that October day after Ian doused me with his cheap cologne. And that brief scuffle as I scurried away held the danger of linking us to their disappearance.

So Everett infiltrated Ian and the Toad's circle of friends. With them gone, it was easy. The groupies were all too willing to join alliances with an upperclassman who was just as charismatic as Ian. His strategy with their girlfriends required a bit more finesse, however. Sure, he empathized with them, showing concern for their missing boyfriends. But Everett knew Kirsten held some sympathy for me ever since she had apologized to him about Ian's asshole-ish behavior. He used that sympathy to come across as a sensitive guy who was only standing up for his younger, awkward brother.

The police had little to go on. All they knew for sure was the pair was last seen at school that Friday afternoon in October and that Ian's truck was missing. There wasn't even any concrete evidence the two had left together. By the time the police showed up to school, the rumors were at their peak. The police were likely just as perplexed as the students had been, wondering which of Everett's clever vignettes were true. They searched lockers for clues. They interviewed teachers, guidance counselors, and of course students. But since Everett had won over the groupies and smoothed things over with Kirsten and the Blonde Eagle, we were in no way associated with the twosome—as friends or foes. And so Everett, Phillip, and I evaded the inquisition. Only one piece remained: Everett's white Grand Am.

I returned from the cornfield cradling the cat in my arms like a baby. I burrowed my cold hand in the warm fur of his stomach as he purred contentedly.

"You came back just in time. We've finished," Everett said with a smirk.

I shrugged and joined them in examining the car. It looked like complete crap. Even after ten cans of spray paint, the work looked shoddy. The blue color was uneven, some patches darker than others. It didn't go on smooth. It bubbled over the layer of paint beneath. Yet Everett seemed pleased with the outcome, so I wasn't about to critique it. Besides, our goal had been accomplished: the car was no longer white. With the job finished, Everett's mood was lighter than it had been all week. "We're done for today," he announced, finally relieving us of our duties.

"Thank God. No more bus," I said, relieved.

"Not so fast," Everett replied. "We're keeping it out here for a while. Until this blows over. But if you don't want to ride the bus anymore, Phillip could drive us." Phillip looked past Everett to the weeds. He didn't confirm nor object, just simply took what was thrown at him. "And, Phillip," Everett continued, "before you go, I need to borrow your car for about a half hour."

"You can do whatever you want. Clearly," Phillip replied as he began to collect the scattered paint cans.

19
COLD, DARK WiNTER

Phillip waited with me in the basement for Everett to return with his car. I had carried the cat back with us. He sat on my lap purring loudly, happy to be inside from the cold. Cable wasn't hooked up to the old television in the basement, and the reception was spotty. Our choices were limited to a religion channel and a home shopping channel. Much to Phillip's annoyance, I habitually switched between the two.

I got a kick out of the exuberant televangelist bragging about how many people were watching the program from around the world and about how he had already saved millions by bringing them to the Lord Jesus Christ. He implored us to call the number at the bottom of the screen, promising that one of his prayer counselors would help us receive Jesus. Wondering what receiving Jesus would've entailed exactly, I reached behind me and jokingly picked up the phone. Phillip only rolled his eyes.

On the shopping network, an equally exuberant woman was selling a sixty-five-piece gold-plated silverware set. It was on special for seventy-five dollars for the upcoming holidays. She kept repeating how classy the set would look for special occasions, while also pointing out that the pieces were durable enough for everyday use. "What better way to make your whole family feel special than sitting down for a meal and seeing these utensils shimmering on the table? Absolutely stunning!" She beamed.

They were similar in their approach, the woman selling silverware and the evangelist selling Jesus. I was intrigued by their skills, their ability to convince people to pick up the phone. And who were these people calling the numbers at the bottom of their screens? Naïve people. Easily influenced. Quick to be taken in by charm and empty promises.

Phillip grabbed the remote and abruptly switched off the television. "You're gullible," he announced. The cat, awoken by his sudden voice, lifted his head and blinked glazed-eyed at Phillip. He stood from my lap and arched his back before stepping off my legs and rubbing against Phillip. Phillip ignored the cat and leaned toward me. "You believe everything he tells you. But he tricks people. That's his thing. I don't know how he does it. He's tricked you into believing things that don't exist. He's tricked me into doing things I'd normally never do. He controls people." He anxiously scratched the side of his face. His fingertips were stained blue, just like mine. Finally, Phillip was letting me in on what had been going on behind his vacant eyes.

"No one's trying to control you," I promised.

"He's a fucking murderer. He'll do what he has to so he doesn't get caught. He's even tried feeding me the same bullshit he's filled your mind with."

My face became hot. The cat became restless. He jumped from the couch and paced back and forth in front of the door. When he realized neither of us was going to let him out, he began reaching his paws beneath the crack. "What'd he tell you?" I asked, focusing on the agitated cat instead of Phillip.

"That it was you, through your dreams, who found that money hidden in the tree. And through your dreams, you knew about the Indians buried in the woods." I was shocked Everett had exposed those secrets to Phillip. Yet at the same time, I was pleased. It meant he wanted Phillip to join us—completely. I did too. Yet based on

Phillip's reaction, perhaps it hadn't gone so well. Perhaps Phillip wasn't quite ready. "Everything he said was so ridiculous. I don't buy any of it. Not one word."

"But it's true," I vowed.

"Think about it for just one minute. Those coins you found? It could've easily been sleight of hand. He could've been carrying them all along and then pretended to pull them out of the tree. The Indians? He might've already known they were there and then planted the idea in your head about people buried in the woods. You say he comes to you in your dreams? Well, he knows that. He knows you dream of him. Maybe the real Everett is taking credit for the Everett in your dreams. You have to admit, you are a bit— impressionable. But c'mon. Spaceship rides in the middle of the night? Monsters in the corn?"

"The tree woman in the woods?" I interrupted. I was stunned how much Everett had revealed to Phillip. But if he could've admitted the tree woman's existence, then surely he could've believed it possible there were such things as monsters. Yet Phillip retreated to that same vacant stare. I had every intention of forcing the issue and making him confess what he experienced in the woods. But for once, I stopped myself. Perhaps Phillip had buried her deep within his mind. Perhaps to validate her existence would be too frightening for him to handle. He seemed determined to stay in his world of logic, where there wasn't any room for women with twisted branches in lieu of hair. If he didn't acknowledge she actually existed, she could remain relegated to a fantasy world.

Phillip's eyes veered away from me and became lost in the blank television screen. "My God. You two are crazy. And you're making me crazy too."

"You're not crazy," I assured him. "And we're not either," I added with some measure of defiance.

"I just wish you'd stop following him so blindly. I get it. He's your brother. I know you can't really get away from him. But you know what? I can. I will no longer allow him to manipulate me. I will no longer do whatever he says just because I'm afraid of what we've done."

"Are you going to tell the police?"

"No. It's too late for that now—unless I want to get arrested for being an accomplice to murder. But I'm telling you this: After he brings my car back, I'm not coming over here anymore. I'm not speaking to him at school. And in the spring, if he decides he still wants to work at RJs, I'll find another job."

I began feeling as agitated as the cat clawing to be let out. I sprang from the couch and snatched the cat. I placed him firmly in my lap, but he struggled away from me. He finally settled on the back of the couch behind Phillip. "What if it's not that easy?" I asked. "What if Everett doesn't *let* you go?"

"He doesn't need me anymore. I've helped clean up his mess. Helped spread his lies. Helped disguise his car. There's nothing left for me to do."

I wanted to plead my rebuttal but was silenced by the sound of the door swinging open upstairs. The cat twisted his ears and stared intently at the ceiling as the stomps descended. Everett burst open the door. To our surprise, he was not alone. Oddly, there was an arm wrapped around his waist. I could tell the way Phillip's eyes widened that he was just as shocked as I was when her head popped up from behind Everett's shoulder.

"Hi, Phil!" She smiled at him, displaying her gap-toothed grin. She then lasered in on me. "Hi, Ayden," she said, using a voice as if she were talking to a child. She bent over to greet me, and strands of her hair fell forward, tickling my forehead. I felt trapped within her hair. My skin began to itch under my sweater. After finally tossing back her head, she used her hand as a temporary ponytail holder. With her full face revealed, I noticed how much her deep brown eyes complemented her auburn hair. She didn't wear makeup. She was pretty in a natural way, I supposed.

"Hello," I quietly replied.

"Kirsten has horses," Everett announced. "You like horses, don't you, Ayden?"

"Yeah." He knew I liked horses. He didn't have to ask. The way she whipped her long hair in circles behind her head reminded me of a horse's tail. "You kind of look like a horse," I told her. Phillip chuckled cautiously while Everett produced a firm frown.

"Kirsten's dad has fifteen horses on a ranch in Texas," Everett continued.

"Yes. And I have three quarter horses and two Appaloosas here," she boasted. "You can come over and ride them if you want."

I couldn't respond. I didn't know what was happening. *What's he doing with Kirsten? Why'd he bring her into our basement?*

"So let me get this straight. You two are an item?" Phillip bluntly asked the question I was too afraid to ask.

Everett wrapped his arm around her waist. "You could say that," he said, flashing his devilish grin.

It was so strange. Was I supposed to congratulate them? I hadn't ever seen Everett with a girl in that way. It was something I had never even imagined. Their affection toward one another made me feel embarrassed. And nervous. I found myself producing a fake cough.

The plastered-on smile left Kirsten's face. Suddenly she became solemn. She clasped her hands and bowed her head as if she was going to pray. "Everett means so much to me," she gushed with a quiver in her voice. "He's been my rock. My best friend, helping me through everything that's happened." She looked to him adoringly before giving him a small peck on his stubbled cheek. Clearly, she was under his spell.

Phillip shifted uncomfortably. Perhaps he too found her as pathetic as I did. There she was fawning over Everett for helping her cope with her loss—when *he* was the one who had killed her boyfriend. And what was Everett thinking? Was she his ultimate revenge against Ian? There was no way he genuinely liked her. There was no way he truly fell for her big, dumb smile and her long horse hair. *Was there?*

"So you're over him now?" I asked Kirsten. "Ian?" I felt the question was a legitimate one, seeing as it had been only about a month since he had gone missing. Yet I realized my mistake when the room filled with a terrible silence and Everett shot a glare my way so powerful it felt as if he were burning a hole right through me.

Kirsten clung tightly to Everett as if she needed protection—from me of all people. She looked about to burst into tears. But before she could let any stream down her face, she unlatched herself from Everett, took in a deep breath, and tossed her hair back once again. Her eyes were glazed, yet she smiled triumphantly through her pain. She turned to the cat, which had been watching her the entire time with intense curiosity. "Is it yours?" she asked.

"He doesn't belong to anyone," I replied.

"Can I pet it?" Without waiting for my answer, she reached for the top of the cat's head. Already agitated, he displayed his fangs and hissed at her. Droplets of his saliva sprayed her hand. Before she had a chance to pull back, he clamped himself on to her arm, digging his claws into her skin. She attempted to pull away, but that only caused his nails to hook in deeper. He stood on his hind legs to tighten his grip. He then bit down on her like a snake injecting venom. Blood trickled from the fresh punctures. She whined for Everett, who came to her aid, scowling at me disapprovingly as he unclamped the ornery, growling cat from her arm.

"He's wild." I shrugged. I opened the door. The cat shot out of the room and galloped up the stairs. I followed him, no longer wanting to be trapped in the basement myself. I let him outside, and he darted into the bushes.

I stepped onto the driveway. The burst of chilly air felt good on my flushed face. Phillip too emerged. He stood beside me, hugging himself in the cold. "What's Everett doing?" I asked, looking to the swaying bushes. "Why does *he* have to be the one to help her?"

"Do you mean to say you're questioning Everett?" he replied sarcastically.

I didn't answer. But it was the truth. Everett confused me that day. Before Kirsten entered our basement, I had never questioned Everett—not even after Phillip's passionate tirade. It was strange. I never thought one person could change things so much. But Kirsten the Horse Girl did. "I just don't understand why he is with her."

Phillip laughed. And with all the wisdom he possessed at that age, he simply replied, "Relax, Ayden. As fucked up and crazy as he is—he's growing up. What'd you expect? Him to never have a girlfriend?"

The wind was suddenly no longer refreshing. It began to sting my ears and nose. As my face went numb, I watched Phillip climb into his car. I followed it to the end of the drive and watched it turn the corner. Tiny frozen crystals began to gently sprinkle over the neighborhood. It had been threatening for weeks, and the sky had finally given in. It was time for cold, dark winter. And there was nothing that could be done to stop it.

PART IV
KIRSTEN THE HORSE GIRL

20
NEVER-ENDING BLACKNESS

My fingertips squeaked over the paneling as I circled sunken, hollowed eyes and traced curved horns. The man with the melted face eyed me with his sinister, unrelenting gaze. But I knew there was nothing behind those eyes. It had been years since the monsters had separated from my walls and roamed free. On that night, I had an inkling they were searching for a way back in. It was most likely the horned monsters I heard scratching at the side of the house. Digging like dogs. Perhaps they were burrowing, searching for weaknesses in the foundation.

Phillip had been wrong. I realized that as my panic escalated. The monsters *were* real. I wasn't dreaming. Everett wasn't there to suggest their existence. In fact, they came for me *because* Everett was gone. For years, they had been waiting for the moment I'd be left unprotected. And finally, on that night, they had me right where they wanted. Alone. Vulnerable. Dad was on his route somewhere in Indiana. Mom was at the hospital. Not that it would've mattered much had they been there. Neither possessed Everett's expertise. Versus one of the demons, they would've been devoured in seconds.

Shadows, black as oil, swelled from the corners. One climbed up on the foot of the bed. I pulled my limbs closer to my body. Another stretched across the ceiling. When it reached the light overhead, it began draining the bulbs. Tiny pops erupted until the bulbs were completely overpowered. In total darkness, all I could focus on was the scratching and digging, which morphed into rancorous clawing and pounding. The sounds intensified and overlapped, culminating in a single horrific hum. It was so violently loud, so unrelenting, I began to shake. And just when I thought I could no longer stay inside my skin—it stopped. Silence. My heart raced, but I didn't dare move a muscle. And then, through the heating vent, came growling and low whispers. The monsters were in the house.

Finally compelled to move, I stood briskly and blindly fumbled for the doorknob. Once I assured that the door was locked, I rushed to the window and threw open the shade. I used the pale moonlight and the distant glow of Mr. Newberry's ever-faithful lamp atop his pole barn to find my jeans. I slipped them on and felt for the keys in the front pocket. I looked over the driveway. Outside, the wind had picked up. It lashed the tall bushes. There sat Everett's old Grand Am. It glowed under the moonlight like a jeweled chariot, with the promise of whisking me away from danger.

The steps began to creak. The demons were making their way upstairs. As they crept down the hall, their eager chatter filtered beneath the door. Gently, politely, the doorknob twisted back and forth, producing a series of clicks. There was no doubt the demons could've easily burst through and ripped me apart in seconds. Yet they savored my fear. They could smell it. They wanted me marinated in it before they ate me.

I lifted the window. The warm night air poured freely into the room. I was ready to remove the screen, lift my legs over the edge, and jump—when curiously, the doorknob became still. I turned back. Only for a moment. The weak light from outside couldn't even begin to penetrate the infinite black hole that had become the room. And out of this blackness, a twisted face appeared. Caught off guard, my body jolted. It climbed from the shadows and flipped its cloak over its shoulders, exposing its chest and stomach, which were invisible against the black backdrop of the room. Clever demon, it had found a way, through a dark portal, to beat the horned monsters to the prize. It sneered, bringing its melted face before mine, allowing me to view its leathery skin up close. It was pulled in extreme positions, like invisible pins holding down the hide of a dissected animal.

I frantically shoved the screen, and it popped out of the frame. The cloaked monster, however, was not about to let its prey escape. I felt its powerful hands clamp on to my shoulders. It spun me to face it. All I could see was black as it shoved me into itself, forcing me into its body of darkness. I struggled, grabbing the edges of its cloak, kicking my legs like a helpless frog being eaten headfirst by a hungry snake.

Inside of it, the darkness was overwhelming. I tingled like my blood had stopped circulating. This sensation took over my entire body. It felt as if I were slowly transforming from organic matter into static electricity. I became dizzy. Disoriented. I began to see shapes that were even darker than the dark and vast space before me. The shapes danced closer, morphing into beings with thin bodies and large, oblong heads. They floated in front of me as if they were treading water. Their bodies had no bones. No flesh. They were just—dark matter. They warped and twisted into odd formations. Some had limbs stretching more than twice the length of their bodies, appendages so thin, they became nothing more than faint wisps across the deep space.

It became all-consuming, this world of never-ending blackness. It would've been easy to just let go, to join the dark beings that had gathered to witness my arrival into their world. Yet I could still feel my bedroom wall with my bare feet. I could still feel the wind blowing up the back of my T-shirt. It took all my strength, all my concentration, to brace my heels against the wall and begin stepping up its side. I knew if I were to slip, my attempt at escaping would surely fail—and I'd be swallowed whole. I climbed until I felt the window's ledge. And then, I stretched my legs as far as I could before hooking my ankles to the other side. The cloaked demon tried pulling me deeper inside it, but I flexed my feet tightly, holding on as long as I could.

The black-as-ink beings crowded me. Their bodies overlapped, merged, and split apart again. They caressed my neck and face. Their touch was electric. Wherever they touched, the tingling sensation intensified. I realized, as they wrapped around my neck, that they wanted me to join them, that they were helping the demon devour me. They choked me as they coiled and tugged with their electrified limbs.

So that it could finish its meal, the monster lunged forward to unhook my feet. Yet as it did, I stiffened my legs and held tightly on to its cloak. Instead of my being absorbed further into it, it inadvertently pushed me forward. My shins and kneecaps scraped over the ledge. Just as it was about to push me out the window, I let go of its cloak and transferred my grip to the windowsill. I squatted for a moment with my feet planted against the siding. And then, I pushed away from the house. The dark beings lost their grip on my neck, and my head separated from the demon's body. I imagined that I had kicked off the edge of a swimming pool to perform a backstroke and that I was gracefully floating over the driveway. But in reality, I fell to the grass with a thud, my head narrowly missing the cement.

I dug the keys out of my pocket while hoping to God my legs still worked after the fall. I twisted my neck to see Everett's car and the bushes thrashing beyond it. I wasn't so sure the thrashing was caused by the wind. Just as likely, there were monsters lurking within the bushes. I scrambled to my feet, ignoring my pain as I stumbled across the drive. I jumped in the car and sped down the road, not brave enough to look in the rearview mirror.

I drove through Ruthsford and past its cemetery hidden by the pines. I drove far into the country until I spotted an old wooden barn. Isolated and lonely, it was surrounded by a vast field of weeds and clover. I pulled off the road and drove straight through the field, listening to the weeds tickle the underside of the car. I parked beside the sad barn. Its paint had long since faded. Its sagging roof threatened to cave in. The planks that made up its outer walls had buckled. I wondered how many more years it could stand before collapsing under its own weight. I figured we could keep each other company for a while.

After assuring the doors were locked and that there were no demons in sight, I reclined the seat and rested my eyes. I had escaped, but my mind hadn't. Occasionally I saw flashes of its stretched face and of the dark beings that dwelled inside it. I had never been so afraid in my life. But my fear was overshadowed by my anger. I knew why I was attacked. And I knew exactly who was to blame.

21
CLIP-ON TIES

Surrounded by horses, I fed them carrots, apples, and tall grasses I had pulled just beyond the fence. I pretended I was one of them. That I could communicate with them. Our telepathic conversations were simplistic, consisting of such topics as which apples were the sweetest and how soothing the sun felt on our backs.

Everett and Kirsten had just returned from her father's ranch outside Houston. They had spent two weeks riding horses and exploring the city before making the cross-country trip back to Michigan with two new colts. Her father had given them to her to keep at her mother and stepfather's ranch. I hung out with the older horses as they got the new ones settled.

"You should be a trainer!" shouted Kirsten as she and Everett appeared at the far gate.

As they made their way across the pasture, the grouping scattered. I stood exposed with my bucket of treats, peeved they had interrupted us so soon after we had just gotten acquainted. "They don't need to be trained," I replied quietly. "They're fine the way they are."

"But you're a natural," she insisted, completely missing my point. "It's amazing how you can get the most timid horses to come up to you."

I had to squint into the afternoon sun to see them. They were holding hands. Whatever it was—maybe the glowing sun or the ranch as a backdrop—they looked as if they were straight from some postcard or magazine ad featuring the perfect married couple. Phillip had been right about one thing: we *were* growing up. The seasons seemed to change at a faster pace than when we were younger. Three years had passed since the disappearance of Ian and Todd the Toad. I was seventeen, about to graduate from high school. Everett had graduated the year before. He worked fulltime at a lumberyard driving a forklift, stocking wood, and loading it into the beds of pickups. Any spare time he had, he spent with Kirsten. She had started her own business giving horse-riding lessons and breaking in colts for novice equestrians. After work, Everett would help her with her stable chores.

It remained inconclusive whether it was the spirit of revenge or an initial infatuation that sparked Everett's interest in Kirsten. Whatever the reason for their strange union, I thought they would've grown tired of one another. They hadn't. Because of Kirsten, everything was different. Ever since that cold November day she had infiltrated our basement, my vision of Everett continued to waver. I was stuck between an Everett whom I trusted totally, unconditionally, and one who, as Phillip suggested, had manipulated my mind. Yet if the latter was true, he had since had his fill, had grown tired of the novelty.

Everett was no longer eager to hear my dreams. No longer interested in running through the cornfield in the middle of the night. I begged him to fly the spaceship with me just one last time. And the next day, I found a stack of job applications in my bedroom. Job applications! He had collected them from gas stations, fast-food restaurants, and grocery stores.

Everett had plans to buy a new car for himself with his paychecks from the lumberyard. So he promised that if I got a job, he'd give me the Grand Am. It was a nice enough gesture. But with him being so insistent I get a job, I was onto him. The message was clear. He wanted me occupied so he and Kirsten could spend more time—alone. True, wherever they went, I pretty much tagged along. I hated it. But what else was I supposed to do? With Kirsten always around, hanging out with Everett—without her—was nearly impossible. As hurt and annoyed as I was, by habit, I still did as he said and filled out every stupid application he had given me.

He took me for a haircut and let me borrow the clip-on tie he had used for his interview at the lumberyard. He said it was important I looked clean-cut for my interviews. "It doesn't really matter that you have no experience as long as you look clean-cut and come off as polite. Say you're a hard worker. Tell them you'll have your own transportation. It's that easy," he promised. And it was. In a couple weeks, I had a job bagging groceries.

There was a lot to remember: Don't pack soaps, detergents, or anything poisonous with food. Heavy items go on the bottom. Refrigerated items together. Ice cream in the special freezer bags. Don't bag milk unless requested. Eggs packed separately with breads and placed last in the cart so they're on top.

If a customer wanted carryout, I had to load the bags into their trunk. Petrified by conversation, I trailed far behind as I followed them to their car. But the distance wouldn't keep everyone from talking, mostly about the weather. "Now if I could just take you home with me to carry these bags into the house" was the typical parting statement. I'd force a laugh as if I hadn't already heard the same lame thing a thousand times. Aside from the small talk, I looked forward to carryouts. On my way back, to escape the frenzy inside, I'd take my time wandering the lot collecting far-off stray carts.

"We'd better get going," pushed Everett. I dumped out the remaining carrots and apples from the bucket before reluctantly leaving the horses. Mom was preparing a meal to welcome Everett and Kirsten back from their trip. Although it was early spring, she was having summer fever, so the menu was corn on the cob and barbecue chicken on the grill.

I was feeling the change of season too. Everything was melting. The ground was moist. Worms were making their way to the surface once again. The first of the robins had arrived and were hopping across lawns, pecking the muddy ground. Buds had appeared and were beginning to unfold. In the woods, the snow and ice had melted, flooding the low areas. Tadpoles and mosquito larvae were already swimming in the pools of murky water. In a few weeks, the higher grounds would be covered in the lush blooms of white and purple wildflowers. Everything was coming alive. It made me want to run through the field and into the woods. I wanted to balance across the logs connecting the Indian mounds. Build a fort. Sit on the roof all night long looking over the neighborhood and up at the stars. But I couldn't do any of those things. I was no longer a kid. I was graduating from high school. Soon I'd no longer even be a teenager.

When we came into the house, Mom was sprinkling paprika on her famous deviled eggs. Dad was on the patio putting the final coat of barbecue sauce on the chicken. The rich smoke blew through the screen door and saturated the house with its sweet aroma. "Kirsten, your hair's getting so long and so pretty," gushed Mom. "I wish I could find that shade of auburn in a box."

"Aw, thanks, Angie."

"Dinner's almost ready. Would you and Everett please set the dining room table? And, Ayden, go in the basement and bring up some pop," Mom said.

"We're not eating outside?" I asked, disappointed.

"We were going to. But when I went to take the cover off the picnic table, I noticed the side of the house was just covered with flies." She shrugged.

When I came back from the basement, I found Kirsten and Everett nuzzling beside the table. They giggled at being caught. I dropped the assortment of two-liters in front of them, prompting them to finish setting the table.

While we ate, Dad told us about the freezing rainstorm in Illinois he had to drive through a few weeks before. "The rig ahead of me smashed into a Celica. Bam!" We jolted as he clapped his hands together and then slid his palms over one another. "Boy, did that tiny thing go rolling across the median." But the bulk of the talk was about Everett and Kirsten's Houston trip. And after hearing every minute detail about that, we had to endure an endless update on Kirsten's horse-training business. I tuned her out and instead focused on the rays of light coming through the sliding glass door and warming the table. I was picturing the flies sunning themselves on the side of the house — when it happened.

With a hint of apprehension, Everett cleared his throat before scooting his chair closer to Kirsten's. He wrapped his arm around her shoulder. "Kirsten and I have been seeing each other for three years now. It's no secret how I feel about her." I didn't understand what was happening. But Mom immediately did. She stood from the table without pushing back her chair and produced a grin that rivaled the grins Everett and Kirsten had been flashing all day. She clasped her hands together in excitement. With only a few words, Everett had turned her into a giddy child. He finished by simply saying, "We're going to be married in June."

With that, Mom rushed to wrap Kirsten in her arms. She then moved to Everett and kissed his forehead. "I'm so happy! I'm so happy!"

Even Dad put down his cob of corn to dole out hugs. "I knew something was going on the way you two couldn't keep off each other," he said. Kirsten turned bashful, gazing to her lap with a shy smile while Mom, Dad, and Everett broke into laughter. It was hard to tell if they laughed because of Dad's remark or because of Kirsten's modest reaction to it.

"That's the good news," Everett warned.

"What could possibly be bad?" asked Mom. "Sure, it's a short engagement. My gosh — only a couple months! But it's right. It just feels right, doesn't it?"

"We're moving to Texas," Everett announced. Mom returned to her seat, the light drained from her face. As quickly as it had rushed in, the energy in the room dissipated. "When we went to visit Kirsten's dad, we looked at houses down there," he explained. "The cost of living is so much cheaper. Here, we'd have to move into a trailer or some crappy apartment. But there, even on our budget, we can afford a decent house. Kirsten's found a stable that wants to hire her. And the weather's so much nicer. You guys can visit in the winters to get away from the snow."

"But what will *you* do there?" Mom asked.

"There're plenty of lumberyards. I'm sure I'll find something." Mom shoved a spoonful of bean salad into her mouth, looking unconvinced. Kirsten pulled a section of her long hair behind her ear, her eyes nervously darting between Mom and Dad, attempting to read their faces. "It'll be all right," he promised. "And Kirsten's dad is down there if we need anything."

"They're young, Angie. Let them learn by trial and error," Dad piped up before starting back in on his corn.

"Oh. You're right," she conceded, forcing the return of her smile. "You've always been bold, Everett. It's just who you are. And things always seem to have a way of working out for you. So if you think this is the right choice for you and Kirsten, then I'll trust your judgment."

I didn't say a word as I watched it all unfold. On the outside, I was silent. But on the inside, I felt like a ghost no one could hear even though I was screaming at the top of my lungs. At some point, my brain had switched into protective mode. Parts of it shut down. The faces around the table became unfamiliar. I felt the sensation of seeping out of my body. I tried to keep it from happening, but my mind desperately wanted to evacuate, to flee from what it couldn't handle. And so I separated from my body, through the top of my skull, and found myself floating several feet over my head in a kind of vacuum. My body stood from the chair, but I was not controlling its muscles. I was no longer behind its eyes, although I was tethered to it, pulled along by it like a balloon on a string as it left the dining room. Nobody called after me. Nobody cared as my body lumbered through the side door and into the backyard. It marched instinctually through the field.

Parts of the ground were still frozen, while other sections were beginning to thaw. My feet stumbled over the earth without feeling the textures beneath. At the back of the field, the weeds from last season were still there, dingy and matted. Yet the forest was awakening, with tiny buds that had begun dotting the tree limbs. Being there was comforting. It was a familiar place. A special place. Where were the cats? I hadn't seen them in so long. I checked behind the log where they had appeared years before, but they weren't there.

My body crossed the property line and entered the cornfield. Dad had found out from Mr. Newberry that he wasn't going to plant corn that season. He was going to let the soil rest for a season or two, let it become rich again before planting a new crop. So without the land being tilled, a healthy growth of dandelions had taken over the landscape. They grew up the slope. Their heads were covered in that fuzzy, white down, waiting for strong winds or passing critters to shake loose their tiny parachutes and send their seeds airborne.

With each breath of spring air, I felt myself lowering. Calming. Merging back with my body. And when I found myself once again looking out from behind my organic eyes, when I once again had regained control of my limbs, I kicked the nearest cluster of dandelions. I watched the parachutes break loose and float away before cascading back to the earth like a gentle snowfall.

In the brush pile behind me, I heard sudden movement. I spun to see green eyes fixed on me. After darting his head out to say hello, the pure black feline bounded toward me. I couldn't be certain, but it sure seemed to be the same slender black cat that introduced himself to me the day we spray-painted the Grand Am years before. He followed as I began making my way through the field of dandelions. Not too far into my trek, I checked to see if he was still behind me. Not only had he followed closely, but behind him, three more cats had emerged from the brush. Each had identical black coats. Their emerald eyes sparkled in the afternoon light.

We marched up the slope, knocking loose and dispersing the dandelion seeds as we went. Each time I looked behind me, more black cats had joined the procession. They were multiplying. The small group of four became twenty. Then fifty. As I neared the top of the hill, I looked again, and there were hundreds of black cats trampling through the field of dandelions.

I stopped at the highest point. From directly behind me to the base of the slope, the landscape was dotted with black felines. As soon as they recognized I was standing still, they halted as well, observing me attentively. The seeds they had kicked up made it appear to be snowing from the ground upward. The particles eventually fell back upon them, delicately painting their black coats with white speckles. Some sat on their hind legs. Some lay with their paws crossed regally in front of them, while others began grooming themselves, checking intermittently to assure I was still within view.

I knew what it meant. They had come to say goodbye. My vision became blurred. The field in front of me became a watery, impressionistic landscape of black splashes against a muddy backdrop. I wiped the tears from my eyes so I could more clearly take in the beautiful scene.

Crossing over from our property, a figure stepped into the field. *Everett.* He looked up the slope while shielding his eyes from the sun. Having identified me, he cupped his hands around his mouth and shouted something I couldn't make out in the distance. The cats nearest him seemed to pay him no attention. They continued to focus in my direction. Frustrated, he began charging through the congregation. The cats did not waver as he stepped between and over them, his shoes kicking up the fallen white flakes.

When he finally reached the top of the hill, he didn't say a word. There was nothing he could've said except to say he was not leaving. Instead, he stood beside me in silence, looking over the content felines. After some time, he sat on the moist ground. I sensed him looking up to me, so I did as he asked without words and sat beside him. My jeans immediately became soaked from the damp soil. Together, we took it all in one last time. The woods. The fields. And the mystical cats that sat patiently before us. As the sun set over the landscape, I still couldn't believe what was happening. I couldn't believe he was abandoning our magical world.

22
LiTTLE BLUE HOUSE

With Everett gone, buildings were taller. Hallways were longer. The universe itself seemed to expand. The sky was vast, and the stars that speckled it moved apart from each other, creating gaps the size of galaxies composed of nothing but empty space. Without Everett, the world was overwhelming. He wasn't there to explain it to me. Protect me. Tell me what to do. How to act. I realized quickly I didn't know who I was. He held my identity and took it with him wherever people go when they *grow up*. And I was left an empty, isolated abnormality.

The world wasn't to be enjoyed but endured—and if I was lucky, in small doses. I was afraid of being around other people. Everyone was so much more intelligent than I, their words much more articulate than the surely erroneous words I would've uttered—so I avoided eye contact and stopped speaking. Driving became too heavy a responsibility. There were too many components to remember. Too many opportunities to make a mistake, get in an accident, become lost, break something I couldn't fix. So I started riding my bike to work.

Work. I dreaded going. I had been reassigned to the bottle room in the back of the store, sorting pop and beer cans. The machine had eight slots, each corresponding to a bottling company. My job was to slide the cans into the correct slot. The machine would crush and drop them into the bins below. It became too complicated. Too often I stood in front of the growling machine, watching earwigs crawl out from cans that hadn't been rinsed, unsure of which slot the can in my hand was supposed to be dropped into. *Does Coke or Pepsi make Mellow Yellow?* I'd agonize over these choices as more and more bins filled with cans to be crushed piled up behind me.

Nature became my only solace, a sanctity in a world that spun so fast I couldn't keep my eyes focused. I studied its microsystems. I stared into puddles. Peered into foxholes. Sat among weeds. I examined the bones of a dead raccoon I had found at the back of the field. I stared at them for so long, imagining them gathering and fusing, that I wouldn't have been at all surprised had the hollow carcass stood and scurried into the forest. I'd hike to the far end of the woods, where there was a small pond. If I sat long enough, turtles would come out of the water to say hello. Some days, it'd be five at a time. I'd pet their heads with my finger. I'd grip their shells and sail them around the edges of the pond as if they were miniature spaceships. They came to love hovering in the tall weeds, chewing on foliage they couldn't otherwise reach.

Even though I found comfort escaping into the countryside I knew so well, I had to be careful not to lose track of time. It was crucial I be back to the house before dark—because when Everett left, it was not just my identity and confidence that were taken; my protection was gone as well. Strange how at one time I had welcomed the monsters. I'd become excited when Everett suggested we search them out in the cornfield or deep within the woods. We'd tempt them. Tease them. It was like poking at a tiger through a cage. With Everett, there was no real danger. Yet without Everett, the cage had been removed. The tiger was loose, and it was looking to kill.

Each night, they dared come closer to the house. I lay awake listening to their tapping. Scratching. Digging. Their grunts. And their moans. Nobody but Everett could've stopped them. He promised he'd visit. And he'd say, "You can visit me when Mom and Dad come to Texas. And when you save up enough money, you can come on your own." But promises of seeing him in some vague future weren't enough. I lived with the ever-present feeling of impending doom.

And soon, just as I predicted, evil came to me in the middle of the night. It didn't shatter the windows or claw through the doors. It was through a portal of darkness that a cloaked demon found its way into my room. I narrowly escaped being eaten alive by jumping out my window. That night, I slept in my car beside an old barn. Only when the sun rose did I make my way back home. Still too afraid to go inside, I sat on the log in the field where Everett used to sit, staring into a sea of tall weeds.

The tallest golden strand became my focal point. I studied its subtle sway. I concentrated all my energy, fear, and desperation into the tip of the thin plant. I stayed locked on it, and eventually everything else went black. All that existed was the swaying plant. Noises from the woods were erased. My sense of touch was removed. I became numb. The weight of my body was gone. It was a strange sensation, being in the field while at the same time feeling as if I wasn't even there. At the peak of this vibrating duality, I knew I no longer needed the swaying weed. I was ready to let go.

I closed my eyes and traveled high above myself. It wasn't my first time. I had done it before in that very spot as Everett looked on. I had never gone much higher than the trees. Yet no longer did our hiding spot in the field offer the same comfort and safety it once had. No longer did I feel compelled to stay tethered to it. I rose to the clouds and flew through their foggy dampness. I was afraid I'd lose control and float forever past the stratosphere and into the ozone layer. I was afraid I'd be catapulted into space and become trapped somewhere beyond our solar system, unable to find my way back. But I concentrated on my breathing. I could breathe at that altitude just like I could breathe underwater in my dreams.

And slowly, I relaxed. Being sure to keep within the safety of the clouds, I allowed myself to ride the wind.

When it felt right, I exhaled deeply and dropped below the billowing wisps. No longer was I above the woods and the field. Instead, I hovered over a neighborhood I wasn't familiar with. In this particular neighborhood, I singled out a particular house. It was a little blue house. The grass wasn't mowed. The fence that outlined the tiny backyard had collapsed in one section. Strangely drawn to it, I began to drop at a rapid pace. Unable to slow my descent, I entered through the roof in a swift motion. Passing through the shingles, two-by-fours, and drywall was as simple as blinking. I barely felt a thing.

I steadied my breathing while orienting myself from my wild ride. I found myself looking over a small living room, my back stuck against the ceiling. Above the couch was a painting of two nuzzling horses, with ribbons tied to their manes. I slid forward and noticed that above the television was a large frame that held various-size photos. There were photographs of Everett and Kirsten's wedding day. Pictures of my parents, Kirsten's parents. And in one of the frame's tiny circles, I even saw a picture of me. It was odd, looking at myself while not in myself—thinking of my body sitting far away in a Michigan field near a pile of old raccoon bones.

They still weren't settled in. Boxes were strewn along the entryway. Cans of paint sat on top of a tarp in the corner. Half of one wall was a faded shade of yellow, while the other half had been freshly painted bright white.

I was startled by sudden loud bangs. "Goddamn it!" I heard from another room. Everett! I quickly scooted into the kitchen. His shirt was off but apparently was doing little to cool him. He was red-faced and dripping sweat. The August heat of Texas was suffocating the small house. He stood over an air-conditioning unit. Tools were scattered about. At the end of his rope, he began attacking the unit with a wrench, denting the dilapidated thing. On the other side of the kitchen, Kirsten held open the fridge door.

Wearing a thin nightgown, she had her hair bundled up and was letting the cool air flow over the back of her neck.

A series of clicks filled the room, followed by a sound similar to gushing water. Everett and Kirsten heard it too and began searching for its source. Everett's eyes fixed to the ceiling. And eventually, on me. Kirsten too seemed to have spotted me. Everett scowled disapprovingly as he reached up. I cowered in the corner, not knowing how I was going to explain my long-distance intrusion. "Motherfucker!" screamed Everett. As he held his hand up to the vent, I realized it wasn't me he was reaching for. "I cannot fucking believe this! It's heat!" He raced to the thermostat, attempting to stop the hot air from gushing through the vents.

Kirsten rushed to the window and desperately tried to lift it open. She wanted air, even the dry air Texas had to offer. But the window wouldn't budge. "It's not gonna work!" Everett screamed to her. "They're sealed shut! All of 'em—except the one for the air conditioner." She held back tears of frustration as she gave the window one last futile shove. Everett charged to the hallway. He opened the metal panel that concealed the furnace. He cussed at it, not knowing what to do. Giving up on the window, Kirsten swung open the kitchen door. Two large cockroaches, which had been clinging to the curtain, dropped near her feet with a clack. She let out a short scream before kicking them out the door. Desperate for air, she left the house with them.

Everett had left for this? For a dump of a house without a working air conditioner? For a possessed furnace? For that awful horse painting above the couch? Still, in his presence, I felt safe. No longer did I sense the evil that had been relentlessly pursuing me. As I hovered on the ceiling, watching him tinker with the furnace, I wondered why I couldn't just stay there. Live with him in the tiny blue house. He wouldn't even have to know. I'd leave my body behind. I didn't need it. I'd let it rot in the field, let it wither and become a skeleton like the raccoon's.

Yet just as that thought penetrated my mind, I became distracted by the sound of shuffling beneath me. I looked below.

But the noise wasn't coming from inside the blue house. It came from a place far away. I reached for Everett. But he didn't even notice as I was sucked through the roof and back into the atmosphere.

Abruptly, I opened my eyes. It was unbearably bright, even with a thick cloud passing overhead. My body tingled. It took a moment for my circulation to kick in, for the rest of me to fill back into my cells. Once again, I heard the rustling noise beneath me. I stood dizzily from the log. One of the cats, I assumed. It had probably been hiding in the log the whole while, had become restless and wanted to play. But when I knelt to peer inside, what I saw was not the welcoming face of a frisky feline. Instead, I found a pair of glowing red eyes glaring into mine. It gave a low, sinister growl. I jolted back as it lunged forward. It charged out of the log, growling, baring its teeth. A claw trap was clamped on the front leg of the raccoon, assuredly set in the woods by Mr. Peterson. The animal was vicious, filled with fury and pain. Had I attempted to unclamp the trap, it surely would've torn into me. It was looking to bite, to attack whatever dared come near. It chased me out of the clearing and through the weeds.

Of course it couldn't have been a friendly cat. It had to be a ferocious wounded animal that pulled me back from Texas. I should've known. Evil never would've allowed me to stay with Everett. It worked to keep us separated so I'd remain an easy target.

The phone was ringing as I entered the house. I answered, out of breath. "Ayden? Is Dad there?" Everett sounded out of breath as well.

"You have to come home," I whispered desperately. "The monsters—they're out of control."

"Ayden—"

"Every night they come out of the woods and the fields and into the yard. They've been clawing to get in. And then last night, the light in my room kept getting dimmer and dimmer—"

"Calm down." He cut me off. I could tell he was agitated. I knew he was already frustrated and sticky with sweat. "Nothing's coming out of the woods. And if your lights are getting dim, change the bulbs, for Christ's sake. Just because you hear noises and your room is getting dim doesn't mean—"

"I was attacked!" I revealed boldly before bringing my tone back down to a whisper. "Last night. I was almost eaten. They know you're gone. They didn't get me. But they'll try again."

"Listen to me. You're completely safe. Now stop it."

"Safe! They're coming after me because you're not here. They won't even let me visit you."

"But you're coming in the fall with Mom, right?"

I was becoming as frustrated with him as he was with me. "When are you coming home?" I asked flatly.

I could hear his breathing become more labored as I imagined the tiny house transforming into an oven. "Not for a while," he said finally. "Please. Is Dad there?"

"I don't know," I replied angrily, "because I just walked into the house after sleeping next to a barn in the Grand Am last night. Want to know why? Because I had to jump out my bedroom window to stop from being shoved into a cloaked monster's black-hole stomach."

"Well, can you see if he's there?"

I was stunned. He wasn't willing to even listen, much less come back and rescue me. He didn't care if monsters devoured me. He was more concerned about his broken furnace than my survival. "At least tell me what I'm supposed to do. If you're not coming home, when they come for me again, how will I survive it?"

I could feel the heat rising through the telephone. He let out a deep sigh. "Fight them," he offered reluctantly. "Just like we did before. Just like I taught you. Fight them like we fought them from inside the spaceship—and on foot in the fields and the woods."

Although my heart swelled a bit at his admission of our past adventures, his proposition was absurd. "How could I fight them alone?" I asked. "I'd be killed in an instant."

"You don't need me. You never did. You could've handled them all on your own." But he was wrong. I *did* need him.

Dad came into the house looking weary after his long haul through the Midwest. With him in earshot, I quickly changed the subject. "Thanks for putting me above the television," I said.

"Above the television?"

"My picture—in the circle." I handed the phone to Dad without saying goodbye. "It's Everett. He needs help with his furnace," I told him before disappearing to my room.

23
THE HYPERBARIC CHAMBER

Sleep pumped through me like a drug. It was the deepest, heaviest sleep, as if I were curled beneath a giant rock. It would've been easy to remain under the spell of the intoxicating rhythms. Yet somehow, in the corner of my mind that refused to give up consciousness, I knew I was being held under by the hot and heavy breath, by the poisonous fumes expelled from the bellies of demons.

I had finally convinced Everett to come home. I had come too close to having him back to be thwarted once again. I had to wake. Warn him we were under attack. So I attempted to force myself out of it. At the bottom of the foggy pit where I languished, I envisioned a spiral. I climbed up on the winding coil and rode it for miles and miles, twisting up, and eventually out of, the murky trap.

With a fierce headache, I oozed from the bed and onto the floor. I lay motionless on my belly, with my limbs sprawled like a twisted scarecrow. I gathered my energy before trying a second move. When I forced myself onto my hands and knees, my muscles felt like leather restraints working to pull me back down. But I pushed against it, arching my shoulders and pressing forward.

My brain pulsated with pain as I slowly made my way out the bedroom door. With each tiny movement, the inside of my head swirled in a million different directions. I was dizzy. Nauseous. But I kept my eye on the phone at the end of the hall. It sat on the stand in the distance like the peak of a far-off mountain. I crawled along the carpet like a half-tranquilized animal, determined to make it, determined to contact Everett.

When I finally reached the base of the stand, the vision of the phone towering overhead triggered a wave of nausea in my head that rolled to my stomach. Gripping the wooden legs, I vomited uncontrollably. When my stomach emptied, I used what little strength I had to jerk the stand forward. The phone crashed to the floor. The receiver fell off its base. The sound of the dial tone permeated the air. Yet instead of prompting me to start pressing digits, the endless drone began pulling me back under. I rolled to my side and lay in my vomit. But I didn't care. I couldn't focus on anything but the monotone hum. I became lost in it. Forgot what it meant. Where it came from. Its purpose had been erased. I could no longer fight it. There was nothing I could do but give in—and sleep.

When I opened my eyes again, all but a trace of the hammering in my head had been alleviated. I felt quite comfortable. Alert. But I was no longer in the upstairs hallway. I was no longer in the house. Florescent lights blazed through the tube of glass that encased my body. I was trapped. Held hostage in a glass coffin. *Am I dead?* Had the hands of evil held me under for too long? Had I finally been snuffed out?

In my peripheral vision, I caught a flash of movement. I didn't dare move a muscle for fear I'd find myself trapped inside a lifeless corpse. I strained to hear. But no sound outside the cylinder could be heard. All I could hear was the sound of my breathing and thunderous heartbeat. *Wait.* If I had a heartbeat, was it possible I was still alive? Or did the dead somehow retain the same sensations as the living? The rhythm of breath? The beating of a heart? A blob of white came closer and closer to the glass. Panic struck. I sprang upright and pressed against the glass, futilely attempting to release myself from the tomb.

Startled, the man in the white lab coat nearly fell over. He dropped his clipboard. Papers scattered about. He scrambled to the glass. Still flustered, he began speaking, although his words were silent to me. It looked as if he was trying to say, "Get down" or "Calm down." Clipped to his coat pocket was his badge. His name was Dave. He looked younger in his photo, which was a version of him without his mustache and glasses. Realizing his communication wasn't being effective, he flashed me the OK signal. He then tapped his forehead in the universal gesture meaning he was an idiot. Finally, he flipped a switch on the wall. The sounds of the surrounding room crackled into the glass tube. "I apologize," he said into a microphone. His voice sounded as if it came from a weak radio station. I spotted the tiny speaker along the bottom edge of the coffin. "It's just that you gave me a bit of a shock. But I want you to know you're OK. Your mother's here. Let me get your mother."

In a few moments, he returned with Mom. She looked exhausted, still wearing her blue hospital scrubs. She clutched her purse in one hand and a tissue in the other. He ushered her to the microphone. "Oh, thank God you're awake. And thank God you're OK," her voice gushed through the speakers. "What happened?" she asked, looking first to me and then to Dave.

He took over the microphone. "You're in a hyperbaric oxygen therapy chamber," he explained. "The carbon monoxide level in your bloodstream was extremely high."

"I was so tired. And dizzy."

He nodded. "When carbon monoxide enters your system, it slows down the ability of oxygen to travel through your bloodstream and to your organs: your heart, your brain, etcetera. Normal levels of carbon monoxide in the bloodstream are around ten percent. A person goes unconscious around forty. When you were brought into the hospital, the level in your bloodstream was at fifty-eight percent. You're lucky you were still alive when your mom found you. While you're in this machine, you're breathing in pure oxygen. And it's pressurized, so you are breathing in about ten times the amount you normally would. This will help restore your levels to normal."

"What caused it?" asked Mom.

"Well, a number of things can cause high levels of carbon monoxide. Fires, for one. House fires. Even the normal burning of wood can cause dangerous levels of carbon monoxide. And then there's breathing in fumes from a faulty fuel-burning furnace. And the fumes from cars if they're left running in an enclosed area. But the strange thing is—" He took off his glasses and rubbed his forehead. "The strange thing is, in your son's case, there was no fire present. And you didn't have a faulty furnace. In fact, the fire department performed a carbon monoxide test. And the results showed normal levels at your residence." He put his glasses back on. "It's as if his body mimicked the effects of carbon monoxide poisoning without any real threat in the air he was breathing. Frankly, we can't make any sense of it."

It was fitting that I, the anomaly, sat encased in glass as they peered at me from the other side with questioning looks on their faces. My own mother looked at me in disbelief. "What happened?" she begged again. I turned away from them and lay back on the white linens that lined the tube. They may not have known what had happened. But I did.

24
STRANGE AQUARiUM

"Where's Kirsten?" I asked as we stood in front of the nuzzling horse painting.

"At the stables," Everett replied. Since we hadn't seen each other in so long, our conversation felt stilted. But I didn't much care. The important thing was that I stood right beside him, that I was in his presence. "Hey, sorry I missed your graduation."

"It's OK." Truly it was. Of course I was desperate for Everett to come home—but not for that. I was certain the crowd would turn against me as I walked across the stage to claim my diploma. I visualized being booed. Laughed at. Awful names shouted from the darkened auditorium. Everett witnessing that would've made the humiliation even more unbearable. I agonized over whether I would even attend. In the end, I may not have received the strongest applause, yet I wasn't publicly obliterated. I couldn't help but wonder how different graduation would've been had Ian Stein and Todd Snelling been at the ceremony.

"So what're your plans now that you've graduated?"

"I don't have any," I answered honestly. "Ask for more hours at the grocery store, I guess."

"But you're just beginning. You can do anything. Try for a better job. Go to college. Travel. Mom and Dad would give you a bit of dough for that. You have a million different choices." I looked to my feet, ashamed for not having a plan. But without him, life was stagnant. And the choices he spoke of seemed so overwhelming, they didn't feel as if they were choices at all. Independent decisions, I was convinced, would be wrong decisions.

I lifted my head when I heard a small explosion in the basement followed by a gushing noise. "What the heck is that?" I asked.

"The basement. It's flooding," he said matter-of-factly.

"*Flooding?*"

"Yup. See for yourself."

I opened the basement door. He was right. A large pipe that ran along the ceiling had burst. Split in two, it spewed an endless supply of water onto the basement floor. It gushed so fast and with such force that within a few moments, the floor was saturated. Everett's barbells and dumbbells were submerged. Empty cardboard boxes began to float yet soon crumpled and sank. A pile of clothes climbed the steps, animated by the rising water.

I shut the door on the disaster and rejoined Everett at his side. Water seeped beneath the door. It made its way across the light-blue carpet in tiny waves. It pooled at our feet and rose past our ankles. "It sure is rising fast," he observed. The door bulged from the pressure. Streams of water shot out from every crevice, adding gallons to the gallons already rushing across the floor. "Go ahead," he said, noticing I was mesmerized by the heaving door. "Open it."

As instructed, I sloshed my way back to the throbbing door. Water showered over me, and I was instantly soaked. With much reluctance, I looked back to Everett through the streams of water. He stood with his hands firmly tucked in his pockets and nodded for me to proceed. I grasped the handle with unease before swinging open the door.

It was as if an entire ocean had been stored in the basement and unleashed itself upon me. In a flash, I was swept across the living room like a piece of sediment, first thrust to the ceiling, then pushed to the floor. My face dug into the carpeting as a strong current bore down on me. Waves rolled throughout the house, crashing against the windows and submerging the furniture. The shelves were swept clean. The kitchen cupboards blew open, spewing cups and dishes into the jostling waters.

When the forceful current finally released its grip, I rose to the surface. My head bobbed in the two-foot gap of air beneath the ceiling. All was submerged except a set of ceramic horses upon a high shelf in the kitchen. Beneath them, I found Everett treading water as he grinned like a mischievous child. "C'mon," he called before disappearing under the water. I felt a tug on my calf. I dipped my head below the surface and opened my eyes. It took me a moment to adjust to the watery world. But when I did, I could see clearly, almost as clearly as seeing through air. And the temperature of the water, I realized, was neither cooler nor warmer than air. It required no adjustment.

Everett swam gracefully about the room in his jeans. He circled above the sunken couch before allowing his body to lower by letting loose a stream of bubbles. As he descended gracefully, he assumed a sitting position. When he settled onto the cushion, he rested his arm over the back of the couch, acting like there was nothing out of the ordinary about relaxing in a completely submerged living room. He grabbed the remote floating nearby and pretended to flip channels while watching the blank screen. I too released air from my lungs and sank to join him. We sat on the couch together, laughing bubbles. He waved his fingers through my floating hair.

He then squatted in front of the couch before springing toward the ceiling. I did the same. At the surface, we took a few gulps of air before dipping back under. We swam from room to room, marveling at how the house had transformed into a strange aquarium. In the bedroom, an ivy plant floated over the bed. Its long vines reached across the room like tentacles. I grabbed the pot and placed it on my head, pretending I was Medusa, the green vines the writhing snakes. Everett laughed and swam to the bed. He wrapped himself in the blanket floating just above it and pretended to sleep. We wrestled. We hid from each other in the closets and behind the overturned furniture. We peered out the windows to the dry yard and sun-drenched sky.

I performed a series of somersaults for Everett. I tumbled five or six rotations until my feet kicked loose the horse painting that had stubbornly stayed affixed to the wall. By the time I stopped, I had made myself dizzy. Needing air, I lunged toward the surface. Only I couldn't reach the surface. I thought maybe my equilibrium was off, that I had confused the floor for the ceiling. Yet I noticed Everett was next to me—right side up. He was pounding his fist against the ceiling, desperately trying to get to air.

The water had risen, closing the gap. Panicked, I too pounded the ceiling in a frenzy. But it was no use. Everett gripped my hand and pulled me deeper. He tried the front door, but the pressure of the water kept it sealed. He grabbed a kitchen chair. It moved in slow motion as he heaved it against the picture window. With its momentum stunted, the chair barely tapped the thick glass. The horse painting, suspended behind us, oscillated back and forth, making the horses appear to gallop toward us, mocking our struggle.

Without air, we became weak. Our desperate pounding turned to light taps. Instead of breaths of air, we inhaled deep gulps of water. Water filled my stomach. It filled my lungs. My head swirled and pounded. I could feel myself begin to slip. Lose consciousness. Go black. I looked to Everett just before it happened. He was the last image I saw. His eyes were closed. His hair waved gracefully in the water. But the rest of his body was still. So still. He floated past me and sank to the floor.

I woke gasping for air. I jolted out of bed and stumbled down the hall to the phone. I didn't even glance at the clock as I furiously dialed the number. When the wounded raccoon dragged me back from Texas, I knew I'd no longer be allowed to visit Everett by leaving my body. But I still had one luxury: my dreams. Everett had taught me that dreams were an impressionistic version of past, present, or future reality. Yet in just the few moments I had to process my latest impression of reality, one thing was horrifically clear: Everett was in danger.

"Are you OK!"

"Do you know what time it is?" he answered groggily.

"I've been good. I haven't called in a long time about the monsters."

"Jesus, Ayden. Are you still sleeping in the Grand Am?"

"No."

"Good."

"Just listen. I know you don't want to hear this. But I had a dream. I dreamt of you in Texas. I don't know what it means yet. But you need to stay away from water. I don't know why, but this water is different from the water in my other dreams. I couldn't breathe under this water. And your basement—it has something to do with your basement—"

"We don't have a basement."

"Are you sure?"

"Of course I'm sure."

"OK. Well. Whatever. You need to come home as soon as possible."

Silence.

"Don't you remember my dreams? Don't you remember how I found the coins in Mr. Peterson's tree? How I found the Indians in the woods? You used to listen to my dreams. You used to look for clues. If I had told you this when I was thirteen, you wouldn't have hesitated. If you were the same person you were back then, you would've gotten on the first flight back to Michigan. Are you that clouded? Have you become that clouded—by her? Aren't you coming home? Aren't you coming home?" I repeated in desperation.

He exhaled deeply. Finally he replied, "Yeah, I suppose I should." *Thank God.* "Give me a few days. I have a couple job interviews, and then I can come up for a visit. Now get some sleep."

"I will!" I happily agreed. Everett was finally coming home! I hung up the phone, cracking a triumphant smile, a smile that felt as though it could've repelled demons on its own. There was power to it, power knowing Everett was on his way to me.

I waited three nights, and each night the dream was the same. Sure, the details differed. Our conversation before the pipes burst varied. We'd play different games in our underwater world. But each night, we'd become trapped. Each night, we'd drown. And each time I woke, I became dizzier. And more nauseous.

"Dreams are tricky," Everett would say. Determining futures from them wasn't simple. In a dream, it was easy to become clouded and unfocused, to miss the clues to how reality will truly unfold. But as I breathed in pure oxygen, it wasn't difficult to unravel the true meaning of my dream. It was the conclusion I had feared from the moment that I attempted to wake myself from my latest and most poisonous slumber. Deep down, I knew the tissue my mother clutched wasn't for me. I had just been too afraid to ask if it was for Everett.

"Is he dead?" I asked quickly to hasten the sting.

Her eyes widened before instantly flooding with tears. She pressed her hand against the glass in an attempt to get closer to me before returning to the microphone. "You've always been so perceptive. I didn't want to tell you," she sobbed. "Not yet. Not until you were out of—that machine." She spoke in a whimper, as if she herself was having trouble breathing. "Kirsten's mother called. She told me. I got ahold of Dad. He's on his way home from Ohio."

"How'd it happen?" I asked with a lump in my throat.

"It's so strange. It's all so strange. It doesn't make any sense."

"How'd it happen, Mom?" I persisted.

She leaned in as close to the glass as she could. "Carbon monoxide," she whispered. "Their furnace. It was their furnace. It was broken and must've been leaking fumes for quite some time. Kirsten, she got out. She passed out in the yard. But Everett, he had been home all day. He had been breathing it in for too long. Dear

God, I don't understand it either, how you came down with it too. I think it's just that you two were always so close. So close . . ."

Of course it was carbon monoxide poisoning. In the dream, we were drowning. Suffocating. I should've known it was the broken furnace. I should've been able to piece together the furnace troubles I had witnessed during my out-of-body trip to Texas with the clues I had learned from my recurring dream.

And of course Kirsten had survived. She had left him in the house to die. She was a monster—just like the monsters that worked to keep Everett and me separated. In fact, if Everett had never met Kirsten, he never would've left Michigan. He would've still been alive. Yes, demons were at play. They tampered with the furnace. They released the poison that caused his suffocation. But I blamed her. Kirsten was just as responsible for his death. And he was so close. So close to coming home.

"Let me out of here!" I screamed, pounding against the glass chamber.

25
WARRIOR OF PEACE

When Everett was in Texas, I was attacked in my own bedroom. I was an easy enough target then. But with Everett dead, I was like an open wound, vulnerable to infection. Finally, the demons had me where they wanted. Full of sorrow. Afraid. Utterly isolated. There was no question they were on their way to reap their reward. It was just a matter of which breed would get to me first.

Plastic tubes blew fresh oxygen into my nose. It helped to keep me alert. I peered behind the eyes of every nurse, searching for monsters in disguise. At night, I'd stay awake anticipating their arrival. I'd stare at the glowing red lights of the machine against the wall, waiting for them to transform into glowing red, sinister eyes. I'd monitor the dark corners for the slightest shifts in tone, attempting to find the outline of a murderous figure before it lurched forward.

Yet it was not during the night when evil finally found me. Boldly, arrogantly, it slunk out of the shadows in the middle of the afternoon. Just after lunch, a low growl began blending with the hum of the hospital equipment. It was subtle. At first, I didn't pay it much attention. My privacy curtain was drawn, so I wondered if I had dozed off and the bed nearest the door had since become occupied. It was possible the noise was my new roommate's respirator or some other equipment. I removed the oxygen tubes to better isolate the sound. Sure enough, it *did* seem to be coming from the other side of the curtain. I stretched to grab the curtain, drawing it back just enough to see that the bed—was empty.

"Hello?" I held hope there was a nurse on the other side of the curtain whom I couldn't see. Yet the only response I received was from the growl. It began to amplify, sounding like saliva or blood bubbling in a raw throat. "Who's there?" I called out meekly.

My heart stopped as a shrill voice answered, "Meeeeee!" It spoke as if it was the first time its vocal chords had been used to produce words. Its voice was high-pitched yet overlaid with a deep, gurgling snarl.

"Nurse?"

"Meeeeee!" it corrected.

"Mom?"

"Meeeeee!"

"Dad?"

"Meeeeee!"

The door creaked shut and latched with a loud click. The shift in air pressure caused the curtain to gently oscillate. The room suddenly went dim as the florescent bulbs were drained of their luminance. Only specks of natural light seeped between the slats and corners of the closed blinds.

What looked like fingers, pointy fingers, began poking at the curtain in a frightening tease. This went on for a few moments before the fingers suddenly rushed forward, sweeping the fabric toward me. The demon on the other side repeated this move, pressing the curtain toward me and then releasing it, each time bringing its claws closer and closer. All the while, it chuckled from its rotted throat.

I knew exactly what it was up to. It wanted to push my fear beyond its boundary. It could gauge fear, smell the amount of it emitted from my pores. To it, the aroma was like seasoning. And there would be no satisfaction eating me without proper flavoring.

"Meeeeee!" its evil voice cackled delightedly as it pressed the tip of one of its large horns into the curtain. It was succeeding. I *was* deathly afraid.

But I knew I had a choice: I could either wait until it had me overcome with terror, completely debilitated, at which point it would finally consume me—or I could act first and at least put an end to its gleeful torment. Determined to make the latter happen, I firmly grasped the edge of the curtain. I took a deep breath before giving it a swift yank. The metal rings along the track slapped together as the curtain was flung open.

And there it was. A horned monster. Exposed. Just as surprised by my bold move as I was, it immediately drew its arms to its chest. It bent its wrists forward as its eyes locked on to mine. It had the eyes of a shark, large and unblinking. Except unlike a shark's eyes, its pupils were deep red. It moved its sharp fingers in undulating waves, as if it were impatiently tapping an invisible surface. Its lips quivered as it snarled. As it stepped closer, its snarl transformed into a grin, displaying its mouth chock-full of sharp teeth.

Though I was frozen in intense fear, I also felt a rush of energy surge through my veins. The combination caused me to tremble. When the monster swiped for me, I briskly swiveled off the other side of the bed. The sense of fear that at first had been paralyzing ultimately released in an explosion. I had followed the impulse that came naturally. I knew I was in danger, and my body reacted. The concept was so simple. So elementary. Yet at the same time, I was astounded I had been able to evade its grasp.

The demon sealed its mouth and curled its lips into a devilish smirk. It brought its fingers to its nose and smelled them while contemplating its next move. Suddenly it dipped beneath the bed. I bent to see it crawling on its stomach, grunting as it made its way toward me. I whipped the bedside table my way. My lunch tray flew off, splattering the cup of juice and half-eaten bowl of soup across the floor. As soon as the demon emerged, I rushed it, slamming the edge of the table into its chest, pinning it against the bed's railing. I heard bones crack, but the creature didn't seem the least disabled. It stretched its neck forward, snapping its jaws. As it thrashed against the table, I felt its breath on my skin. It was hot and stank of blood and decaying flesh. Unsure of how much longer I could hold it at bay, I let go of the table and sprinted for the door.

But the door—wouldn't budge. "Help!" I screamed as I tugged. "Open the door!" Thrilled my daring escape had failed, the demon eyed me with a fresh grin as it crept my way, green saliva dripping down its chin. I knew I mustn't let it get me cornered. I climbed onto the bed nearest the door. But not quick enough. Its claws caught my leg. Blood splashed across the floor.

As I was trapped atop the bed, blood trickled from the gash and onto the sheets. As I clutched my wound, the creature stood between the beds, daring me to make my next move. I was alone. Just it and me. Assuming it had somehow jammed the door, no one was going to rescue me. In the tiny room, I wouldn't be able to evade it forever. It would eventually wear me down, getting in enough slashes until I'd weaken from the loss of blood. Finally, I'd find myself between its massive jaws. Devoured. I had to fight it, I realized. By myself, like Everett had told me to. At least I had to try. My eyes darted furiously about the room—until I had a plan.

Facing the other bed, I squatted while extending my arms in front of me. I closed my eyes and erased the snarling devil from my mind's eye. Instead, I visualized that the space between the beds was the pit down the fifteenth row in the cornfield. I had jumped it before. And I was confident I could jump it again. And so I leapt into the air, curling my legs tight beneath me, intent on once again soaring high above the danger below. I could feel the wind, smell the sweetness of the field as I catapulted among the stalks. I opened my eyes only when I felt my feet touch the ground. They caught the far edge of the bed. I tumbled to the floor, pulling off the top sheet with me. Despite a repeat of my original shaky landing, I made it. I hadn't been ripped to shreds. The eager demon hadn't even grazed me.

I crawled to the window and braced myself upon its ledge. The demon, still intent on savoring me slowly, tiptoed its way to me. I allowed it to get close. It relished my scent, so I let it sniff my bare feet, smell my hospital gown. And as it began to drop its lower jaw, I jerked the blind's cord that I had been discreetly wrapping around my wrist. The slats rapidly slapped together, collecting at the top of the window. Sunlight burst into the room, blanketing the space before the window in a dazzling glow.

The monster slapped its hands over its eyes and shuddered. Its skin shimmered in the light as it howled. I confirmed then that while the monster was not fond of artificial light, natural light actually incapacitated it. It did what nothing else could to a horned monster: halt its relentless charge. There it stood. Immobilized. Vulnerable. I hadn't seen a monster in stark daylight before. I bent over to examine it up close. Its body smelled of mold and of wet soil. Its skin was the palest green, almost white. It reminded me of a tomato that hadn't yet ripened before the season was over and had shriveled and rotted on a cold vine. I touched it, and it felt much like a winter tomato—thick, tough skin, with uneven lumps covering a mushy inside. Its long toes overlapped. I felt its large horns. I ran my hands beneath them and up to their sharp points. They felt heavy, as if they were made of solid rock.

I wasn't sure how much time I had. Perhaps a dark rain cloud passing overhead was all that was needed to release the demon from its prison of immobility. So without wasting another moment, I grabbed the metal lunch tray from the floor. I lifted it high over my head. And with all my fear and fury, I brought it down on the monster. I bashed its head over and over—until it finally took its hands from its face. Thin lines of green liquid oozed from the corners of its eyes as its shocked pupils turned from a deep red to a soft pink. It screamed in shrieking howls as it blindly swiped every which way. But I was relentless. I danced around it, dents forming in the tray as I continued smashing its head with all my might. Its neck bones snapped, forcing its chin to slump into its chest. I didn't let up until it collapsed into a pile of itself like a rag doll tossed carelessly to the floor.

Nearly out of breath, I crawled onto my bed. With a sense of triumph, I firmly pressed the call button. If I hadn't killed it, I was at least certain it had been permanently disabled. Yet in my peripheral vision, I saw it begin to unravel its crumpled arms and legs. Somehow, it stood once more. Its neck was stretched like taffy, its head dangling down its torso, weighted down by its heavy horns. It took quick, shallow breaths through clenched teeth. It wobbled toward me—a blind, determined monstrosity.

I picked up the tray once again and knocked the demon back to the floor. I held the tray over my head for a moment, lowering my arms only when I was sure its body would stay limp. That's when its arm abruptly reached up and flung the tray from my hands. My feet became tangled in the sheet on the floor, and I fell. My tailbone throbbing, I scooted backward, retreating to the corner.

The monster fumbled for the tips of its horns. Once it had grasped them, it hoisted its head back to an upright position. It sniffed the air before thrusting its head forward to sniff the edge of the sheet that lay between it and me. It inhaled the aroma of the sheet. It licked it, tasting my flavor. Satisfied with what it had gleaned, it crawled toward me with surprising accuracy.

I had blinded it. Crippled it. As I cowered from the demented thing, I realized I had underestimated just how resourceful, how tenacious it was. This was no more clearly demonstrated than when it pulled back its horns to unhinge its drooling mouth and lunged toward me, managing to clamp its giant teeth upon my ankle. It pressed down on its horns, forcing its razor teeth deep into my flesh as it growled like a wild dog fighting for a piece of meat. Pain seared up and down my leg. I could feel its tongue lapping the blood that flowed through the puncture wounds.

I spotted my fork in the middle of the floor. With the demon clamped on to me, I dragged myself toward it. I formed a tight fist around its handle before stabbing the monster repeatedly in its face. It growled defiantly. But when I forced the fork deep into one of its dysfunctional eye sockets—and I was unable to dislodge it from its brain—its grip on my ankle weakened just enough to allow me to pry open its jaws.

As I stood in agony, the nasty thing began to twitch and convulse. I couldn't believe it still had life left in it. To avoid its dangerous claws, I grabbed it by the horns and held it at arm's length. But I was helpless, desperately looking about the room for what to do with the twisting devil. It was then I noticed the dark corner outside the bathroom door. It was the only spot in the room natural light couldn't reach. I limped backward, dragging the demon toward it as it cursed at me in growls.

When we approached the dark space, I spun its stout, muscular body. I shoved the monster feetfirst into the darkness. And the darkness ate its legs. So I pushed the demon in further, letting darkness wholly take back what it had unleashed upon me. And when the demon had been eaten up to its waist, I finally let go of its horns. The blind thing reached for me as I planted my foot on the ridge between its horns and sharply kicked the rest of it into the corner.

With my leg split open and my bitten ankle throbbing in unbearable pain, I stumbled back to the bed. Our blood, red and green, stained the sheets and smeared the floor in an impressionistic mural that documented our brutal fight. *Maybe Everett was right after all? Maybe I alone could fight the demons.* Without him, I had eluded a cloaked monster and had successfully vanquished a horned demon. Yet already, I was exhausted. Soon there'd be another attack. And another. They wouldn't stop pursuing me. The horned monster that attacked me that day was likely merely a scout, only a fraction of the evil that brewed in the darkness. More would come and more than one at a time. And after I sent the demon back with a fork skewered in its eye socket, I was certain little mercy was to follow.

Would what happened that day be my future? Would the rest of my existence be spent fighting evil? Living in anticipation of the next attack? Would I end up some kind of warrior of peace? Fighting demons whenever they appeared in dark corners?

Fighting them until one day I'd be attacked when my guard was down and finally overtaken? Perhaps it would be in my sleep. Or as I strolled through the fields. I wondered just how long I could survive alone.

I was securing the oxygen tubes back to my nose when the door burst open. The young nurse dropped her jaw at the scene before her. "What happened in here!"

"Where the fuck were you?" I snapped.

"I came as soon as you called."

"Yeah, right. You never even came to take my lunch tray," I fumed.

"What happened to your legs!" she gasped, rushing toward me as she noticed my wounds.

"I was bit."

"*Bit!* Bit by what?"

There was no sense hiding the truth. "A demon," I replied. I pointed to the dark corner next to the bathroom. "I dragged it over there."

She looked over her shoulder, terrified. "Where is it now?"

"I shoved it in the corner. Darkness ate it."

She returned her attention back to my bleeding legs before scanning the room. "Where's your silverware?" she asked.

"On the floor. But you won't find the fork. I stabbed it right into the demon's goddamn eye."

"I see. Well, here's what we're going to do," she said calmly. "First, we'll get these wounds taken care of. Then we'll get someone in here to sit with you so you don't do any more harm to yourself."

"I didn't do this to myself. I told you. It was a demon. And if you wouldn't have been so goddamn slow getting in here, you would've seen it for yourself."

"And this demon—you pushed it into the corner?"

"Yeah."

"OK. I think I understand now. But still, I'll get someone to sit in here with you. That way, they could protect you in case it comes back."

"No one can protect me. I have to protect myself now. And it's probably better if no one gets in my way."

"It couldn't hurt, could it?"

"If you think being eaten doesn't hurt."

"Hmm. Well, let's give it a try."

PART V
VOICES FROM
THE OTHER SIDE

26
BORROWED ENERGY

"You're pretty tall."

"Thanks," I said, not knowing how else to reply.

"You play basketball?"

"No."

"You should play basketball."

"Because I'm tall?"

"Sure. Don't you like basketball?"

"Not really."

"What sports you play?"

"None."

"What'dya do then? Like for hobbies?"

"I don't have any."

"No hobbies?"

"I like to sit in fields, I guess."

"And hunt?"

"No. Just sit in fields. Or woods."

"Doin' what, man?"

"Hiding, I guess."

"*Hiding?* From who?"

"Everyone."

His badge said his name was Tyler. Tyler was irritating. How could he ask questions of such inconsequence while I was in the middle of a war against evil? Earlier, he had watched intently as I chewed every bit of my food. And when I had to pee, he made me leave the door open. Even though I had to go really bad, I just couldn't with Tyler watching. "I didn't stab myself with silverware," I assured him. "And I'm not going to hang myself from the curtain rod or anything." He should've been more concerned about his own safety than mine. Were a demon to show up during his shift, I doubted he had the skills necessary to survive. "It's OK," I told him. "We don't have to make small talk. I'm going to close my eyes now." With my eyes closed, there was no pressure to talk. I was so sleep deprived from keeping my own watch that despite Tyler's constant shifting in his squeaky chair, it didn't take long before I fell asleep.

By the time I woke, it was late afternoon. The sun dipping behind the towering building next door brought shadows into the room. They may have seemed like ordinary shadows at first, yet they began morphing the room into something different. Bands of darkness stretched across the ceiling from the corner where I had ungraciously returned the horned monster. They carried with them a heavy blackness, a pure darkness that gave passage to sinister things.

Tyler was supposed to be watching over me. Yet despite the glossy magazine in his lap opened to a photo of some guy flying through the air on a motorcycle, his eyes were closed. His chin to his chest. *What an idiot.* He was oblivious to what oozed across the ceiling like an evil, black ink. He didn't see it pave over the lights, snuffing them out as it swelled. Based on its size, it wasn't intended for just a single monster. Dozens of demons could've materialized from a portal of such size. After narrowly surviving the attacks of two singular monsters, I felt foolish for ever thinking I had it in me to fend off several. I'd be lucky to survive the night. Trapped in the room with Tyler, all I could do was wait and see what the black oil pooling above my bed would give birth to. It hung overhead like a dark cloud, full of infinite, wicked possibilities.

A light tap came from the door. So polite evil was. Tyler jolted out of his slumber and slapped shut his magazine. It didn't seem fair he too would be consumed. He blinked wide-eyed as he checked his watch. He straightened his scrubs before swinging open the door. Curiously, he wasn't instantly eaten alive. Instead, he whispered to someone in the hallway. After a few moments, he turned to inform me, "You have a visitor." My visitor casually strolled past Tyler, wearing, what else, a pair of blue jeans and a plain white T-shirt. Tyler tapped his shoulder. "Buddy, would you mind staying 'til Anita shows up? It's just about shift change."

"No problem," Everett agreed. He winked and flashed me one of his sly smiles like he would when we were getting away with something devious.

"Thanks, man." Tyler left the room with his magazine under his arm, softly whistling a tune.

Everett stood beside the bed, his grin still intact. I sat up in shock. Seeing him again, being in his presence, brought forth a rush of indescribable emotions. Instead of speaking, I simply leaned forward and gave him the tightest hug ever. His strong arms hugged me back. My brain told me he was dead. But he was there. He was real.

Immediately he took notice of the blackness swirling overhead. With his arms folded, he sneered at the congealing mass. Within it, he could see the face of evil. And clearly, it could see him. Upon recognizing Everett, it slowly retreated back into the corner from which it had seeped. As I had known all along, Everett's presence alone could chase away demons. He was like a star. By simply existing, he repelled darkness. With him near, my fear began to fade. He glared defiantly until the last of the tainted shadows left the room, until it returned to its natural afternoon hue.

"Soon they'll figure it out," he whispered before sitting on the edge of the bed.

"Figure what out?" I whispered back.

"That I'm dead."

"You mean they don't know?"

He shook his head. "And once they realize that, it won't matter if I show myself or not."

"They can't hurt you, can they?"

"No. They can't hurt me. But I can't hurt them either. I can't fight them. They'll learn that. And when they do, I'm no longer a threat."

It was a devastating thing to learn. The power Everett possessed in life had been taken away with his death. He was my protector rendered useless. My hero in restraints. "But I won't survive much longer. Not alone," I fretted. Everett lowered his eyes, looking ashamed. Immediately I turned red from my own shame. How could I have been so concerned about my own survival when Everett himself had not survived? The important thing was, even in death, Everett cared about me—enough to materialize in my presence. And selfishly, I had yet to even ask what he had been through. "What was it like? Dying?"

He lifted his gaze while searching for the right words. "It was like—going to sleep. There was no pain. People call it 'dying,' but that's not really it at all. It's more like you're *changing*, shifting forms. Like energy shifts forms. I know now that we come from nature. And that we go back into it. As I let go of my body, I smelled it. I could smell nature. I smelled grass. And the sweet leaves of fall. I smelled dirt. Rain mixed with pine sap. Flowers. Do you know the lilac bush in the backyard?" I nodded. "It smelled like that when it's in full bloom. I wasn't dying. I was being reabsorbed by nature. It happens with everything, not just people. A tree dies in the forest and later becomes covered with mushrooms. Everything is just energy changing forms.

"I know it's strange to think about, but I found myself unfolding and sprouting on the maple that overlooks the garden. I couldn't see where I was. I wasn't even sure *what* I was. But somehow, after I fell to the ground, turned brown, and withered, I knew. I then realized I had choices about what I did with my energy. I suppose I could've stayed near my body if I'd wanted, until every bit had broken down and been reabsorbed. But instead, I chose to be someplace familiar. I learned not only could I choose where I'd end up, I could choose what I'd become. I wasn't limited to just plants. I could be as simple as single-celled bacteria or part of a network of fungus. Or I could be more complex. A cricket. A field mouse. But I learned that with these choices, there were also rules. The more complex I wanted to become, the more energy I'd need to conserve. And this meant I'd have to exist for quite some time without any form at all. And in that time, all I'd be able to do is float through the air, drifting invisible, storing and growing my energy."

I leaned forward and touched him again to confirm he was real. "How is it that you're here? Like this?" I asked.

He tapped his chest. "Having this body is a bit like cheating. I'm here now with not much time, not much energy to stay in this form. It's not natural. Basically, it's—borrowed energy—and it has its limitations. It *feels* physical, but I only have fleeting effects on my surroundings. I guess that makes me—a ghost." He laughed, amused by the mortal word for the form he had taken.

I looked to the dark corner. "What about them? Where does their energy come from?"

"It comes from nature too. Like everything does. Well, at least it *begins* in nature." He scratched the hair on his chin. "Sometimes entities create so much energy that extra spills over. That's all monsters are. Extra energy—perverted. They're still a part of nature because whatever created their energy still controls it, manipulates it—and is itself from nature. But because they cannot gather or control their *own* energy, monsters are also once removed from nature. And because of that, they take on the most unnatural forms."

"How do I stop them?" I asked in a whisper.

His eyes fell to the floor once again. His glum look led me to believe there wasn't hope. But as always, Everett had a plan. He leaned toward me and replied, "Phillip."

"Phillip!" I balked. "I haven't seen Phillip since high school!"

"I can't protect you anymore," he reminded me. "And I can't keep showing up in this form. Even if I could, I'd be of no help. Phillip is the closest thing you have to me. He's *all* you have." I had no choice but to accept what Everett proposed. If Everett said Phillip was my only hope for survival, my only hope at keeping the demons in the darkness, then that was that. Still, I couldn't imagine seeking out Phillip and begging for his protection. How in the world would he receive such a request when he already believed I suffered from delusions brought on by Everett's suggestive ideas?

"Will I see you again?" I asked.

"I'm not sure," he replied. "I'll have to rest for a while. And then, I'm not sure where I'm going. But I'll be with you. Just think of me when you smell flowers. Think of me when you see leaves budding in the spring. Think of me when you are walking in the fields. I might be in the air next to you."

There was another light knock at the door. The sound instantly injected me with fear. Had evil already discovered Everett's secret? Had the demons come to consume me while at the same time torture Everett by making him watch? But it was not a demon that stood in the doorway. As if Everett had summoned him as a gift, there stood—Phillip. He looked part grunge, part preppy. His blond hair was long, down to his chin. But typical Phillip, he wore a dress shirt and a pair of khakis instead of jeans. I looked to Everett excitedly, but he was no longer on the edge of the bed. "Everett?" His energy, apparently, had depleted.

Phillip greeted me with a stilted wave and a smile. "Hey, Ayden. What's going on?"

"I wasn't sure how I was going to find you. But look. *You* came to *me.*"

He sat in the chair next to the bed. "I'm really sorry about Everett. You were saying his name . . ."

"You just missed him," I said before realizing it was probably best to keep Everett's visit—and his message—to myself. There was no sense overwhelming Phillip with his daunting responsibility.

It'd be better to ease him into it. "Are you coming to the funeral?" I asked.

"I was afraid I'd already missed it."

"Nope. It's taking a while to ship his body back from Texas. We're still not sure when it'll get here."

"Yeah, I called your house to find out what day it would be, and that's what your mom said. And then she told me you were in the hospital, so I wanted to see how you were doing. You'll be out of here before the funeral, I hope."

"The doctor said I should be able to go home tomorrow. I just have to come back for a few oxygen therapy sessions."

He nodded and looked about the room. "Did someone bring you flowers? It smells like flowers in here."

"No." I smelled it too. "Smells like lilacs, doesn't it?"

"Yeah, it kind of does." It must've been Everett leaving, I figured. "Hey, what happened to your legs?" he asked, noticing my bandages. "I thought you were here for carbon monoxide poisoning."

"I cut myself with silverware," I lied.

"What'd you do that for?"

"I don't know. I was upset."

"I wish you wouldn't have done that! If you're ever that upset again, you need to give me a call before you start cutting yourself, OK?"

"All right."

"So what're your plans when you get out of here?" he asked, hastily changing the subject.

"I don't have any."

"Well, you're done with high school now. Have you thought about going to college?"

"You sound just like Everett."

"It'd keep your mind off things. And it's not too late to sign up for the fall semester at Lanford Community. I could help if you want. It's my last semester there. We could even see if we could take a class or two together. How does that sound?"

Going to college didn't interest me. But going to college with Phillip changed everything. "That'd be great!" I couldn't hide my elation. Everett's plan was already in motion. Phillip was going to rescue me. For the first time in a long time, I felt alive. My legs tingled under the covers. I wanted to stand, to walk down the halls and out into the courtyard. I whipped the oxygen tubes from my nose.

"Whoa. Are you supposed to do that?" cautioned Phillip.

"It's OK. Let's go for a walk. I can go for a walk!" I said eagerly. I tossed the blanket from my burning legs. At first, I thought what flew from beneath the blanket was a wrapper or a leaf. It spun through the air in a dizzying tumble. Yet as it came out of its twist, a pair of wings unfolded from its body, and it fluttered to the window. Upon the butterfly's bright yellow wings was a striking black pattern: an arc above a cluster of black dots, which looked as if it had been applied by a painter's brush.

"Where'd *that* come from?" wondered Phillip.

"Same place everything comes from." I smiled. "Nature."

27
RUTHSFORD CEMETERY

The Ruthsford Cemetery was situated on a hill secluded by groves of tall pines. To get to it, you first had to make your way down a road darkened by the thick, overhanging evergreens. The entrance was at the top of the hill. At the bottom was a ravine, where a small river flowed. Gravestones scattered the slope, which was naturally tiered into three sections. It reminded me of an amphitheater. The tiers I imagined to be balconies, and the bank of the river the stage. On the other side of the ravine grew a forest of tightly packed birch, maple, oak, and pine. Being inside the clearing was like being in the center of the universe. If you looked up, the sky seemed exclusively linked to that piece of earth. Everything else was simply out of orbit. With the constant flow of the serene river and the colorful change of seasons the wilderness beyond it provided, I figured if some soul wished to linger in the air before transitioning into something else, it'd be the perfect place for it.

I unhooked the tape recorder from my handlebar before we dumped our bikes at the top of the hill. "What'd you bring that for, anyway?" asked Phillip.

"Sarah Estep," I replied.

"Who's Sarah Estep?"

"This woman I saw on TV. She goes to haunted places: old battlegrounds, murder sites, cemeteries, catacombs—and she interviews the dead."

"And how does she manage to pull that off?" he asked, full of mockery.

"She records herself asking questions. And sometimes, when she plays back the tape, she'll hear their answers."

"And she's batshit, right?"

"She's a scientist, Phillip," I scolded. "She went to this lighthouse used during the Civil War as a prison camp and recorded one of the dead soldiers explaining how he died. His voice was all staticky. But you could make out some of what he said."

"I bet."

"C'mon," I said. Undeterred by his skepticism, I took off down the gravel path that looped the perimeter. "Let's try it." I made my way to the section of graves nearest the river, where the more recently dead were buried.

As I neared Everett's grave, I noticed that grass was finally beginning to sprout over the fresh patch in the earth. The clump of hawk feathers I had tied to a rock were still there. And although the wire stems had become twisted by the wind, so too were the plastic flowers Kirsten had left before she scurried back to Texas with her father.

It was strange to think that not many years before, Everett, Phillip, and I had tended to the secluded cemetery. I'd trim around the gravestones, daydreaming about the lives of the people buried beneath them. It was different then. I could easily separate us and them—alive and dead. Yet knowing someone who was represented by one of the markers blurred the lines between the two worlds. After talking with Everett, I became fascinated by death, intrigued by its possibilities. I didn't bother stopping by Everett's grave with my tape recorder. I had already interviewed him, knew he was no longer with his body. He had left it and was storing energy so he could materialize into other forms.

Instead, my eye was caught by a shimmer of red beneath the sweeping branch of a pine. As I made my way toward it, I realized it was one of those tiny balloons on a stick used in flower arrangements. "Miss You, Love You," was written in cursive on the face of the bright balloon that had been stuck in the ground above the freshly dug grave. A stone hadn't yet been placed. But there was a card attached to the base of the balloon. I opened it to reveal a handwritten epitaph beneath the graphic of a sun setting behind a glowing forest. It read:

Thomas Allen Gouldman
Loving son and brother
1971—1994

He was twenty-three. Close to Everett's age. "Too young," Phillip declared from over my shoulder. "Wonder what happened?"

"Let's find out," I replied with a grin before activating my recorder.

"Trust me. You're not going to hear anything when you play that back," he chided.

"Maybe not. Or maybe—he's still near his body." I extended the microphone. "Hello, Thomas. My name is Ayden. And this is Phillip. I'm going to ask you a few questions—if that's all right." I waited a moment for his permission before continuing. "First of all, could you tell us how you died? We'd really like to know." I held the microphone just above the balloon. Phillip shoved his hands in his pockets as the branch over Thomas's grave bobbed gently. Aside from the slight wind that drifted through the needles, the cemetery became silent. The animals, even the river, seemed to hush as we all strained to hear Thomas speak.

When I felt I had given him enough time to respond, I brought the microphone back to my lips. I was interested in learning how Thomas's experience might've differed from Everett's. "What did it feel like to die? Did you smell flowers? Lilacs? Are you inside your body? Or are you hovering near it? Do you still have vision? If the answer is yes, can you see me now? Can you feel yourself building up energy? Did you know you can choose where you go next?"

Phillip had snuck away, clearly not as entertained as I was. When I finally stepped away from the grave myself, I continued recording. I held the microphone out to the headstones I passed just in case others had something to say. The low branches slapped against the dusty ground as a gush of wind swept through the cemetery. The wind fed a rush of noises into my microphone, noises that may have very well contained voices from the other side.

I spotted Phillip up the hill wandering about, reading inscriptions. He was in the old part of the cemetery. The gravestones there were pale white. They looked so delicate, as if made of chalk. Many were cracked. Some had fallen over. I joined him before a tombstone that was split in two. The top half rested on the ground against its base. I felt the subtle grooves where lettering had once been defined and legible but had become weathered and erased over time. Pieces of sediment rubbed onto my finger like sparkling grains of sand.

A few rows ahead stood two tall, skinny stones. Although most of the lettering on these had also worn away, I could faintly make out the years. On each, the date of death was 1859. I noticed in the row behind them were three more stones in the same style yet smaller. They too had the same faint year of death etched into them. "A family," I announced. "All died within the same year. Must've been the plague."

Phillip laughed. "You're only off by a couple centuries. Not to mention the wrong continent."

"Oh."

"More like a fire. Maybe tuberculosis."

He wandered off into another section, where the dates of death ranged from the early to mid-1900s. He examined them closely, walking up and down the rows as I followed silently. He stopped short in front of a cluster of markers. "Look." He pointed. "All these people died toward the end of 1929. You know what that means, right?"

"I have no clue," I said honestly, feeling like an idiot.

"Black Tuesday."

"Oh. OK." I didn't know what Black Tuesday was but nodded as if I did.

"The stock market crash," he thankfully explained. "People lost everything overnight. The rich were all of a sudden poor. There were riots. Mass suicides. People jumping out of buildings. It was the start of the Great Depression."

"You're so smart," I marveled. My tone may have come off a tad sarcastic. But I meant it.

We eventually circled our way back to the river and sat at its edge. We threw rocks to the other side while Phillip told me what to expect from college when the semester started in a couple weeks. As for him, "I just want to be done so I can start making money as soon as possible. I take classes straight through the summers so it'll only take me three years total. And when I'm done, I'll take my CPA exam and start makin' the big bucks," he jokingly boasted. "Oh yeah, I'm gettin' a big house. A boat. Two jet skis. And a giant RV because I'll be goin' on cross-country campin' trips."

The future frightened me. Even listening to Phillip's playful version of it made me uneasy. The future meant change. In the future, familiar things could very likely no longer exist. In that moment, I felt content. Safe. Comfortable in my body. I tape-recorded his voice as we sat by the river. That day in the cemetery may not have meant much to him. But I never wanted to forget it. I wanted the feeling captured. I wanted to be able to relive it should moments like it no longer exist.

28
PAUL'S CASE

Against the wishes of my academic advisor, I took only English and humanities courses. I had some choices for the science requirements. Geology. Biology. Anatomy. But none of those interested me. And math, with all those numbers and symbols swirling about, was too intimidating. I was warned not to put off the core courses I dreaded. Otherwise, I'd be stuck with a punishing final year. But seeing as my intention was to simply be near Phillip, I didn't see the point in any long-term planning.

College was different than high school. It was bigger for one. I could hide. Become part of the crowd. Disappear when I sank in my chair. There was relief in being anonymous. No one knew who I was, so there were no snarling faces waiting for me each day like there had been in high school. Occasionally I'd run into someone from high school. Mike Scheppers, one of Ian's and Todd's former groupies, spotted me in the hall. He held up his hand and shouted my name as if we had some sort of camaraderie just because we went to the same high school. I walked straight past him, ignoring him as if I were famous and couldn't be bothered by some random fan. It felt good.

On my nights off from the grocery store, I'd hang out with Phillip. He was into cardio, so we continued biking to the Ruthsford Cemetery well into late fall. Visiting the cemetery with Phillip was one of my favorite things. I always brought my tape recorder with me, even though Thomas Gouldman proved to be uncooperative. The cemetery was at least fifteen miles from his house, but I was used to biking and could pedal forever without getting winded.

Unfortunately, on most nights, Phillip preferred jogging. Mortified that in the darkness I'd crush spiders or baby frogs, I'd keep my eyes intently on the sidewalk. When I spotted innocent creatures, I'd jump over them. Phillip would laugh. "You look like a deer leaping through the woods," he'd joke. Running would quickly cause me shortness of breath and sharp cramps to shoot up and down my side. I'd often take a shortcut back and wait for Phillip on his porch. On nights he'd jog, he'd offer to let me off the hook. But I never skipped an opportunity to spend time with Phillip.

Between school, work, and evening cardio sessions, I'd come home exhausted. I'd lie in bed and fall completely asleep within minutes, not waking until the alarm forced me to. The bony fingers that had once gripped the back of my neck had weakened. The demons were distant. Silenced. As always, Everett had been right. Without my even having to ask for his help, Phillip kept the monsters in the shadows. I was happy then. It was a new feeling for me, getting through my day without fear and anxiety.

Sure, sometimes I'd feel like a balloon whose string had been let go of by a hapless child. Alone. Out of control. It was then that the campus, its long halls and unfamiliar faces, overwhelmed me. These feelings of insecurity were fleeting, however, confined to moments when Phillip wasn't near, moments when I didn't feel Everett in the air next to me.

Our schedules overlapped closely enough so Phillip would give me a ride downtown most days. Unfortunately, we managed to get only one course together: studies in fiction. He needed English credits, and it met the requirement for his transfer program.

In class, Phillip sat between me and Ginger. He wasn't entirely subtle about glancing her way. Throughout the hour, he'd cock his head in her direction. I couldn't blame him. She had smooth, olive skin. Full lips. High cheekbones. And chestnut hair that occasionally fell over her cheeks in loose curls. Her face was oval-shaped. I heard once that people with oval-shaped faces didn't age as much as people with longer facial structures, something to do with how the skin doesn't stretch as much over time.

Yes, Ginger was beautiful. Yet more than that, you just knew she was more intelligent just by looking at her. It was in the way she sat with her back perfectly straight. And when she looked at you, if you should be so lucky, her lips sort of pouted, and she brought down her thin eyebrows. There was something about her that made you feel inferior. Yet rather than displaying her status with dominance, she looked upon you with sympathy, which was even worse. It was as if she felt sorry for you because you had to be in her presence. Sorry because, being next to her, your faults and flaws were only magnified. She was simply perfection in the form of a human being.

One day, my insecurities regarding Ginger slipped into the open. It began when the young, enthusiastic instructor's voice boomed, "OK, you young scholars! Willa Cather. *Paul's Case.* I hope you read it. Because we are about to discuss it!" I switched on my recorder. I had a tough time concentrating in class, so I'd listen to the lectures later.

Something connected me to Paul. He had escaped the doldrums of Pittsburgh for New York. Through an expensive hotel room and the beautiful music of an orchestra, he became a small piece, if only a glimmer, of the culture there. I listened as the class discussed the symbolism of flowers in the story. How they stood for all things appealing about high society. How they were an extension of Paul himself. And how near the conclusion of the story, when his time in New York had come to an end, the carnation in his coat drooped.

The discussion then focused on the possible reasons why Paul had jumped on the tracks in front of the oncoming train. That's when Ginger delicately raised her hand. Her fingers curled until they made a partial fist and only her index finger was left pointing to the ceiling. It was as if all the knowledge in the world dwelled in that finger. "I see Paul as a coward," she proclaimed. "He steals two thousand dollars to fund his journey and is then overwhelmed with shame. Though that's not the part that makes him a coward. What makes him a coward is that he believes facing his father and coming clean would be more unbearable than killing himself."

The instructor squinted and nodded, processing Ginger's comment. Ginger curled her lips upward slightly, satisfied with her interpretation. But I knew there was more to Paul than that. It was more than guilt that drove his premature transformation. "Very thoughtful analysis, Ginger," praised the instructor. "Is there another young scholar who would like to speak of Paul's decision?"

I became hot. My fingers tingled. My arm was weak as I raised it over my head. Phillip turned to me, shocked. I had yet to voluntarily participate in any class discussion. And I'd sink in my desk and avoid eye contact with the instructor in hopes of never being called upon. "Ayden!" She pointed. "We don't hear from you enough. Please. Enlighten us."

"Paul's not a coward," I countered. I started out softly, my voice trembling. "There's more to him than that. More than what she said. All he wants to do is escape reality. He uses Carnegie Hall, and art, and music, and theater to escape. Actors and opera singers." I began to speak faster, forgetting to pause as Phillip held his look of astonishment. "And when he was forced to wake up, forced to separate his fantasy world from reality, he had no other choice but to throw himself on the tracks. Why would he go back home? He wasn't happy there. He knew his future there would be miserable. It had nothing to do with feeling shame for stealing the money. He was defeated, just like the dying carnation in his coat. He *had* to end his life. There was no other way!" I took deep breaths, as if I had just run a mile.

Ginger's brown eyes widened, just slightly, as she adjusted herself in her seat. I didn't dare look at her for longer than a glance as I waited for her retort. And sure enough, she was quick to clarify her original response: "Yes, it's true. There was nothing Pittsburgh could offer him in terms of aesthetics, which he craved. So in Paul's eyes, going back would mean he had failed. He couldn't bear to face his father, his teachers, the people of Cordelia Street. But instead of addressing his failures and legitimately working his way back to the world he loved, he took the easy way out."

"Jumping in front of a train doesn't seem that easy to me," I snapped.

The class began to murmur and shift uneasily in their seats. Phillip jabbed me with his elbow and whispered, "OK. You can stop. You're never going to win an argument with a woman. So you might as well not even try." *But I did win!* Why couldn't Phillip see that?

I looked to Ginger, to her perfect lips. Her white, fluffy sweater was so soft and feminine. It contrasted with her skin, accentuating her healthy glow. She sat perfectly calm, with her fingers curled around her pen. It was then I understood. Phillip was right. I was never going to win. Not really. My tape recorder reached the end of the tape and shut itself off. I sat through the rest of class without documenting further discussions. Like Paul and his carnation, I was defeated.

29
GiNGER THE METEOR

"She likes me, huh?" Phillip asked as we tossed food on our trays.

"*Who* likes you?"

"Ginger. C'mon. She likes me, don't you think?" He shoved his face in front of mine and cocked his head, forcing his wild grin on me. "You know she wants me," he persisted.

I couldn't help but laugh. "I'm sure she does," I agreed.

Phillip was the first to spot her. I could tell something had grabbed his attention the way he suddenly went mute and put away his nutty grin. She appeared as if summoned by the mention of her name. She was alone. People like Ginger had no need to travel in groups, I figured. We watched as she confidently strode into the cafeteria, her loose curls gently bobbing. There was a certainty in the way she slid open the glass door to the cooler and selected a sandwich and bottled water.

Phillip waited until she stepped in one of the checkout lines before dashing across the cafeteria. My plate of fries nearly slid off my tray as I hurried after him. "Hey, Ginger," he said as he stepped smoothly behind her.

She spun toward us, her lips lifting in a gentle greeting. "Phillip, right?" she asked.

"Uh, if you think I'm a tool, then it's Chad," he said with a smirk. "If you don't, then yeah, I'm Phillip."

She bit her bottom lip and laughed delicately. "Hey, you're taking statistics, right?" she asked.

"Yeah. How'd you know?"

"I saw you had the book."

"You taking it this semester too?"

"After lunch. Who do you have?"

"Manglitz."

"Me too. He's tough. But it's not that difficult if you actually pay attention." She rolled her eyes. "A lot of people are dropping already. There are some real weak students in that class."

"*I'm* not weak." He grinned. "I know what you mean, though. I don't really mind him either. In fact, I'm sure I'll ace it," he said with a touch of that faux boastful charm of his.

I slouched behind Phillip, resisting the temptation of peering into her brown eyes, as if her gaze would turn me to stone. I was so sure she hated me after our sparring over *Paul's Case*. Yet when I finally looked to her, the look she gave back didn't seem like one of hatred. More like perplexed curiosity.

"Are you eating here?" asked Phillip.

"Yeah. I have a half hour to kill." As she approached the cashier, she had her money ready, exact change included.

"So are me and Ayden. Want to sit with us?"

I stepped out from behind Phillip, officially exposed. And Ginger, in turn, officially set her soft eyes on me. "Sure," she replied and then bestowed upon me her customary look of pity.

Ecstatic she had accepted, Phillip eased his playful smile into one of sincerity. I did my best to smile too, but my stomach—it burned with acid. It felt like a tiny meteor had crashed into the tender lining. It was Ginger. She was lodged there, burning my insides.

Phillip led us to a table next to the full-length windows overlooking the roof of the activities center. Despite all the smokers who congregated on the roof, he knew I liked sitting there. Beyond the smokers were a line of bird feeders bolted to the ledge. I enjoyed watching the birds while eating. And with the awkward silence that day, I desperately needed their company. Focusing intently on the birds, I was well on my way to joining them, becoming one of them, when Ginger's voice brought me back to the table. "So, Ayden, you're a fan of Willa Cather, I take it?"

I should've known it was coming: retribution for challenging her in class. She just couldn't resist. My face became flushed. I wished I hadn't ever opened my mouth about *Paul's Case*. I wasn't prepared to debate her in the cafeteria—again in front of Phillip. "I guess," I replied. "I haven't read anything else she's written besides that story." I braced myself to be destroyed.

"You should read *My Ántonia*," she suggested. "It's considered her masterpiece. There're parts that read just like poetry. I think you might like it." I couldn't believe it. She had her chance to finish me off. Yet she didn't take it. Instead, she offered me a book recommendation?

She then turned her attention to Phillip, who had yet to avert his attention from her. "What's your major, Phillip?"

"Accounting," he answered. He puffed out his chest. "I'm going to be a CPA."

"Mine's business management. I'd love to manage a nonprofit like a hospital. Or a charity organization like United Way. What's your major, Ayden?"

"I don't have one," I replied before sheepishly returning my gaze back to the birds. Surely Ginger couldn't relate to someone so unsure of themselves. I was willing to bet she had her entire future meticulously mapped out. All she had to do was follow her plan. Must've been nice.

"That's smart," she responded. "Might as well take some classes here and figure out what you're into before going on to a university."

Her responses weren't what I was expecting, but they had me flustered just the same. "Why's your name *Ginger*?" I blurted. "You have brown hair. It doesn't make any sense."

She let out a laugh. "Well, I'm named after my grandmother's sister. And actually, she wasn't a redhead either. So I think it's OK for just about anyone to be named Ginger."

I shoved a fry in my mouth and bowed out of the conversation at that point. I wouldn't have been able to offer much anyhow as they began discussing finance classes and where they wanted to travel abroad. "No way! Me too!" Ginger exclaimed, raising her voice beyond its typical reserved tone when she found out she and Phillip had the same plan to finish college early by taking classes year-round. I rolled my eyes. Both overachievers hardly touched their food. Ginger just kept sipping her water, somehow making it look seductive without even trying.

Slowly, so as not to disturb their riveting conversation, I pulled my tape recorder from my backpack and held it under the table. I flipped the tape over and pressed play. I strained to listen, trying to block out the sounds of the cafeteria and focus only on the noises coming from the tiny speaker. "*Hello, Thomas. My name is Ayden,*" my voice from the tape said. The volume was turned up a bit too loud, causing Ginger to stop midsentence. "*I'm going to ask you a few questions—if that's all right.*"

"Is that your voice, Ayden?" she asked.

Phillip let out a light laugh and answered for me. "Yeah. It's him. He was screwing around in the cemetery."

"*In the cemetery?*"

"Yeah. Hey, Ayden and I are going to the movies tonight." Phillip quickly changed the subject to save me—or perhaps himself—from embarrassment. "Would you like to come?" I laughed to myself at the proposition. Why would Ginger, the intellectual beauty queen, want to go to the movies with *us*?

"Well." She thought a moment. "It depends what you're going to see."

"We were thinking *Natural Born Killers.*"

"It's a satire," I added.

"A satire of what?" she asked.

She had me right where she wanted. I swallowed hard while providing her only a vacant stare. I may have had an idea, but I wasn't confident I even knew what a satire was, much less what the movie was supposed to be a satire of.

"I think it's supposed to be a satire on how the media sensationalizes violence," responded Phillip, saving me. Bravely, he asked her again: "So. Do you want to see it with us? Or . . ."

"Sure. I'll go." She smiled.

I could feel her burning, burrowing deeper—when suddenly my voice on the tape interrupted again: "Could you tell us how you died? We'd really like to know."

Wind came through the tiny speaker, sounding as if someone were crumpling a piece of paper too close to the microphone. Yet through the interference, from behind the wind, a faint voice called out. "I Wa. Sss," it said. It was barely audible, so I turned the volume up even louder and brought the recorder to the surface of the table. The light voice repeated with just a bit more clarity, "I Wa. Sss. Ca. Ar. I. Wa. Sss. In. Ca. Ar."

"Phillip? Is that you?" asked Ginger.

"No," Phillip answered in shock. For the first time since she had entered the room, Phillip's attention had successfully been drawn away from Ginger.

The voice continued to break through the wind. "In. Ca. Ar. It. Hap. End."

"Holy shit!" shouted Phillip, his cheeks turning red from pure astonishment.

"A. Lone. It. Hap. End."

"Who is that?" Ginger looked to Phillip, to me, and back to the tape recorder.

"I thought you listened to that tape a hundred times!" said Phillip.

"I did. I mean, I guess I didn't have the volume turned up loud enough. We have got to listen to the whole tape again!" I shouted. "And we've got to get back to the cemetery. Right away!" I leapt to my feet. My enthusiasm forced Phillip to his feet as well. We gathered our backpacks as Ginger looked upon our sudden upheaval with a look of bewilderment.

"I'm so sorry," Phillip apologized. "I'll call you tonight about the movie, OK?"

"But I didn't give you my number," she replied calmly, in stark contrast to our rushed exit.

"Right," he realized, embarrassed. He handed Ginger his notebook while he fished for a pen. But before he could find one, Ginger flipped to a blank page and used her own pen to jot her number. She then closed the notebook, smiling as she handed it back to him. I could tell Phillip was fighting the urge to flip through every page to find that number while he still stood before her. But after a moment, he grudgingly shoved his notebook back into his bag.

We then left beautiful Ginger sitting alone in the cafeteria with our half-eaten lunches. At least she had a nice view of the birds on the roof.

30
THE VOICE OF
THOMAS GOULDMAN

It didn't take long for Phillip to become weary standing over Thomas's grave before he'd wander off and start exploring. But thankfully, I wasn't left to investigate on my own. A few weeks before, I never would've believed I'd find myself kneeling over the grave of Thomas Gouldman—with Ginger Young. But there we were. At first, it was strange talking to Ginger about Thomas. I was so sure when we ate lunch together that first time that Thomas would've repelled her. I'd assumed sitting in a cemetery all afternoon having a one-way conversation with a headstone would've seemed dull and childish to someone like Ginger. Yet she was full of surprises. After being let in on where the voice on the tape had come from, she was immediately on board.

For her, it was a scientific experiment. Something to hypothesize about. Something to prove or disprove with the support of evidence. For me, the intrigue in Thomas was fueled by my visit from Everett. Making contact with Thomas made me feel closer, in a way, to Everett. Even though I could no longer communicate with him, at least I was doing something to keep one foot in his world. I was doing more than just remembering. I was *reaching*, trying to touch hands.

We relentlessly interviewed Thomas about his life and his experiences in death. We spent hours before his grave. And even more hours analyzing tapes. Yet frustratingly, he had yet to speak again. All we really knew about him was that "it happened in the car." And sometimes, we couldn't even confirm that. Despite marking the position on the tape where his voice was heard, we'd often only hear wind and static upon playback.

After several weeks of trying, even I had to admit that Thomas might no longer be the optimal subject. As we hiked back up the cemetery's hill one evening, I reluctantly offered, "I bet he's moved on. He's probably changed forms. Transferred his energy into a plant. Or become a cricket or something."

Ginger squinted and nodded politely while absorbing the concept. "That's an interesting philosophy. How'd you come up with that?"

"I didn't come up with it. It's what happened to my brother, Everett, after he died."

"Is this what your family believes? Were you raised to believe in this kind of reincarnation?"

"No. He told me that's what happened to him."

"He *told* you? You have *his* voice on tape too?"

"No. He came to me with borrowed energy. But only for a few minutes." Ginger exchanged a brief glance with a befuddled Phillip. I knew what it meant. They didn't believe me. They thought I was nuts. But it didn't matter. And I didn't care. It was the truth.

Ginger thought a moment. "So then, if energy converts into different forms after death, then it stands to reason he'd be somewhere nearby—in his new form, that is."

"He *could* be close," I affirmed. "But he could also be somewhere familiar to him. And if he *did* transfer forms, I'm pretty sure we wouldn't be able to capture his voice on tape anymore."

Ginger's reaction to my revealing Everett's experience was surprisingly refreshing. She didn't patronize me. Rather, she seemed genuinely interested in exploring the possibilities.

Phillip, on the other hand, remained silent. He indulged us, allowed us to continue to speculate on the whereabouts of Thomas. But he merely tolerated it, occasionally shaking his head skeptically. I couldn't figure it out. Like Ginger, he too had a scientific mind. But I wondered if maybe he was only suited for grounded sciences, sciences that dealt with observable physical and chemical reactions. Maybe Phillip and paranormal research just weren't a good fit. But the reason he played along was obvious. It was clear he was more interested in Ginger than in the mystery of Thomas Gouldman.

It became no more evident than later that evening, while listening to our tapes in Phillip's bedroom, that the attraction was mutual. We took turns listening on a pair of headphones. They allowed us to better isolate sounds from the breeze and rushing river. It was my turn on the headphones. When I thought I might've heard a faint voice, I spun around to find Phillip's hand on Ginger's knee. Embarrassed, I turned back to the stereo, pretending I didn't notice.

The meteor named Ginger had since dissolved. I had wrongly assumed someone like Ginger would see someone like me as inferior, insignificant, weak—especially when she was the embodiment of perfection: beautiful, confident, smart. But she was on my side. So when I saw out of the corner of my eye that she and Phillip were holding hands, it felt right. It was natural.

I was forced to overcome my bashfulness concerning their burgeoning affection for one another—as the voice in my ears could no longer be ignored. With much elation, I yanked the headphones from the stereo. The tape crackled throughout the room before a voice sharply stated: *"Fi! Er!"* Phillip and Ginger stood from the bed, astounded. *"Ov. Er. Ed. Ge."*

"Where are you now, Thomas?" my voice on the tape asked. We listened in frozen silence. Afraid to move. Afraid if we broke our concentration, we wouldn't hear him again.

"Da. Ark," his voice finally hissed. *"Be. Low. I. Was. Here. Ri. Ver. Now. Tr. Eee. Sss. Wi. Thhh. You. See. You. Tr. Eee. Sss."*

We listened several more minutes to the chirping birds and rushing river. Only when it was clear he would say no more, when his silence became unbearable, did I speak. "He hasn't transitioned yet," I whispered.

"Apparently not," Ginger agreed. "At least not as of this afternoon. It's unbelievable!" She allowed herself a moment of giddiness before grabbing a pad and scribbling excitedly. "Now what did we learn? You asked him where he was now. And if I'm making it out right, he said he had been somewhere in the dark. But that he was with us. Near the trees. Near the river. And we know from what he said before that he died in a car. But now he's added 'fire' and 'over the edge.' So was it an explosion? Did his car catch on fire after being pushed over the edge of something? You know what?" she asked, pounding the tip of the pen to the paper. "That's actually testable. He didn't die that long ago. All we'd have to do is a bit of research to find out exactly how he died. If it matches some of the details of what these tapes are telling us, then—oh my God." Her eyes widened. "It means we'd have proof of life after death."

"That'll be easy," I offered. "I know right where they keep the old newspapers in the library. All we have to do is look for any articles about car crashes a day or so after the date of his death. We won't even have to look on microfiche since it's been less than a year."

"Let's not do that yet," cautioned Ginger. "We have to do this right. If we read all the details about his death now, it could bias our findings. Cloud our research. We might start interpreting the voice to match the article without even realizing it. No. We should double our recording sessions. First, we need more data. Then, we look for the article."

"Sounds like a plan," I enthusiastically agreed.

Poor Phillip didn't know what hit him. He looked like a dog that had been stranded in the middle of nowhere. I only confused him more when I squeezed his shoulder and shook it in a failed attempt to transfer my exhilaration to him. I felt alive in so many ways, and I owed it all to Phillip. Without him, I wouldn't have gone to college. I wouldn't have met Ginger. Or had anyone to help me study the case of Thomas Gouldman. Unbeknownst to him, he had also saved me the humiliation of going to a psychiatrist. The doctor encouraged it after my so-called *episode* in the hospital. However, Mom and Dad decided not to force me to go after witnessing my success at college. And of course, most importantly, Phillip remained my appointed protector. My guardian against evil. He was the shield I hadn't had since before Everett left for Texas.

I struggled with a way to thank Phillip. But it wasn't as if I could've talked to him about any of these things. He was oblivious, unaware of the power he possessed. Besides, how could I have even begun to thank someone for basically keeping me alive? And then it came to me, through of all things, a dream. I hadn't dreamt in so long, at least that I could remember. I began getting used to sleeping deeply, uninterrupted by dreams—and nightmares. So it was startling when one invaded my peace. And when I woke, it didn't take much interpretation. Although shocking, its meaning was clear: Phillip and I would meet certain death. But I had a plan. What better way to thank Phillip—than saving his life?

31
EVERGREEN HiLL

"Why is it that the sun always seems so bright in the fall?" Phillip asked, squinting, as I jumped in his car.

"Because less leaves are blocking it," I reasoned.

"Ha. Maybe. Hey, I forgot my sunglasses. Got any extra?" I didn't. But I bolted to Mom's car and grabbed a pair off her dash. Until Phillip hastily threw them on, I hadn't given a thought to them being giant women's sunglasses. The lenses overtook his face. Plus, they were crooked. One rim jutted well over his eyebrow, while the other jammed into his cheek. "Thanks a ton," he said sarcastically, followed by a goofy grin, capitalizing on how ridiculous he looked.

"Let's go," I said with a snicker. "You keep coming later and later."

"That may be. But I keep driving faster and faster!" With that, he tore out of the driveway and sped down the road with forced urgency.

"Where the hell are you taking us?" I yelped as we bypassed the entrance to the expressway.

"Look at that ramp. It's a parking lot. I'll get you to class a lot faster if we take Evergreen."

That's when I knew, for sure, that it was coming. We barreled up Evergreen's mammoth hill. It was a peculiar landscape. To the right was a plummeting canyon filled with a thick forest of deciduous trees. The colorful treetops appeared to float just above the height of the road. In the distance, up the steep incline, was a pine forest. The way the far-off pines jutted into the horizon, they looked almost like miniatures from a movie set.

The ride that morning, I had been on it before. It was the same as in my dream: the bright morning sun in my eyes, the colorful splashes of leaves racing by. Yet more than simply giving me a sense of déjà vu, it was as if the dream had penetrated reality, had formed a bubble around us from which we couldn't escape. We moved forward in snapshots, like a video camera recording only one second out of ten-second intervals. Under this influence, we jolted skyward at an unnatural pace. Oncoming cars blinked past us. Houses were superimposed over trees.

I had been determined to thwart the conclusion of the dream but instead found myself helplessly paralyzed inside of it. It tethered my limbs and kept my mouth sealed shut. As we zoomed toward oblivion, all we could do was perform what had already been prescribed for us. No, we weren't going to make it to class. No, we weren't going to survive. What was destined for Phillip and me was final.

Monroe Avenue was at the peak of Evergreen's hill. From there, it was a straight shot downtown. As Phillip turned into the intersection, I watched the bright leaves copy themselves as a reflection on the window. Gold. Red. Copper. Orange. The real and projected leaves danced as they met, overlapped, and came apart again. I was easily seduced by the kaleidoscope of swirling hues as the dark blue Buick appeared out of nowhere. It took the squeal of tires and Phillip shouting, "Holy shit!" to remind me that I was in fact awake.

I shot forward and was abruptly halted as the seat belt locked. The strap gripped my chest and rib cage, and my breath was forced from my lungs. I knew the face of the teenage girl in the other car.

I had seen it before. Her wide eyes. Her clenched teeth. She gripped the steering wheel for dear life and jerked it sharply to her right, futilely attempting to stop the damaging chain of events that had already been set in motion. Her blonde hair was swept forward and froze for a millisecond before her car was sent into a violent spin, blocking our path.

Phillip's silly sunglasses were tossed from his head as he whipped us back into the other lane. He managed to save us from a head-on collision. Yet the front of her spinning car smacked the rear of his, sending us fishtailing across Evergreen. We veered off the pavement and into the gravel before bursting through the guardrail. Phillip desperately pumped the brakes. But it was no use. The tires had left solid ground.

We sailed above the canyon, through the tops of the oaks and maples I had been admiring only moments before. The car filled with the smell of exhaust and burned rubber. I gripped the dash as the branches reached for us like giant, crippled fingers. They scraped along the sides of the car, making the metal shriek as we glided through the treetops. Giant oak leaves slapped against the windows, pressing so tight I could see the veins that pumped the blood beneath their suffocating orange and red skins.

The entire ride, I had been struggling to break free from the toxic trance. And finally, by focusing intently on those majestic leaves, I had found what I needed. They weren't false images. They weren't superimpositions. They were organic. They forced me, in that instant, to become sober. And in my sobriety, I simply could not accept what was to happen. With only seconds to act, instead of panic, I felt incredibly calm. I knew exactly what I had to do.

I pulled the lever that engaged the parking brake. Pressed on the hazard lights. And punched the following buttons on the radio: 2-6-3-4-1. Only these were *not* the parking brake, the hazard lights, or the radio. Not at all. They were the controls in a brand-new spaceship. Instead of old farm machinery repurposed into a flying machine, Phillip's car was the latest model. And the sequence, the lever I pulled, and the buttons I pushed caused the craft to halt in midair.

We hovered silently among the treetops as Phillip clung to the steering wheel in a mix of terror and disbelief. Keeping his back completely straight, he slowly leaned forward, petrified, and peered over the hood to the crater below. He then cautiously turned to me, looking as if he was trying to speak a hundred words at once but was unable to utter one syllable. The leaves wrapped us in a cocoon. They gave me a feeling of comfort and safety. With this sense of protection, I confidently unbuckled my seat belt. "What're you doing!" cried Phillip, breaking the silence. "Do not move!"

"It's OK," I assured him and patted his shoulder. "Remember when Everett told you me and him would fly a spaceship in the middle of the night? Well, this isn't your car anymore. Now it's—a craft." I swiveled on my knees so I could peer through the rear window. I couldn't see between the thick leaves well enough to know if anyone had stopped on the road. But I figured it wouldn't be long before gawkers would be peering over the edge, hoping for a macabre glimpse of a crumpled car that surely had become a death trap to its unlucky passengers.

I plunked back into my seat. Phillip remained stiff. His upper lip was perspiring. "We're safe. I promise." Unlike Phillip, I felt quite cozy in our private hideout among the trees.

I gave him a sympathetic smile as I casually rolled down my window. The bouquet of leaves pressing against the glass popped into the car like giant flowers blooming instantaneously. Phillip allowed only his eyes to follow my movements as I reached my arm outside. I let my fingers feel their way down the stem of the largest red leaf. When I found the thick base, I plucked it from the branch. The branch snapped back, reverberating like a piece of struck metal. I brought the leaf inside. As I twirled it by its stem, marveling at its size and brilliance, the craft began to rock—and slip through the branches.

Admittedly, I had been a bit overconfident regarding the improvised craft's hovering ability. Thinking quickly, I grabbed the lever and began lowering it gently. Limbs bowed and snapped as we crashed through the canopy. Leaves rushed by in a collage of swirling colors. Apparently concerned about my lack of a seat belt, Phillip threw his arm across my chest. But because the car was not a car at all, it thrust against the force of gravity, easing the intensity of our drop. Even so, when we hit the earth, the impact was violent enough to blow the windows out of their casings. I threw my hands to my face as the glass imploded.

"Are you OK!" shouted Phillip. Fragments of glass had shot into our skin. Blood trickled down Phillip's face and my arms.

"I'm all right."

He kicked open his door and lumbered outside. My door wouldn't budge. "We could've been killed!" he shouted angrily as he tugged on my handle. When the crumpled metal finally gave way, I too staggered out. The car had smashed onto a pile of rocks. The tires had been blown apart. "We could've been killed!" he repeated in my face.

Phillip was absolutely right. If the car had propelled off the ridge as I had foreseen, we would've smashed straight into one of the thick trunks and been knocked unconscious even before crashing to the ground. A hot piece of metal would've severed the fuel line. We'd have been snuffed out from smoke inhalation before finally being eviscerated by the flames. There would've been no escape. I knew it. I saw it.

"But we weren't. We weren't killed." I grinned heartily, twirling the red leaf I had yet to let go of. Phillip gaped at me as if I were from Mars. He then rested against his dilapidated car, lowering his head.

It was ironic. I had credited Phillip for keeping my dreams to a minimum. Yet there we were, our lives saved by one. I was quite proud of myself. The dream had tipped me off to the crash, and combining the information I had gleaned with my spacecraft piloting skills, I had found a way to outsmart evil—and save Phillip.

Shouts came from above as several first responders began to slide their way down the steep hill to assess our lives. "Hello! Help is on the way!"

32
REJECTING THE NULL

Even though Phillip wasn't yet back from his night class, his mom let me into his bedroom to wait for him. I was flipping through his biology book when Ginger burst into the room clutching a folder. "I thought I'd find you here," she said, nearly out of breath. She beamed with an equal measure of excitement and intensity. "I've found it," she declared. Without warning, she slapped down a photocopy of Thomas Gouldman's obituary, as well as a brief accompanying article. And suddenly Thomas was real. At least as real as he could get in grainy black and white. His photo was of a young man with moppy hair and an endearing snaggletoothed smile.

After several weeks of not hearing from him, Ginger and I had agreed there was little possibility Thomas was still hovering about in the Ruthsford Cemetery. Although our plan was to collect more data, clearly he had chosen to transition. Reluctantly, we had no choice but to conclude our study. The time had come to factually confirm whether or not the bits and pieces we had learned about Thomas through our voice recordings matched the circumstances of his death in any way.

The headline of the article read, *Local Student Killed in Fiery Crash.* That alone was a direct hit. Not only did it in fact "happen in the car" as Thomas had told us. But his demise also involved fire.

"We did it," I said, satisfied. "The voice on the tape really is Thomas. Has to be."

"Yes. Yes. I think we're safe to reject the null and accept our hypothesis." I had no idea what she was talking about, but I assumed *rejecting the null* had to be a good thing.

"But there's more to it than that. Listen to this," she said and began to read from the article.

> *Gouldman was a junior at the University of Michigan in Ann Arbor. He had been driving back from the eastern part of the state to visit family in the suburbs of Lanford.*
>
> *Police report Gouldman attempted to avoid an oncoming car when his vehicle slid off the road and was propelled into a heavily wooded area. The vehicle struck a tree before falling down a steep gorge. Investigators speculate Gouldman became unconscious either upon impact with the tree or due to smoke inhalation, which would have made it impossible to escape the flames.*
>
> *Several residents who live near the crash site were critical of the city for not installing a traffic light at the intersection. Records confirm dozens of accidents per year have taken place at Evergreen Road and Monroe Avenue since the thoroughfares were connected during a road commission project in 1981.*

"Did you hear that? *Evergreen and Monroe!* That's the same intersection where you and Phillip were almost killed. Just think about it. If Phillip's car hadn't wedged between those branches the way it did, the same thing could've happened to the both of you."

"Is that what he told you?" I fumed. "That we were stuck in branches?"

"How else could you have survived? It's amazing, really. Must be kismet."

"*Kismet?*"

"Fate. Destiny. There's no other way to explain a coincidence like that. All this time we were talking to Thomas, and his fate was so close to what yours could've been."

"Yeah. That's wild," I agreed. But in that moment, I was less enthralled with all the kismet swirling about. I couldn't get past the fact that Phillip had thought *branches* were what was holding us above the canyon—when we were clearly hovering in the craft.

"Even though Thomas is gone, we should keep listening for other voices," I suggested.

She tapped her index finger on her lip. "You're right. If this were a real study, one case wouldn't be enough. We'd need more subjects. But the Ruthsford Cemetery is pretty small. The odds of capturing more voices there is probably pretty low. If we really wanted to continue, we'd need to expand. Go to other cemeteries. Bigger cemeteries."

"Everett told me about this huge cemetery up north. Grand Hallow. He said it's the size of a city."

"That's perfect. We'd need better equipment. A professional recorder. And microphones with filters on them so we're not recording so much wind."

Talking about the next phase of our research got me excited. Yet when Phillip came home and we ran the plans by him—he promptly dumped a bucket of ice water over them. "Uh. C'mon, guys. Let's give the voices from the other side a rest for a while," he groaned.

33
SPACE JUNK

"You're floating," he said. I looked to the floor in case he meant literally. But my shoes remained on the carpet. When I lifted my head, I didn't meet his eyes. Instead, I focused on his mouth and short goatee. Out of the corner of my eye, I kept track of the large orange-and-white fish swimming circles in the aquarium. "In space," he clarified. "You have no gravity. No balance. No direction. Your course is dependent upon what objects you happen to hit. You hit something . . ." He slapped his hands together to provide me a visual and then quickly separated them. "And then you're off spinning in another direction. You're like a wayward piece of space junk. Bombarded by random objects. Allowing gravity to take you where it may. You're reactive. Not proactively steering your own path."

Dr. Griffin was young for a psychiatrist. Maybe in his late twenties or early thirties. Actually, he wasn't a psychiatrist. He was a psychologist. I wasn't really sure of the difference except he told me he wouldn't be able to prescribe medications should I need them.

"You're making your way through," he continued. "You're functioning. But you're on autopilot. You're not in control. You're not an active participant in your own life." He stopped for a moment to chew on his nails, which were nothing more than stubs. I let out a muted chuckle, wondering how seriously I should be taking advice from someone who was supposed to be an example of mental stability yet was an obsessive nail-biter. "Ayden, does that make sense? Are you listening?"

"Yes."

"Do you agree with that assessment? If it's not an accurate representation, then let me know. You know yourself better than I do."

"No. I mean, yes. I do agree with that assessment."

"OK then. So what are you going to do about it?"

I turned my attention to the aquarium. Each time I looked to the tank, I attempted to will the orange-and-white fish away from the coral at the bottom. It looked real, and I was afraid he'd rip one of his fins should he brush against it. "You mean how do I stop being space junk?" I asked.

"Yes, if you're not offended by that analogy."

"Well, I've decided to go back to school next semester."

"Fantastic. That is definitely a move proving you can steer your own ship. I believe you're on your way to becoming a total independent thinker."

"Let's not rush things," I replied sarcastically.

He jotted a few notes and then flipped to a fresh page in his notebook. "How have your dreams been?"

"Not so bad."

"And Everett?"

"You mean, in my dreams?"

"In your dreams. Or otherwise."

"When I dream, if things get bad, if I'm attacked—he's there. He helps me escape from the demons. But he can't fight them, even in my dreams, because they know he's dead. In one dream, monsters were chasing me through the woods. But I saw Everett above the trees. Floating. I followed him, and he led me out of the forest and to a cabin. I barricaded myself inside and stayed there until I woke. Outside of dreams, no. I've only seen Everett that one time at the hospital."

"As long as he remains confined to your dreams, I'm not too concerned. In fact, if your progress stays on track, I believe you could expect him to even further regress until he makes only the occasional appearance. And eventually, I expect he'll be limited to ordinary memories. What about the other hallucinations?"

"Mostly animals. Cats. There was a cat in my bedroom. It jumped from the dresser and crawled under the bed. But when I looked, it wasn't underneath. And birds. A blackbird flew into my windshield while I was driving home from the dentist."

"But it didn't really, did it?"

I shook my head. "I flinched when it hit. I closed my eyes. But when I opened them, there was no bird. Oh, and did I tell you about the pop can?"

"Not that I recall."

"There was a pop can on the kitchen table. For some reason, I found myself staring at it while daydreaming. And then, all of a sudden, it started spinning by itself. I'm still crazy," I assured him, followed by an uneasy laugh.

"I'd say those are still relatively mild. Interesting, but mild. As I've said before, I don't believe you need medication or other forms of treatment for these types of sightings. As long as they're not frightening to you or interfering a significant amount in your day-to-day activities, I say just enjoy them for what they are. They may just always be that something you have that's different from everyone else."

He scratched his goatee. "Now, would you like to tell me more about Phillip and Ginger? If I remember correctly, at the end of our last session, you were telling me the point at which you began to feel—I think the word you used was—betrayed."

"All right," I agreed half-heartedly and began to tell him about the night I helped Phillip look for a new car.

Phillip had been without a car since the accident and was getting tired of having to rely on Ginger and me for rides, so I drove him to the used car lot one evening. The lot was closed. We were alone, just us and the frosted cars. The sky was a thick, dark gray. It was one of those nights where it seemed too cold to even snow. He was unusually silent as he examined the vehicles in his price range. We moved from car to car with our hands in our pockets and our coats zipped to the collar.

"The semester's almost over," he finally said, wiping ice crystals off the window of a red Grand Prix. He peered inside as I stood at its rear, barely pretending I knew what to be looking for when choosing a car. "Final exams are coming up already."

"I'm not worried about exams."

"That's good," he said before heading to the next car. "You know, it's my last semester before transferring."

"I know." How could I have forgotten?

"And Ginger—it's her last semester too, you know."

"Yeah, I know," I said, becoming perturbed by the unnecessary reminders about what already had me filled with anxiety.

"And good news. You know how Ginger was going to go to that school in Chicago? Well, now she's decided to go to Western with me."

"Yeah. Good news." I pressed my thumb onto the trunk. I watched as the frost slowly dissolved around my skin, creating a halo on the dark-blue paint beneath.

"You've enrolled for next semester, right?"

"Nope," I replied bluntly. The thought hadn't even crossed my mind. I couldn't imagine it without him and Ginger.

"Well, I think you should keep at it, even if your degree *does* end up being liberal arts," he teased.

I thrust my fists back into my pockets, attempting to relieve the sting of the cold. I looked up to the sky. It was vast yet hung low over our heads. Thick and murky. It blanketed the earth, attempting to suffocate it. My eyes stung from the cold and began to tear. "I'm not sure what I'm going to do now."

"Well, you should go," he persisted. "Even if it means you have to go alone. But you won't be alone. You'll make new friends. Maybe even someone you can share rides with."

I turned my gaze to the old Grand Am parked near the entrance. It hadn't yet become frozen like the other cars. I had the sudden urge to climb inside and drive away. I imagined just driving and driving. I rubbed my stinging eyes. "It's fucking cold out here."

"Yeah, I know." He gently tugged my coat toward the car. "We can go." The seats were freezing. I turned the key. The car struggled to come to life. I switched the heat on high, but cold air blasted us through the vents. "I talked to your mom," he announced. "She thinks you should keep going to school too."

"You talked to my mom?" I asked, perplexed.

He rubbed his hands together. "We talked about something else too," he hesitantly revealed. "We talked about you seeing someone."

"*Seeing someone?* Like a girlfriend? You talked to my mom about me getting a girlfriend?" I was horrified.

"No. We were thinking you should—see a psychiatrist." Lukewarm heat began to blow through the vents, but I had already started to perspire. My face burned. I was stunned and humiliated. I couldn't look at him. I couldn't speak. "I was hoping you would, but you never really made any other friends at school this semester. Your mom and I just thought that with Ginger and me gone, it would be good for you to have someone else to talk to."

"What? I can't talk to you anymore?" I managed to croak.

"Sure. You can. It's just that Ginger and I are going to be living in dorms at Western. So I doubt we'll be back here that much. And talking to someone else could help you."

"*Help me?* With what?"

"For one thing, I know it hasn't been easy for you coping with Everett's death."

"I'm coping just fine."

"C'mon. It's obvious with all the fantasizing about Thomas that—"

"*Fantasizing!* You heard the tapes. You heard his voice. That wasn't fantasy. That was real."

"Yeah. OK. But I think you need help sorting through your relationship with Everett. You already know how I feel about him. It doesn't mean I'm glad he's gone. Not at all. Who knows? After I stopped hanging around him, he could've changed. He could've become an entirely different person. But even if he did, that doesn't change the fact that at one time he controlled you with his crazy ideas. And you have to agree that he and his death had a huge effect on you. I think if you could learn to understand that, then you could be more—grounded. You could be more social. And you could be—less dependent on Ginger and me."

What was it with him deserting me on cold November days? My mind instantly flashed to the time Phillip had left me to deal with Kirsten on my own. Not only was he abandoning me a second time, he was trying to push me off on some psychiatrist, which felt even worse. I put the car in drive and pulled onto the street as my insides began to splinter. "I can't believe you talked to my mom" was all I was able to utter.

"I'm sorry. But she checked into it, and it'd be covered by your insurance."

"Stop," I commanded. I couldn't take any more. All I could think of was that I had saved Phillip from certain death—that if it hadn't been for me, he would've perished in flames like Thomas Gouldman. For the first time, I didn't want to be near Phillip. I wanted to shove him out of my car.

"My guts felt like they were in a blender," I painfully revealed to Dr. Griffin. "When Phillip and Ginger left, I didn't reenroll that semester. I couldn't. But after a while, I forced myself to at least try to understand why Phillip said what he said. And that's when I came to see you."

"Well, I'd say Phillip was a very good friend to you—even if it didn't feel that way at the time." I nodded in agreement. "In fact, it seems his theory on your psychological state is similar to mine. We both see Everett as the figure central to your problems. It started easily enough by him casting himself in the role of rescuer in your dreams. He encouraged fantastic delusions. Forced you to accept a fantasy world fabricated by him, which ultimately progressed into three-dimensional hallucinations. Because of this, understandably, you had tremendous difficulty interpreting reality, participating in it. The frequency at which you had become accustomed to escaping—through dreams, hallucinations, through the sensation of leaving your body, by indulging in the intricacies of nature—is, frankly, astounding. You relied on these mechanisms as a way to cope with suffering. Yet constantly escaping in so many ways, you weren't truly a whole person. It sounds as if you've spent more time floating outside your body than living inside of it."

At first, I didn't want to admit it to myself. But after many sessions with Dr. Griffin, the past started to become clear. It began to make sense. Ultimately, because of Phillip, there was logic to it all. Finally, the sparks that fed Everett's flames began to die, until he was reduced to nothing more than a fantasy himself. Just like the monsters, his legend had been fabricated. I no longer viewed him as my protector. I was his puppet. His joke. He had taken advantage of me. Manipulated me. Betrayed me. He was evil. And I hated him. And as I switched my brain to seeing Everett in a new light, the hallucinations began to fade. I no longer needed Phillip to keep demons away. With my newfound knowledge, I was able to chase them back into my own mind, reduce them to harmless characters in dreams.

Still, from time to time, I'd indulge myself. I'd visit Phillip and Ginger. I was there when they graduated from college. I was there when they moved into a house together in a new development where only saplings lined the streets. I watched them from the ceiling, from inside the walls. I knew it wasn't real. Had he known, Dr. Griffin would've certainly deemed my behavior unhealthy. He would've told me that I was only disassociating again, creating a barrier that would make it more difficult for my mind to function properly in reality. But after even the cats disappeared, the secret visits were all I had. They gave me comfort. They were my security blanket.

As I watched Phillip and Ginger become adults in my mind, I realized I too had to do the same. So I did. I slowly made my way through college. I finally quit the grocery store for a part-time job taking calls as a patient services representative at the hospital. And when I graduated, they hired me on full-time. I didn't earn much but managed to move into a modest apartment.

Dr. Griffin praised my independence but warned of inadequate social interaction. Yet as much as I craved being with others, I declined and chose a solitary way of life. It wasn't because I was afraid someone like Everett would attempt to control me again. The truth was, I didn't dare risk associating with others because I couldn't bear the thought of once again being abandoned.

PART VI
WHERE THE CATS
WiLL NOT FOLLOW

34
TOUCH OF EVIL

The second night, sleep was a field of blackness. Dark. Infinite. Clear and silent. Void of trepidation. Funny how in the most turbulent of times, I was able to find peace. I woke to the sounds of birds foraging in the bushes. Before opening my eyes, I stretched my arms freely over the edge of the bed. Though I was not restrained, I sensed him watching. Sure enough, when I opened my eyes, there Phillip sat on the wooden stool. "Sorry," he murmured, not intending to duplicate the awkward events of the previous morning.

"I slept really well," I cheerfully reported.

His blue eyes met the floor. "Meaning you didn't find Ginger," he assumed. I too lowered my head, attempting to find the same spot where his eyes were fixed. Accepting my silent answer, he replied, "Well, I had to ask."

"I'll keep trying," I promised. But the truth was, I had yet to try. As it turned out, my peaceful sleep was void of Phillip's anguish as well.

"Will you?" He seemed to beg and ask politely at the same time. "Even though I know it has to be confusing for you. After all these years, me believing Everett."

"Well, you *are* threatening to undo a lot of expensive therapy," I joked dryly.

"I'm sorry I did this to you. Really, I am. Because the thing is, I don't really know. I don't know if I'm right. When I called you, when I brought you here, it seemed like the only thing to do. It seemed to make the most sense. All I could think of was what Everett had told me: that it was you, through your dreams, who found those hidden coins. That it was through your dreams you knew where to find the buried Indians. It became a clear solution. I thought if I could get you to muster just a bit of whatever he had gotten you to muster, then maybe it'd give me a place to look. Maybe you could find Ginger like you found those coins. But today—I don't know."

I filled my lungs with a deep breath and slowly let them deflate. "It's worth a shot, I guess. I'll help you, Phillip. I will."

He cracked a half smile and then suddenly looked as if he had been punched in the stomach. "You know how I told you Ginger and I planned to get married, but that each time something would come up?"

"Yeah."

"Well, that's not totally true. She wanted to get married. She even proposed to *me* for Christ's sake. But I just—didn't. I'd make excuses. Avoid the subject. I love her. Absolutely. But I always kept myself from making that final commitment. I can't even say for sure what it was. I don't know. I guess I was feeling I didn't have a chance to sow my wild oats or whatever. It seems so stupid now. Shit, was I a fool."

Although I was the least qualified person alive to be giving Phillip relationship advice, I found myself saying, "Don't be so hard on yourself. Ginger was the only serious girlfriend you had after high school. It makes sense you had cold feet. You're both still young. There's plenty of time."

"But it made her furious. Made her feel—unwanted. And the worst part is the night she left, the night she never came back, we had a terrible argument over it." He held his head in his hands.

"She was going to leave me if I didn't marry her. She went for a jog to let off some steam. And by the time she came back, I was to have an answer. I should've held on to her right then and there. But I let her go. How goddamn stupid. I should've begged her to marry me at that very moment. But instead, I opted for the time to think about it. My God. I had to *think* about it! And now, because of that, I may never see her again."

"You don't know that."

"Even if things were going to end, they can't end like this. No matter what, I have to find her." His eyes began to glaze until tears spilled down his cheeks. He didn't make a sound. He just let the tears stream.

His silent cry made me uncomfortable and embarrassed. I pretended not to notice. I looked beyond him and into the living area. It was then I saw movement, a quick shadow pass in front of the door. "Phillip," I said as calmly as possible, hastening his lament, "is there anyone else in the cabin?"

"No." My question put him on alert. He lifted his head and focused.

"Because I just saw something move," I whispered.

"What?"

"Past the door. Into the kitchen."

He rushed out of the bedroom. His fingers twitched as he staggered backward in uneven steps. "What're you doing here? How'd you get here?" he asked, stunned.

I threw the covers from my legs. Before I could reach the doorway, the intruder had tackled Phillip in a blur. The two hit the wooden floor with a thud. I swiftly rounded the corner to see a man on top of Phillip. He slugged Phillip in his side and then brutally in the face. Phillip's bashed lip gushed blood down his chin. Even with only being able to see the attacker from behind, immediately I knew who it was.

"Stop it!" I begged. Everett halted while keeping Phillip pinned. He sucked in deep breaths, his torso heaving as he turned to face me. The flash of his famous grin was out of context in the moment but nonetheless proved he was in fact my brother, Everett.

I had been conditioned to feel nothing but hatred toward him. To be frightened of him. And I knew if I was to ever see him again, it would only mean one thing: that I had fallen off the deep end and had lost my mind. Yet in that moment, I couldn't force myself to be angry. Or afraid. And I didn't fret over whether or not I was sane. Instead, all the memories, all the feelings I had suppressed came back in a rush of emotion, and I felt—relief, relief knowing that everything I had buried and denied, everything that I had held a secret affinity for, was not dead. In that moment, I understood the awakening Phillip had spoken of the day before, the realization that things in the past you thought impossible were probable again. And like Phillip, I suddenly didn't care about logic. I didn't care about all the supposed clarity I had gained from Dr. Griffin—because Everett was right there in the room with me. I was not imagining him. Phillip, pinned beneath him, certainly could've attested to that.

Acknowledging what he had done to Phillip, I said to Everett, "You must've been saving up energy for a very long time."

"I have. For a long time. Collecting it. Waiting." He stood, his white T-shirt smeared with Phillip's blood.

"So you being here, coming to the cabin—it must be important," I assumed, seeing as the last time I had seen him, he had materialized to give me the key to surviving without him.

"It is," he assured, stepping toward me. "Now go put your shoes on." I did as he said and hurried into the bedroom. By the time I reemerged, Phillip had regained his footing. Physically, he was hurt. But what impeded him more was the awe he experienced from the otherworldly appearance of his former friend.

"Phillip's girlfriend is missing," I explained to Everett. "I'm here trying to help him find her."

"Is that true, Ayden? Because from what I could see, floating outside these windows among the perfume of lilacs, it seemed pretty clear to me you had been kidnapped, tied up, abused."

There was an awful silence. Phillip didn't protest. He couldn't have. "It started out that way," I admitted. "It did. But I *want* to help Phillip now."

"Don't protect him," snapped Everett. "When I was alive, he ran away from us with his tail between his legs. It took my death and you lying sick in the hospital for him to even visit. And don't give him too much credit for saving you from the demons. He never even believed they existed, never acknowledged you were truly in danger before scampering away a second time, leaving you unprotected. And now he has the balls to force you to listen to his incessant guilt-ridden droning about some so-called lost girlfriend?"

"Her name is *Ginger*," Phillip said, defiantly stepping forward.

"Well, you're not going to find her. Not alive anyway." Phillip looked sickened as Everett turned to me and declared, "Because Phillip killed her."

"Liar!" Phillip burst. He clenched his fists and began to shake.

"Who was the last to see her alive?" Everett shot back. "Who had a 'terrible argument' with her before she went missing? And who do you suppose is the number one suspect the police are looking for right now?" Everett grabbed my wrist. "I will not let you harm my brother any longer just so you can go on lying to yourself, pretending there is a chance she is still alive." He tugged me toward the door and whispered in my ear, "This is it. Are you ready?"

I looked into his eyes. It was Everett. My brother. My protector. But he had abandoned me for Kirsten. For Texas. For death. Phillip was my friend, appointed by Everett to be his surrogate. And for a time, he was. But he had also abandoned me. The first time, Everett had driven him away. But the second time, he had left for the life of a certified public accountant—and had taken Ginger with him. I was torn. I wanted to go with Everett. And yet, I didn't want to leave. I had promised Phillip I'd help him. He stood before us, hurt. Confused. I didn't fear him. But I wondered if I should've. Was what Everett said true? Was Ginger dead? Had Phillip killed her?

Was he really only keeping me there as a way to circumvent his guilt?

"I'm ready," I finally whispered back, cementing my decision. It happened so fast. Before I knew it, we were out the door and running across the field.

"I didn't kill her!" Phillip shouted after us. "I *know* you know that, you asshole!"

I didn't look back to see if Phillip was following us. Everett's grip remained tight as we ran toward the woods in the distance. It felt good to be running with him again. I had missed it, running with him from—or to—danger. When we finally entered the woods, we barely slowed our pace. I was so full of adrenaline, I couldn't even feel the branches scraping against my skin. We pushed through thick brambles. We jumped over logs and depressions filled with water. Everett glided with ease over the obstacles. He'd take one leap that seemed to carry him the distance of three. He moved effortlessly, soaring over the forest floor. My heart pounded as I raced to keep up with him. It wasn't long before our bearings became murky. I had no idea how far away we were from the cabin or in which direction it was.

Yet my bearings weren't all I was losing. After one of his giant leaps, Everett's feet failed to reconnect with the ground. And suddenly, it was only I who ran. He was still clamped on to my wrist, and I pulled him along as he hovered beside me. When he began to rise, my arm was wrenched above my head. I stopped, gasping for air, as his body rotated over me, the soles of his shoes facing the treetops. The veins in his neck and forehead became swollen as blood rushed to his head. I wrapped my fingers around his wrist, squeezing as tight as I could. There was no need to discuss what was happening. We both knew his time was limited. We both knew he had to return, be absorbed back into nature at the molecular level. Speech became difficult for him. He was only able to utter syllables upon his exhales. "You. Have. To. Es. Scape," he managed to get out.

I looked behind me to the maze of trees. "Where do I go?" I felt awful for asking. He had rescued me from the cabin. Had gotten me that far. The least I could've done was figure the rest out for myself. I shook my head, attempting to erase my question. He released his grip on my wrist. And reluctantly, I released my grip on his. I shielded my eyes from the sun as I watched him rise into the treetops. He pushed branches out of his way on his journey to the sky. Once clear of the trees, he extended his arm and pointed west. I knew it was west because it was the opposite direction of the rising sun. I watched as he became smaller and smaller until finally he disappeared, dissolved into the blue sky.

I began to head west as Everett had instructed. But without him, I lost the sense of urgency. I meandered past a pond surrounded by patches of enormous ferns, their leaves a deep lustrous green. I stepped carefully among them, not wanting to disturb the critters that surely made their homes in the slick mud beneath the broad canopies.

A pine forest began where the ferns ended. Stepping into it was like crossing the boundary into another world. The lush green was replaced by a rust-colored floor composed of fallen needles. The dried needles created a soft carpet that kept the floor barren of any new growth. The massive conifers were in perfect rows. Their thin trunks were bare of branches except at the very tops. It felt strange, a bit eerie, to be inside of what felt like a giant cathedral with towering pillars—outdoors.

Near the center of this forest-within-a-forest, I came upon a faint two-track that had been borne into the soft floor. I stood on the path debating if I should cross it and continue heading west. Or whether I should travel the path in hopes of finding—something. I wondered if the path led back to the cabin. In that case, I'd risk coming across an angry Phillip. Yet I also wondered if perhaps Everett had pointed me west for the purpose of discovering the path. Maybe it led to a main road, where I'd be able to flag down a vehicle? I decided to take it. Eventually, its twists led me out of the pine forest and into yet another ecosystem.

I followed the path carved through an overgrown field as it wove between thick bushes and weeds that stood well over my head. The smell of wild carrots mixed with the lingering scent of the nearby pine forest. As I wound along the path, in between the scattered birch and a bramble of overgrown shrubs and sumac, something caught my eye: a glimpse of faded red. I pushed aside the dense brush, revealing broken headlights and a busted grille, with saplings poking through.

A tinge of horror suddenly rushed over me. The tires had long been deflated, causing the body of the pickup to slump. It was a sad, weathered version of its former self. I moved to the side of the truck and pulled off the clinging vines that had choked it over time. Rust had eaten the lower half of its frame, no longer a vibrant, metallic-red. Still, I could clearly see the deep gash that ran the length of its body. I ran my finger over the gouge. Instantly, images flooded my mind: The high school parking lot. The chase through the cornfield. Ian mutilated at the bottom of the pit. Everett covered in blood after battling Todd.

"Afterward, we hid the truck here." Startled, I spun to see Phillip behind me. "It was Everett's idea. He knew my parents owned a bunch of acres up here. He insisted it'd be the best place to hide the truck. I was so—outside of my mind—that I just followed his instructions as he spit them out." He came forward and placed his hand on the hood. "First, I helped bury Ian," he continued. "We pulled him out of the pit and dragged him into the woods. Everett said the cornfield was tilled every other season, so if we just covered him in the pit, eventually his body would've been brought to the surface. He said the woods would be perfect because the Indians were already buried there. Who'd question one more grave? We did the same with Todd, although that wasn't so easy — seeing as parts of him were scattered across the cornfield. After they were buried, we showered. Burned our clothes. And then Everett followed me in his car while I drove the pickup here.

"It was on the ride home when he told me about you. About how you could entrance animals. And about your dreams. He told me how he had been trying to use them to predict the future. Use them to find out things no one else could know. I kept my mouth shut as I listened to all this—bullshit. I figured he thought I was just as gullible as you and was telling me these things to try to distract me from what he had done. But by that point, all I could think of was that I was sharing a car with a murderer. I was in no mood for his games. So I finally told him to shut the fuck up and demanded to know what had happened. I asked him point-blank why he had killed Ian and Todd. Well, that question *did* finally shut him up. He didn't say a word for the longest time. It wasn't until we were almost back to the city that he finally opened his mouth. He told me that he *didn't* kill them. He told me it *wasn't* him who put the metal pieces in the bottom of the pit. And when he and Todd were fighting in the cornfield, he said there were others there."

"*Others?*" I asked.

"'Creatures,' he said. 'With horns. And fingers that came to points like knives.' He claimed *they* tore Todd into pieces. Not him. He told me that he and you had fought with these monsters in the cornfield before. That you'd blast them with the lasers of some kind of craft you rode in the middle of the night. Well, after that, I figured not only was he a murderer, but a batshit *insane* murderer. He said, 'You can believe what I'm telling you about the pit and about these monsters. Or you can believe that I killed them.' Either way, he didn't care. And that was the end of it. He was right. It didn't matter. What was done was done. And I was a part of it. But one thing I was never able to shake from my head was his easygoing way of dealing with it all. It made me feel like—"

"There was a touch of evil in him?" Phillip nodded. I knew that vibe Everett exuded all too well. I didn't recognize it myself until I was older and looked back at the mischievous smirk he gave as he introduced me that first time to the diabolic monsters in the corn. It gave him such delight.

"Still, he was so protective of you. It's strange." Phillip searched the sky, seeming to contemplate the complexities of our fraternal relationship. "How is it that Everett was here?" he asked.

"I saw him before. In the hospital. After they let me out of the hyperbaric chamber," I revealed. "Dr. Griffin had me convinced he was a hallucination. But he was wrong. I guess it's not much different from how Thomas Gouldman was able to communicate with us on a tape. Everett's able to store his energy and communicate with us as his former self."

"I'd prefer he use a tape," Phillip stated dryly.

I should've been afraid of Phillip after what Everett suggested he had done to Ginger—not to mention what I knew he had done to me. But in his presence, without the influence of Everett, I couldn't see anything but the gentle Phillip I had always known. "Don't worry about Everett," I said. "He was only acting on what he had seen through the window. Or bits he had picked up in the wind. He didn't know the whole story. And after everything today, Everett won't have the energy to come back for a long time."

Phillip let out a sigh of relief and then slumped onto the hood of the pickup. "When Ginger disappeared, I began to reevaluate everything about my life. And it goes without saying that if anything deserved further examination, it was that night we had planned to prank Ian. For once, I tried remembering it without blinders on. I tried to see it as it truly was. And there was one thing I couldn't reconcile. One thing I could never explain. When we waited in the woods while Everett and Todd were fighting, I saw something." He scratched his head. "It was a woman. From the trees." My heart began skipping in double beats as Phillip spoke of recalling her. "I thought it was some kind of false memory. That I must've been crazy."

"You weren't crazy," I assured him.

"No. I wasn't. And when I realized that, I had an awakening. I thought if she was real, then the creatures Everett spoke of being out in the cornfield that night could be real. And if they were real, then *everything* Everett said to me on that ride home was possible, including your abilities." He lifted his head. "It all came down to that memory of her. It's why I brought you here," he revealed. "It was my link to the idea that you could help—because I saw her.

Touched her. Felt her skin. And her hair made of branches." He paused to concentrate, still processing recovered bits of information. He was slow to draw out his words. "I kissed her. And there was something else . . ." He stopped short of fully recounting what I knew had actually taken place. "If only I could go back. If only I could do it again, I'd pay more attention this time. Make sure my mind stayed clear."

I leaned closer to him. "Do you want to?" I asked. "Do it again, I mean?"

Phillip shook his head as if he were sobering up from a dream. He restated the mission: "I want to find Ginger."

35
ANOTHER VERSION OF ME

I stood on the outside with the sun warming the back of my neck. Tall weeds and wild oats danced in the breeze, scratching my legs. I felt incredibly small before the massive black curtain that enveloped the entire woods. It draped over the treetops like a giant magician's scarf waiting to unveil some wondrous trick. I walked its perimeter, curious, wondering just what secrets were hidden beneath. I came across a narrow slit in the heavy fabric exposed by the wind. I peeked inside but could only see darkness. I turned to the scene behind me: the sun blazing on the overgrown field, my parents' house in the distance. It felt like I had been placed back in time to my favorite summer so many years ago. Yet as much as I wanted to, I knew I mustn't linger. I gripped the edge of the curtain and plunged into the void.

There was breath upon my face. As my eyes adjusted the best they could to the near darkness, I began to make out the faint outline of a white T-shirt filled by broad shoulders. Slowly, the details of his face emerged. *Everett.* We stood so close that his breath began flowing into my mouth. As if plugged into the same machine, we began exchanging breaths in a symbiotic rhythm. As he breathed in, I breathed out. As I breathed out, he breathed in. We were two parts of one whole, each sustaining the other.

"Ev. Er. Ett," I said, each syllable carried by an exhale. "I'm. Look. Ing. For. Ging. Er. Do. You. Know. Where. Ging. Er. Is?"

"Do. *You.* Know. Where. Ging. Er. Is?" he questioned back.

"Where. Is. Ging. Er?" I pressed, confused.

"Where. *Is.* Ging. Er?" he asked, repeating the question back to me.

"Cut it out," I said, pulling my head back, breaking the reciprocal pattern. "Is it true what you said? Did Phillip kill Ginger?"

Refusing to give up our rhythm, he sucked me in again and asked back, "*Did.* Phil. Ip. Kill. Ging. Er?" With that, he abruptly turned away and disappeared into the darkness. I held my hands in front of me trying to feel for him. As I stepped forward, I nearly slipped—on ice.

"Where are you?" I begged.

Overhead, there was a sudden loud pop that echoed throughout the forest. A spotlight had been switched on. I looked up to see that it was attached to rafters, which were affixed to a black, metal sky high above the trees. The spotlight began scanning the forest until it ultimately settled—on me. Shielding my eyes and squinting, I could see that Everett was only a few steps ahead. Surrounded by the trunks of shiny, metal trees, he stood with his back to me. Yet something about him wasn't right. Even though I was seeing him from behind, I knew the person before me was no longer Everett. He didn't have his broad shoulders, his sculpted muscles. He was too slim. His hair too dark.

The spotlight followed me as I took a step toward him. And as I did, he took a step forward as well. I took another step. And again, he did the same. I touched the back of my neck. And so did he. He then took off in a mad dash across the ice, zigzagging between the metal trees. "Wait!" I shouted as I ran after him. I wanted nothing more than to catch him, grab him by the shoulders and spin him around so I could see his face.

In my pursuit, I began hearing clicking sounds in the distance. It was evident he was leading me toward the noises. The more we ran, the more intense they became. It sounded as if we were heading toward a group of exuberant children banging potlids together. As we got closer, another sound emerged above the clamor. What started as incoherent wails began hitting my ears with terrifying clarity.

"Help!" she screamed over the maddening clashes. "Is anybody here!" As if we were the main characters in some demented stage show, a second spotlight switched on from above, illuminating the young woman behind the voice. Wearing only shorts, a T-shirt, and running shoes, she was tangled in a web of branches, trapped in the center of a grove of angry metal trees. The branches twisted and stretched to reach her. Their metal joints snapped as they took turns jabbing her, their sharp tips piercing her skin.

She boldly pushed past the maniacal branches, enduring painful gashes as a consequence for such a daring escape. For a moment, she was free. She ran to the edge of the darkness, attempting to force her way through the black curtain. But there was no opening, and the curtain was too thick and heavy to lift. As she frantically searched for a way out, the trees nearest the edge snatched her. Their limbs worked like mechanical arms to drag her, kicking and screaming, back into the fray.

Seeing us approach, she raised her arms. "Over here! Help!" Her chestnut hair had fallen into her eyes but could not mask the terror on her face. Blood gushed from the cuts on her arms and legs. Still, even with the torture she had endured, she had not given up. Her eyes darted back and forth, constantly looking for an opening so she could try again.

Everett's imposter had gotten to her first. He stood at the edge of the grove, casually watching her assault with his arms folded. I passed him, running as fast as I could over the slick ice. In the land I was in, being brave seemed less of a risk. But for the first time ever, *brave* is what I felt as I shielded my face and slid into the cluster of trees.

Metal limbs slashed at my arms and swung at my legs. I managed to grab hold of a thick limb about to strike Ginger. The mighty thing easily tossed me backward across the ice. But my move had given Ginger a chance to avoid its blow when it swung back for her. I slid out of control—until I was stopped, stabbed in the back by the tip of a low-hanging limb. I lunged forward to dislodge myself. Crawling on my stomach, I desperately worked to maneuver back to Ginger while branches snapped at me overhead. The thinnest limbs beat upon me like metal whips. I rolled side to side, trying to evade them. The ones that missed cracked all around me on the thick ice.

While enduring this gauntlet, I managed to catch a brief glimpse of the man who was content to merely watch us, the man who had dared replace Everett. And to my astonishment, that man—was me. Or another version of me, at least. It was unnerving, seeing myself looking back at me, especially when, as he observed our torment, his expression was too serene.

Somehow, I had made it to Ginger in one piece. Trapped together, I prepared to endure the torturous onslaught along with her. Yet as soon as I stood at her side, the branches took their resting positions. Suddenly, miraculously, all was still. I looked about for my mysterious clone. But he had left along with the violence. Ginger held her arms in front of her defensively, too afraid to relax. When she was finally satisfied the limbs weren't going to reanimate, she gave me a hug. "Ayden, thank God you're here. What's happening? Where are we?"

"In the metal forest," I replied simply. "Phillip—he sent me. He's been looking for you." Hearing his name, she looked as if she was going to cry from happiness, relief. I was happy too. Seeing her again, I realized I had accomplished my mission. I had found Ginger. All we had to do was escape.

But escaping wasn't going to be easy. Like an alarm suddenly being tripped, an unbearable high-pitched blare came from the metal sky. Glowing orange sparks cascaded from above. The sparks reflected off the shiny metal trees and the glassy ice floor. As they met the cold ice, they quickly extinguished. I was enchanted by the beautiful scene, even though I knew it was becoming increasingly dangerous. The mass on the other side busted through the sky like a drill puncturing sheet metal. As a coiled tip emerged, the metal sky surrounding it broke into chunks, ripping off tree limbs as it fell.

"How do we get out!" screamed Ginger over the terrible whir.

"I came through an opening on the other side of the forest," I shouted. "But I don't think I could find it again."

"If there's one opening, there could be more. We need to split up and look. You go that way. I'll go this way," she instructed. "If you find an opening, wave your arms—and yell!" With that, she ran to the curtain and began running her hands over its dense fabric. As we separated, her spotlight followed her, and mine followed me. I did as she said and made my way along the curtain in the opposite direction.

After edging along a large section of the curtain without any luck, I turned to scan for Ginger. When I spotted her, she was shouting to me with her hands cupped around her mouth. Yet her words were indecipherable over what sounded like a freight train. She pointed to the sky. And that's when I saw the spiral had dropped into full view. Its base much wider than its tip, it had torn through the metal sky and was shredding the treetops. The massive thing twirled at such a rate, it was difficult to see that it was made of one single strip of giant, coiled metal. As the tornado continued to lower itself, fragments of metal whipped across the forest. "Watch out!" I shouted as a severed limb was propelled in Ginger's direction. Luckily, she saw it coming and dove out of its way just in time.

The flying debris subsided for a moment as the tornado settled, its tip hovering just above the iced floor. There was at least some sense of safety pinned to the sidelines, hiding in the perimeter. But then, it began moving through the center of the forest, spinning recklessly as it chewed apart the frozen wonderland. The seemingly sturdy trees were easily dismantled. As metal ate metal, deadly chunks were flung at dizzying speeds.

The tornado's trajectory put it on a path for the cluster of trees that stood between Ginger and me. Knowing we'd be obliterated along with them, we met on the other side of the trees and, together, sprinted across the icescape. Running in this war zone was a true obstacle course. We had to think fast and move fast, all while balancing on ice, in order to avoid the treacherous shrapnel. The smaller, unavoidable pieces stung as they pelted our skin.

When we should've been well out of the cyclone's reach, I glanced over my shoulder. To my horror, I realized the thing had not only altered its path but was directly behind us. Clearly, the whirring beast had a brain. A purpose. It spun deliberately behind us, threatening to slice through our soft bones with ease. I stopped running. There was no use. It having a brain meant there was no escape. It could hunt and kill us at will.

Realizing I had stopped running, Ginger stopped too. Her mouth opened wide in amazement and terror as she met, up close, the tornado that stalked us. The cluster of trees that had been behind us seconds earlier was gone. Gobbled up. Its ferocious appetite did not go unpunished, however, as its coils had become mangled from the metal it had chewed up and spit out. Its rotation was no longer smooth. It spun unevenly, growling angrily before us as it churned through the forest's cool air.

Ginger, the most self-assured person I had ever known, knelt in defeat, her bare knees pressed to the ice. She clasped her hands before her. Without words, she begged the metal monstrosity for mercy. It, however, did not grant Ginger mercy. Instead, the sinister tornado bore into the ice. Ice shavings sprayed into the air as the forest's floor began to splinter. Freezing water rushed onto the surface and over Ginger's legs. We were blasted by a mix of water and shards of ice. As the cracked ice began to cave into the waters below, I stepped off the unstable ground and clung to the closest tree.

The rush of frigid water woke Ginger from her despair. In a panic, she attempted to scramble back to her feet. But the ice she knelt on was no longer stable, and she promptly slipped upon it. She lay still for a moment, stunned, on her back, partially submerged in the unearthly pool. The freezing water crept over her torso and up to her neck. Sparks formed underwater as the twister continued to bare down, hitting metal tree roots. As a fountain of water, bits of ice, and tiny metal shards showered Ginger, she struggled to once again stand. But the chunk of ice beneath her had slipped away.

I reached for her with one arm while clutching the tree with the other. "Ginger!" I screamed to get her attention. She reached up to me. But the swirling vortex sucked her closer toward the metal demon. Screaming deliriously, she was pulled beneath the churning waters. The current lodged her struggling body among a mass of metal roots and vines. Her dedicated spotlight allowed me to see her clearly beneath the surface, where she became entwined in the twisted mesh. Her arms flailed desperately as she attempted to claw her way out of the metal restraints. Her hair stood on end, bobbing in the turbulent waves.

She was still alive when I left her. Still fighting for her life.

36
EFFECTIVELY PUREED

"Ginger!" I shouted as I sprang upright. I grabbed the truck's door handle and studied my surroundings. I didn't know how long I had been asleep in the cab of the old pickup until I realized it was nearly dusk.

"You found her?"

"Yes."

Phillip slapped his face in a mix of elation and disbelief. "Is she all right!"

"No."

"Is she dead?" he asked, fearful of my response.

"I don't know. But I know where she is."

Phillip bolted out of the truck and ran down the two-track. I followed not far behind, although it took a moment for my blood to begin circulating again. Running with Phillip through the fields and forests was almost as exhilarating as running with Everett. With the warm summer breeze rushing past my face, I felt electric. Full of energy. I barely noticed the limitations of my adult body. I was like a kid again. I felt that if I could've just picked up a bit more speed, I could've galloped over the highest treetops with ease.

The path eventually led us back to the field where the cabin sat. We were about to emerge from the trees when Phillip threw his arm across my chest. He pointed to the gravel drive leading up to the tiny cabin. There, three police cruisers were parked. I squinted in the growing darkness. The lights were on inside the cabin, and at least two men walked the yard. "Fuck! Fuck! Fuck!" Phillip cursed under his breath.

As we watched them invade our hideout, there was no need to discuss the seriousness of the situation. With his live-in girlfriend missing, Phillip disappeared during the height of the investigation. If he hadn't been the prime suspect already, he surely was that evening after having been found living in secret at his parents' cabin in the middle of nowhere. To compound his problems, if they were to perform a detailed search of the grounds, eventually they'd discover an old pickup, which would link him to the unsolved disappearance and possible murders of Ian Stein and Todd Snelling. And then there was me. His former friend from high school and college. Had anyone noticed I had gone missing too? And if so, did they believe I was his victim? Or his accomplice?

Phillip motioned for me to follow him. In the cover of darkness, we scuttled along the perimeter of the trees until we rounded the backside of the cabin. He eyed his pickup across the yard. "We've got to get to Ginger," he declared with a heavy dose of desperation. "Dammit! My keys are inside." The truck was so close but might as well have been a million miles away.

The wind began to pick up, first bending the tops of the trees in the distance and then rustling the branches behind us. With the wind came a low growl. It could've perhaps been thunder. Yet a tingle that ran from the base of my spine to the back of my neck told me that something old and familiar had been stirred. I moved closer to Phillip. I tried reading his face to see if he too had sensed this presence lurking in the air, but he was too preoccupied with his predicament.

A branch snapped behind us. Phillip jolted, finally taking notice of the creeping darkness. However, what lunged for us was not at all what I had anticipated. From out of nowhere, bright lights flashed into our eyes. "Don't move!" a deep voice bellowed sternly. "Don't you dare move."

"Show your hands!" commanded another voice.

I wasn't sure how we were supposed to show our hands without daring to move. Defying the orders of the first voice, I opted to slowly open my palms at my sides.

"We have Phillip Rosemann here!" shouted the deeper voice. Three officers rushed from inside the cabin to assess the catch, and we were surrounded. "You had been told, Rosemann, not to leave Lanford. What're you doing this far north?"

"Looking for Ginger," he barked, squinting into the light. "And you're just slowing me down."

"Bring them out front."

We were escorted to separate ends of the front yard. Two officers began interrogating Phillip, while I was given to a young officer with a round gut that matched his round face. He kept his lips cocked to one side as he anxiously chewed a piece of gum. "You're Ayden Dezelan, right?" he asked.

"Yeah."

"I'm Officer Barnes."

"Hello."

"How'd you get here?"

"Phillip drove me."

"Did Mr. Rosemann bring you here against your will?"

"No."

"Uh-huh. Well, we have a statement from a resident at your apartment building that says you were dragged, unconscious, across the parking lot by someone fitting the description of Mr. Rosemann and then placed into a vehicle with a license plate matching a vehicle owned by Mr. Rosemann."

"That's right," I confirmed.

"Can you explain that?"

"I was really tired."

"You were so tired, he had to drag you across the parking lot in order to get you into his vehicle?"

"Yes."

Calling the look he gave me skeptical would've been an understatement. "I'm going to ask again. Were you held against your will by Phillip Rosemann at any time?"

"Against my will? No. I want to be here," I affirmed.

"Uh-huh. OK. Do you know the whereabouts of Ginger Young?"

"Yes."

"Is she on the premises?"

"No."

"Where is she?"

"Ginger's — in the woods."

"*Where* in the woods?"

"Not *these* woods. I have a pretty good idea she's in the woods behind my parents' house."

He pulled a small notebook from his pocket and briefly flipped through the pages. "And your parents' house is in Lanford?"

"Yes. Well, actually no. On the outskirts. Between Lanford and Ruthsford. The woods there aren't as big as these woods. Just a small patch of trees, really. I wish they were bigger. But farmland has taken a lot of the trees. And houses have too. It's kind of sad, isn't it?"

"Yup."

"I mean, where are the deer and the owls supposed to live?"

He switched his wad of gum to the other side of his mouth. "How do you know Ms. Young is in those woods?"

"Because I saw her there."

"*When* did you see her there?"

"This afternoon."

"You were in the woods behind your parents' house this afternoon?"

"No. Hey," I said, pointing behind him, "look at those trees." Dark, rolling clouds charged across the sky in the distance. And beneath them, the trees began taking a battering from the wind.

"I need you to focus, Mr. Dezelan. You just told me you saw Ginger Young this afternoon in the woods behind your parents' house. Is that the truth or not?"

"Yes. It's the truth."

"How could you have seen her in those woods this afternoon without being there?"

"Because," I pensively replied, "I saw her—in my dream."

He leaned closer as if he had trouble hearing. "*In your dream?*"

"Yes," I quietly confirmed.

He adjusted his cap and peered into my eyes as if he thought no one was at home inside my skull. He did his best to continue his questioning, pretending as if I hadn't said anything unusual at all. "To your knowledge, did Mr. Rosemann have anything to do with the disappearance of Ginger Young?"

"No." At least I didn't think so.

"Did *you* have anything to do with the disappearance of Ginger Young?"

"No. All I know is she's probably out there. In old Mr. Peterson's woods."

"Mr. Dezelan, do you know whether or not Ms. Young is alive?"

"She was when I saw her in my dream. But is she alive right now? Hard to say."

He brushed his moustache with his finger. "All right. I need to call this in. And we'll need to bring you and Mr. Rosemann into the station for further questioning." He placed his hand on the back of my shoulder and led me to one of the squad cars. On our way across the yard, we passed Phillip.

"Yes. But I didn't hurt him!" Phillip argued. When I saw his feet start to shuffle, I knew they had whipped him into a mighty panic. Sure enough, seconds later, he broke from the officers and bolted for the cabin. A brawny officer charged after him. He slammed Phillip to the ground and used his weight to subdue him. "I don't care if you believe me! Just go look for her! Please!" he wailed as another officer assisted in handcuffing his wrists.

The sight of poor Phillip tackled and handcuffed made me sick to my stomach. He had come so close to finding her only to have his mission squelched. It wasn't clear if they were going to send anyone to search for Ginger in the woods or not. Yet even if they were, they had ruined everything. It should've been Phillip and me searching those woods together. Not some cops. We didn't need their help. It wasn't fair we wouldn't be the ones to find her.

After shoving me into the back of the squad car, Officer Barnes radioed the station. I peered through the window to the burly officer who had handcuffed Phillip. He had stepped away from the others and stood several yards into the field, his attention held by the trees in the distance. There was something peculiar about the way they thrashed, the way their limbs violently bent and snapped. Suddenly, several of the tallest trees disappeared from the horizon as if removed by a giant eraser. With the commotion surrounding the cabin, the two of us were the only ones aware that something alarmingly powerful was out there mangling and devouring trees. Then—it showed itself. Bursting into the organic landscape from another world, the spinning coil of metal leapt over the treetops. It touched down in the field and barreled toward the tiny cabin.

Jarred out of his frozen amazement, the officer turned to the cabin. He cupped his hands around his mouth and screamed his terrible warning: "Tornado!" The wind, however, easily stole his voice. He ran toward the cabin for cover, but the metal beast quickly closed the distance on him. It had set its sights, and he didn't stand a chance. The spinning blade effortlessly sliced through his flesh and bones. His body was swiftly divided into pieces, which were flung every which way. His head landed in the lilac bushes. With a loud thud, a chunk of his torso slammed onto the hood of the squad car I was stuck inside of.

Startled, Officer Barnes rushed outside and reflexively drew his gun. While attempting to process the sight of the mutilated torso, he failed to sense the tornado whirring directly overhead. When he finally looked above to the otherworldly cyclone, his jaw went slack in disbelief. His screams were quickly muted as the tornado lowered itself. First, it plucked off his head. Then, it sucked him into its body, where he was effectively pureed. His liquefied body sprayed over the gravel driveway and covered the squad car in a layer of red mucus and pulverized bone. Through the gore-tinted windows, the world suddenly appeared a dull shade of red.

The still-hungry tornado began chewing on the squad car. A shower of dazzling sparks flowed over the windshield as the twister drilled into the hood. Behind the mesh divider, I was trapped. I tugged on the locked door. "Get me outta here!" I pounded the glass. "Phillip!" But Phillip was still in custody of the remaining officers, who huddled near the cabin, too afraid to approach the tornado.

Halfway across the field, two more metallic cyclones dropped from the sky, crisscrossing as they charged toward the cabin. I only caught a glimpse of their terrifying approach, however, as the car began to spin. With the car rotating faster and faster, I gripped the armrest to keep my head from hitting the ceiling. Just when I thought the turbulent ride couldn't get any more nauseating, I was flung across the field. After spiraling through the air, the car crashed and rolled until it settled on its side. The tornado chased after the vehicle like a cat after an injured bird. It pounced back onto the car and began grinding it into the soil. A series of loud pops rang out as the windows shattered.

Slammed against the driver's side door, I grasped the seat belt and hoisted myself between the ground I was being crushed into and the deadly metal drilling above. The tornado churned aggressively, intent on completely destroying the vehicle. It crushed the interior while simultaneously working like a vacuum to suck up the wreckage. The airbags released and immediately ruptured, sending a flurry of white powder up the tornado's shaft.

I knew if I stayed wedged where I was, I'd soon be shredded and vacuumed up with the rest of the debris. So I made a desperate move. Using all my strength, I began clawing my way up the back seat, determined to escape through the blown-out rear window. With the car spinning, it wasn't easy. I was dizzy. Nauseous. But little by little, I climbed my way up—and miraculously out of—the whirling car. Outside, I gripped the window's edge for dear life. It was like being on a demented Tilt-A-Whirl. Blood rushed to my feet as I spun in dizzying rotations, with hot sparks spraying over my body. When it became clear no moment would be any less dangerous than another to disembark, I let go and was hurled into the field.

I lifted my throbbing head just in time to see the car crumpled like a piece of paper and then sliced into thousands of flying pieces. I tried to stand but vomited at once. Queasy, I limped toward the cabin. The field was scarred with zigzagging trails of overturned earth. While the tornado that had eaten the car began drilling into another police cruiser, the other two were busy hunting the scrambling, screaming officers. One of the tornados chased two of them into the woods behind the cabin. It sliced through the thick trees, pursuing them relentlessly.

I dodged my way through the pandemonium and crept around the backside of the cabin. It was there I found Phillip. With his hands cuffed behind his back, he cowered on his knees, pressing himself as tightly as he could against the cabin's foundation. "You're alive," he said upon seeing me.

"So are you," I said, relieved.

"It chased me back here. I was sure it'd kill me. But then it took off after one of the cops." The awful sound of metal buzzing was in the air all around us. "We have to get out of here. We have to get my keys."

I cupped my hand beneath Phillip's elbow and helped him stand. We cautiously made our way to the side of the cabin and hid behind the porch. The tornado out front had already destroyed the second cruiser and was enjoying the third. It flung the vehicle across the field, chased after it, and then tossed it in another direction. Each time the car slammed down sounded like a small explosion. "Let's hope that thing doesn't get bored with that cop car anytime soon," said Phillip as he eyed his pickup.

All we had to do was slip inside the cabin, grab the keys, and bolt for the truck. The distance to the door seemed short enough, so I decided to go for it. Phillip, however, ordered me down as soon as I started climbing the railing. "Wait. Over there," he said and nodded to the other side of the yard. I jumped down and peered around the side of the porch.

Across the yard, the third tornado had one of the officers pinned on his back. It had twisted his shirt right off him. He let out low moans as the metal tip penetrated his chest. Upon drawing blood, the twister let up. The man slid backward in a panicked attempt to escape. But the playful twister pinned him once more. His moans turned into screams of agony as it burrowed deeper into his chest, punishing him for his disobedience.

"It's OK," I said. "It's busy with him. I think I can make it."

"I'm going too," Phillip declared.

"Phillip . . ." I motioned to his handcuffs.

"All right then," he relented. "The keys are on a hook in the kitchen. Be quick. And be careful."

Feeling as brave as I had when I burst through the grove of metal trees to save Ginger, I alone crawled onto the porch. Slowly, I stood erect. Yet as I rose, the tornado pinning the officer rose as well. It had noticed me, was curious what I was up to. It spun in midair, hesitant, deciding which of us to pulverize. Spotting me on the porch, the gored man stood. He wobbled, clutching his wounded chest before limping toward the cabin. His limp turned into a feeble run as he desperately sought safety. The tornado whirred with fury, prompting me to dash for the door. I heard the weight of the heavy metal drop to the earth behind me. It roared across the yard as I flung open the door and raced for the kitchen. The officer, not far behind, entered with his breastbone exposed, looking more dazed than in pain. He scurried past me and hid in the back bedroom.

I grabbed the keys off the hook and clutched them tightly just before the tornado ripped into the front bedroom. The entire structure shifted off its foundation. The roof caved. The floor sloped. I dove behind the counter for shelter from the flying wreckage. With the bedroom obliterated, the metallic monster tore through the bathroom. It sounded like a thousand circular saws buzzing at once as it chewed through wood, pipes, and porcelain. It then charged into the second bedroom. This room it demolished with purpose and precision, spinning the tip of its funnel into each corner. There was no mistaking when it had gotten what it was after: a blunt scream rang out before a thick fountain of blood sprayed into the hall.

248 • Stephen Stromp

37
SUMMER'S PEAK

When the deafening roar went silent, I crept out from my hiding place. The cabin had been sliced in half. The rooms on the other side of the living area no longer existed. A new roof had formed that slanted dramatically toward the exposed foundation and resealed the gap. The front door was wedged shut, partially crushed beneath the weight of the buckling walls.

I had assumed I was trapped, yet I felt a breeze from the back of the cabin. I followed the airflow, climbing over fallen boards, chunks of plaster, and a severed pipe gushing water across the carpet. It led to an opening created by a stubborn wall that refused to give in to the weight of the ceiling. I poked my head out only to find my escape route blocked. It was nearly silent as it spun, rotating just above the cement foundation. Only a light whoosh could be heard as the coiled blade swirled through the night air. That's how it breathed, I reasoned—by constantly rotating. I retreated back into the dilapidated cabin. Truly trapped.

As I cowered like a scared rabbit, the front door began to heave. Finally, it burst open, and Phillip literally fell into the cabin. His hands still secured behind his back, he had used his shoulders to ram the door. "Are you all right!" he shouted.

"Still alive," I affirmed, stepping out of the darkness to help him to his feet.

"What about the cop?"

"Dead. They're all dead," I assumed.

"Did you get the keys?"

I had to open my fist and look. "Yeah." I had been clenching them so tightly, they had dug into my palm.

"All right. Let's go!"

"Not yet," I said. I tugged his sleeve and led him to the opening at the back of the cabin. I gestured ominously to the tornado purring over the cement slab.

"Jesus," he whispered, in awe of seeing it up close. "I saw two of them take off into the sky. I thought they had all gone." As if to join our conversation, the tornado lurched forward, biting at the collapsing roof. "We need to leave out the front door. Right now. And get in the truck as fast as we can," Phillip insisted.

"No." To his surprise, I refused. I had a thought. The tornados were from my dream. Yes, my dream had warned of their arrival. But there was something else. Somehow, I knew they had a deeper purpose beyond the death and mayhem they had brought to the cabin that night. I grabbed Phillip by the shoulders. Gently, I pushed him backward toward the tornado.

"What the fuck, Ayden!"

The tornado thrust forward several feet, eager to meet Phillip. He pushed against me, but I wouldn't relent. "Trust me," I said, my hands trembling as I offered him to the metal monster.

"Jesus Christ!"

I placed him as close as I could without allowing the beast's sharp coils to slice him. Then I stepped back, praying my instinct hadn't been a colossal misjudgment. There Phillip stood, apparently trusting me. Or simply too afraid to move. His hair was tussled by the slight wind the tornado created. He closed his eyes and breathed short, nervous breaths. His forehead and upper lip perspired. His lips were slightly apart, quivering. The way they jittered, it looked as if he was talking to himself. Or praying. The tornado leaned closer.

"Lift your arms," I instructed from a safe distance. He opened his blue eyes and looked to me. Afraid and looking bewildered with himself for trusting me, he slowly raised his shackled wrists. He held them apart, keeping the chain linking the cuffs taut. With a small eruption of sparks, the tornado easily sliced through the chain without so much as nicking his skin—and Phillip was free. He swung his arms forward and quickly leapt to my side.

The tornado lifted straight into the sky, taking chunks of the roof with it. I ran through the opening and gazed upward, marveling at the twirling creature as it ascended into the vast darkness. I tingled all over from the rush of the exhilarating encounter.

With the tornados gone, it felt as though we were free to leave. Yet the hum of the spinning metal was slowly replaced by a different sort of hum. I listened closely, parsing it out until I discovered this new hum was composed of a cacophony of overlapping, low groans. I couldn't see them. But I imagined them watching from behind the trees, waiting for the perfect moment to step into the yard. And sure enough—lured by the gruesome slayings, energized by the smell of terror that wafted in the air—the small yet lethal beings trotted out from the woods. Shadows of their wide horns and pointy fingertips stretched across the yard, allowing them to appear colossal.

Phillip saw the shadows too and motioned for me to get back inside. We bolted for the front door. Phillip closed it to a crack, and we peered outside. One of the green demons had discovered the officer's severed head in the lilac bushes. It lifted the head and uttered a gleeful howl as it sniffed the dead man's face. It licked the mouth before rolling the head up and down its torso, slowly at first, and then with increasing feverishness. Its growing excitement was telegraphed with an extra-wide grin. It culminated its act of depravity by rolling the head between its legs, which would've been even more disturbing had the creature possessed genitals.

Even with the unnerving sight going on before him, Phillip couldn't take his eyes off his truck. He wanted so badly to get to it, to get to Ginger. He opened the door just a bit more and turned sideways to slip through. "Wait!" I warned. But Phillip was resolute. He managed to get halfway onto the porch—before a horned demon's jaws swiftly clamped on to his arm. It had been patiently waiting on the wooden bench beside the door. Phillip cried in pain while attempting to pull himself back inside. But the demon wasn't about to let go, and its large horns jammed in the opening.

The commotion enticed more monsters to gather on the porch. Soon, dozens charged the front of the cabin, their horns stabbing into the walls. In a frenzy, I heaved open the door, allowing Phillip to bend his elbow and slip the creature inside. To secure the door, I hauled over a kitchen drawer and propped it against the handle. I then grabbed a loose floor plank and began bashing the growling thing that clung to Phillip. I bashed it until its face was flattened, until its eyes were pushed deep into their sockets. Yet even after its body went limp, its powerful jaws remained affixed to Phillip's arm.

It was a surreal sight, Phillip standing with the lifeless creature dangling from him. He eyed the mangled thing with a look of shock as his blood flowed from its jaws. I grabbed the monster's upper lip with one hand and its chin with the other. Phillip winced in agony as I attempted to pry its jaws apart. It wasn't easy, but finally, its mouth opened like a spring trap, and the lifeless demon dropped to the floor.

Using their brute force, the monsters easily busted through the door. While they clambered over one another to be the first to get inside, others had discovered the opening at the back of the cabin. They stepped over the rubble, daintily holding their pointy fingers beside their horns.

"I'm dizzy," Phillip announced. Even for his fair complexion, he looked pale.

"C'mon. You should sit down." I guided him to the couch. I sat beside him with my hand on his shoulder. He didn't acknowledge the monsters entering from both ends of the cabin. He didn't say a word when they began to encircle us. Perhaps his shock was too great. His pain too much. Or perhaps he didn't want to face the fact that there would be no escape, that death was surely upon us—and that death meant he was never going to see Ginger again.

His somber defeat permeated my mind in those moments. I looked to his blood dripping onto the cushions and to the vicious demons flooding the cabin. They bared their teeth. Licked their lips. Couldn't believe their luck at the sight of Phillip and me offered up so perfectly for a feast. Knowing we were trapped, they closed in on us slowly so they could savor our fear. Make it last. Bask in its aroma. It wasn't fair, especially for Phillip, that this was the way it would end.

I closed my eyes and pictured the spaceship that had often aided my and Everett's escape from the horned monsters. *If only we were in the spaceship.* Inside the craft, we would've been safe, hovering above the terrorizing fiends.

Like Phillip, I too began to feel light-headed. I took a deep breath, and as I exhaled, I cupped my hands beneath the seam of the cushion and lifted upward. I imagined the cushion struggling to rise with me on top of it. After a few moments, I felt the sensation of slowly lifting from the couch as if I were being repelled by the opposite end of a magnet. I clutched the cushion as my feet spilled over the edge, all the while concentrating on my slow rise and the cushion's ability to support my weight.

When I opened my eyes, I found myself with my head nearly touching the crooked ceiling. I held on tight, afraid to fall, yet astonished to see the room from the new perspective. I blinked slowly, making sure I wasn't confusing the real world with my wishful imagination. "Am I really floating?"

"You're really floating," confirmed Phillip, looking up to me. His face had come alive even though he was within reach of the crowding demons. Upon seeing me levitate, the monsters' creeping movements were replaced by quicker, more determined steps. If I was out of reach, then they surely weren't going to miss the opportunity to devour Phillip. Yet just as they had him surrounded, their mouths opening to taste his flesh, Phillip's cushion also began to float. As he rose to join me, I saw a bit of hope infuse in him once more.

Demons climbed upon the couch. They reached for us. Tore stuffing from the bottoms of our cushions. The cushions weren't a proper craft. Not even close. They didn't provide the same level of protection. No metal construction. No lasers. But as they linked together to form one unit and began to move us through the cabin, they did the trick. The monsters crowded beneath us, slashing their claws into the air as they jumped. But they couldn't reach us.

We rode our makeshift craft through the opening at the back of the cabin. We sailed outside through the warm night air. As we rounded the front of the cabin, we were hit with the overpowering scent of overturned earth mixed with lilac blossoms. There was something comforting about that short ride above the yard with Phillip. I felt safe. Relaxed. Sure, the small devils followed close behind. And sure, the ground beneath us was littered with destroyed vehicles and dismembered corpses. But as long as we didn't look down, there was no need to think of those things.

Upon spotting the truck, I gripped the front corners of my cushion. By adjusting my grip, twisting and folding the fabric over, I was able to steer us in its direction. Phillip, eager to get inside, anxiously stood up on his knees as we approached. I worked to lower us gracefully, but Phillip couldn't wait. He jumped from his cushion and ran the last stretch to the truck. He climbed inside and impatiently watched the remainder of my descent through the rear window.

"The keys!" he demanded as I touched ground beside the passenger door. I climbed in and handed them to him. He had them in the ignition and the truck speeding down the driveway before I even had a chance to close my door. A few of the most zealous demons had climbed into the bed of the pickup, but they were quickly thrown off by Phillip's wild driving.

It was time to say goodbye to the cabin. As we made our way onto the dusty road, I found a rag tucked behind the seat and tied it tightly around Phillip's wounded arm. I rolled my window all the way down, allowing the warm night air to flow into the cab. It was a night to remember. A night filled with wonder and exhilaration. Summer had finally reached its peak.

38
MULTIPLIED BY THIRTY

Phillip plowed the pickup into the first few rows of stalks. We emptied out as if gravity pulled us forward, as if our legs had no choice but to charge through the corn. The stillness of the night was oddly out of sync with the frenetic pace at which we raced. The rough texture of the wet leaves slapping against us felt like being licked by the tongues of giant cats. Phillip led the way, briskly tearing past the stalks, even though it was I who knew where we ultimately had to end. He was getting warmer.

When I came to the spot where I imagined Ian's pit had been, I leapt. My feet left the ground, and I sailed through the air. When I landed, I didn't topple over. I firmly reconnected with the earth. And without as much as a wobble, I was back to running again.

We were almost parallel to the woods when Phillip abruptly stopped. I planted my face into his back, nearly knocking him over. "Do you hear that?" he whispered.

We listened quietly for a moment. From the direction of the road, incomprehensible chatter invaded the corn. It soon overlapped with the sound of stalks being trampled carelessly. I wasn't sure what was happening until blue and red lights began pulsating over the field like a visual heartbeat. "The police!" I gasped.

Before being diced to pieces, one of the officers had obviously gotten the message out that the missing Ginger Young might've been in the woods we ran toward. In the time it took us to travel across the state, it had certainly been discovered that the officers sent to apprehend Phillip had been ferociously butchered. And with his truck parked recklessly beside the road, things were beginning to look much worse for Phillip. "They know we're out here," I warned.

"I don't give a shit. The more people looking for Ginger, the better. All that matters is she's found. That she's safe. I don't care what happens to me. Over here!" he broadcast over the stalks.

"What'd you do that for!" I scolded.

"You can lead us *all* to Ginger," he insisted.

From deep within the corn, the sound of heavy footsteps headed our way. The way the long and powerful strides whipped through the wet leaves, I knew they weren't the same as the clumsy footsteps tromping from the road. I wasn't so sure giving up our position was a good idea. I yanked Phillip into a tight grouping of stalks and made sure he saw my finger over my lips. If what rushed toward us was what I thought it was, I knew we mustn't move a muscle.

Phillip was clearly perturbed but thankfully kept silent—as it appeared from the darkness. Somehow, it had reached us quicker than the sound of its steps. Standing beside us, we could see its face: the stretched skin, the twisted sneer, the eyebrows carved dramatically high into its forehead. Trying to hold completely still, I prayed our impromptu hiding spot would be good enough. We barely breathed as it adjusted its full-length cloak. Lucky for us, it seemed intently focused on the incoming group stomping through its cornfield. In a flash, it charged ahead, its determined strides taking it toward the road. When the sound of its boots hammering the dirt began to fade, Phillip whispered, "Who the hell was that!"

"A cloaked monster."

"Everett didn't tell me about a cloaked monster. Just the ones back at the cabin. With the horns." Another set of powerful footsteps headed our way from the back of the field. This time, Phillip was sure to crouch silently next to me. When the demon passed us, its cloak lingered a moment, the edges fluttering between the leaves of corn. "How many do you think there are?" Phillip wondered.

I thought of the paneling in my old bedroom, how the awful pattern holding the monsters' faces repeated about thirty times. Then I thought of the fully realized demon that had materialized from the darkness in my room, intent on devouring me years before—and I multiplied him by thirty. "Thirty or so," I offered.

It was then that a stampede of the ravenous monsters suddenly began rushing past us, ripping through the corn and toward the unsuspecting police. Still hiding at the base of the stalks, I buried my head in my arms as if protecting myself from crashing waves. Yet when a gunshot blast came from near the road, followed by a scream, I jolted upright. Oddly, the gunfire didn't carry an echo. It consisted of a quick pop, followed by the absence of sound. The scream too was silenced abruptly in midshriek. A moment later, the sequence repeated: stunted gunfire followed by extinguished scream. "What's happening!" Phillip panicked.

I didn't know how else to explain it except to say, "The police, they're being—absorbed."

From the front of the field, the stalks began thrashing toward us like a tidal wave. We took off running as fast as we could. Yet with the strobe of the police lights, it felt as though we moved in slow motion. Reality sliced into unrealistic frames, and we became easily disoriented among the labyrinth of twisting rows. And when the wave caught up with us, we were infused into its pandemonium. Having witnessed their fellow officers being ingested whole, police ran alongside us with their guns drawn and with the fear of death in their eyes.

Out of nowhere, a cloaked demon stepped before us. It held open its cape, revealing a body of darkness. The cop beside us fired his gun, yet the bullet simply disappeared into its chest. The tall demon gave an angry sneer before lunging forward and grabbing the screaming officer. He struggled to free himself, but the cloaked monster quickly wrapped him beneath its cape as if it were a giant cocoon. As it ate, the demon threw back its head and tossed it side to side. Soon the outline of the officer's body was gone. He had been devoured by the black hole the creature carried beneath its cloak, the darkness that caused its voracious hunger.

Clearly, their bullets wouldn't save them. We spun around to see a cloaked monster take a bullet directly to the face. The impact only shifted the grooves in its skin to more intense angles. Cops were grabbed from behind without warning. Devoured by demons charging with open cloaks. Attacks came from all sides, shrinking us to a petrified huddle.

"We can't stay here!" shouted Phillip as, one by one, those around us were sucked into never-ending blackness. Phillip was more exasperated than afraid. He was closer than ever to finding Ginger. Yet he found himself trapped in the cornfield with the relentless demons. To him, the cloaked monsters were a frustratingly inconvenient obstacle, albeit an extremely lethal one. No matter his motivation, he was right. No longer could we take our chances in the corn, waiting to be absorbed. The trouble was, with all the mayhem, neither of us knew which direction would lead us out of the corn versus deeper into it.

Another gunshot rang out. This blast, however, was different. It hadn't been absorbed into a deep and void stomach. It reverberated fully throughout the cornfield. It bounced off the tall trees of the woods, which were somewhere nearby. I tugged Phillip in the direction of the gunfire. The energy in the field shifted as soon as we shifted our course. Several of the cloaked monsters broke from the murderous circle they had formed around the remaining police and lunged down the rows after us. It felt as though we were trapped in an endless haunted maze as we dodged cloaked demons rushing us from clusters of stalks.

Once again, the sound of gunfire erupted. Uninterrupted. Full of power. Strange we ran *toward* gunfire—for discovery, for safety. But that's what we did. And soon, the last leaves of corn licked our faces.

39
NETHERWORLD

We found ourselves in no-man's-land, the limbo between the cornfield filled with the cloaked demons and whatever stirred in the woods. The cloaked monsters did not follow us. They remained hidden in the stalks, opting instead to scowl from the edge of the field. Maybe they were too timid to show their warped faces outside of the corn. Whatever the reason, it was as if they wouldn't—or couldn't—cross the invisible boundary.

There was something incredibly freeing about standing in the small strip where the night wind blew unimpeded. At first, I assumed we stood alone. They blended so easily against the swaying trees. Yet as our eyes adjusted to the open space, we began to make out their massive chalk-white frames looming as tall as the trees. They towered shoulder to shoulder, creating a barrier along the perimeter of the woods. As they swayed, hollow bone clanked against hollow bone. The sound was peaceful, really, like the gentle song of wooden wind chimes in a summer's breeze.

It was then that we saw her, looking insignificant beneath the behemoths. She stood before them, immersed in a sea of tall weeds up to her hips. The evening breeze gently caressed her hair, which came to just above her shoulders. Phillip was especially eager to reach her, to spin her around. Yet when she raised her arms and pointed a pistol at the mammoth skeletons, we stopped to see exactly what she was up to.

She aimed at one in particular, a peculiar skeleton that wobbled out of sync with the others. Upon closer inspection, the skeleton's clavicle bone was shattered, causing its uneven stature. She fired, and the bullet was a direct hit to the center of its spine. It stretched its long arms forward, attempting to maintain its balance. Yet already injured, it toppled easily, crumbling to pieces that scattered among the weeds. Immediately, the skeletons on either side of their fallen counterpart locked shoulders, resealing the gap. Down the line, others followed suit, tightening the brief slack until a fresh skeleton filed in from around the bend.

Sensing our presence, she promptly spun toward us, and we found a pistol aimed at our heads. We raised our hands in surrender. Yet as soon as she recognized us as human, the officer lowered her gun. She was older than I had imagined she'd be. The lines around her eyes and mouth gave the impression she was somewhat stern, yet also wise. Naturally, Phillip was disappointed, having hoped to see another face turn his way.

"Where'd you two come from?" she asked. I answered her by nodding to the edge of the cornfield. "I'm surprised you got out of there alive. I barely did." She looked us up and down. "You're those men we're looking for, aren't you? Phillip? Ayden?" We didn't answer. "Well, it doesn't really matter anymore, considering . . ." She looked back to the giant monsters. "Whatever they are, they certainly don't want us in those woods." She tucked her hair behind her ears. "That woman—she's in there, isn't she? Ginger Young?"

"We think she may be," I said.

"She's in there," Phillip assured her—and himself. "And we could use your help getting inside."

She shoved her pistol into its holster. "You've seen how well my shots have worked. I shoot one down, and another takes its place." She was right. With their numbers seemingly infinite, they were poised to forever secure the perimeter of the woods.

"Call for backup," Phillip pleaded.

"I *am* the backup. The entire department has tried entering these woods. One way or another."

Phillip paced. He looked as if he were coming out of his skin. He didn't know what to do with his hands. He alternated between hugging himself and swinging his arms about. "There *has* to be a way inside. We've got to come up with a plan. We can come up with a plan!" He looked—and sounded—delusional. Yet his intense desperation, mixed with his sincerity, could've drawn sympathy from the most cynical. Besides, what else were we to do trapped in the netherworld between demons with insatiable vortices hidden beneath their cloaks and giant skeletons with the strength to hammer us into jelly? Plus, the cop had the same goal as us: to find Ginger Young.

"It'll be dangerous. But maybe, with the three of us, there's something we can try," she offered. With Phillip more than eager, we heard out her crude plan. And before I knew it, I found myself wildly charging toward the monsters like some foolish barbarian. It was laughable, us with our small statures rushing an armada of giant, swaying skeletons. But we had no delusions of winning a war against them. We merely wanted to penetrate their shield.

The closer we came, the tighter they huddled. Their long limbs swayed side to side in unison, forming a line of swinging pendulums. As we approached, the nearest skeletons bent forward in an attempt to bowl us over. If one were to break out of line, it could've easily flattened us. But the monsters fought their instincts and continued to stand shoulder to shoulder, restraining themselves for the greater cause: to assure no soul enter the woods.

Standing before the wall of powerful, clanking knuckles was as hypnotic as it was intimidating. Phillip and I retreated a few steps. But the officer, her height barely up to their knees, boldly stepped forward. She was closer than she had been before yet managed to stay just out of reach of the closest lurching skeleton. She raised her pistol and began firing rapid shots. She was a good shot before, but at closer range, she fired with precision, concentrating on its neck bones. As she carried out her damage, Phillip and I cautiously moved in. She fired until its massive skull detached from its neck and was sent plummeting through its rib cage. On its descent, its skull fractured its ribs, causing a chain reaction that dismantled the rest of the frame.

That's when Phillip and I made our move. We ran through the shower of giant bone fragments and headed for the fleeting gap the carcass had left in the line. The skeletons on either side of the opening swung for us. From behind, the cop yelled, "Get down!" We ducked just as two giant fists collided over our heads like cars in a head-on crash. Phillip rolled on the ground ahead of me. When he came out of his roll, he leapt to his feet and stumbled backward. He had made it into the woods! He watched from inside as the officer and I attempted to squeeze our way in as well. But in the next instant, bone clashed with bone. Shoulders locked. It was an awful sound. And an even worse feeling—being sealed out of the woods within terrifyingly easy reach of those lethal fists.

The next thing I knew, I was flying. I must've been scooped up and tossed through the air. As I sailed through the cloudless night sky, the moon came closer and closer. I studied its colossal magnificence. At the peak of my arc, it seemed as if, had I been able to reach only a bit higher, I could've touched it, felt its dust and gray craters with my fingertips. I would've been content to forever float beneath the black sky punctuated by the dim glow of the moon. Yet gravity worked to pull me back to the earth. Despite the assuredly dramatic height from which I dropped, my landing was painless. I landed in a deer's bed, a soft and comfortable patch of matted weeds. And like a curious deer, I lifted my head above the tall weeds to assess my surroundings.

That's when I learned I had fared much better than the officer. I spotted her clasped in the hand of a skeleton. Her limbs jerked uncontrollably as it shook her with anger. Then, with all its might, it flung her across the field. She reached into the air, attempting to grab hold of something where there was nothing to grab hold of. She landed on the other side of the narrow field, near the edge of the corn. I knew she was still alive because I could hear her whimpers. I stood and was able to faintly see her on her stomach, attempting to crawl on her elbows. With multiple bones likely crushed, she was too easy a prey for the monsters in the corn to pass up. One dared lunge out from the stalks. It grabbed her swiftly by the ankles and dragged her into the corn without so much as a struggle.

My eye caught the moonlight reflecting off something she had left behind. I approached it cautiously, careful not to step too close to the corn for fear the gathering cloaked demons would grab me as well. I picked up the pistol and brought it back to the lumbering skeletons. Behind them, I saw Phillip waving his arms. He had waited for me. Of course he had. I should've known Phillip wouldn't have left me trapped in the netherworld alone.

The menacing monster that stood between us swiped for me. I leapt back, just enough to stay out of reach, before pulling the gun on the towering thing. When Phillip saw I had the gun, he smartly darted out of the way. Attempting to duplicate what had worked for the cop, I aimed for its neck bones and pulled the trigger. Unsurprisingly, my shot wasn't as precise as hers. Instead of hitting its neck, the bullet flew through its enormous eye socket and struck the back of its skull. The skeleton jolted backward. Splinters crept across the inside of its skull. The strike, however, didn't take it down. It was soon back in line with the other dancing bones. I pulled the trigger again, but there was no blast. The pistol was jammed. Or out of bullets. There was nothing I could do. Phillip would simply have to go on without me.

Yet Phillip wasn't willing to give up on finding a way for me to cross over. He began kicking and pulling random branches until he finally managed to tear off a low-hanging branch from a dead tree. Holding it over his shoulder like a spear, he charged the skeleton that kept us separated. With all his fury, he wedged the branch between the skeleton's ribs. He kept a tight grip as he and the creature fought to gain control over one another. Phillip was lifted off the ground as the monster tried to shake him loose. Yet every chance Phillip got, he wedged the branch deeper into its rib cage. He forced his weight onto it, creating a lever that began cracking its giant ribs. He then thrashed the beast back and forth, smashing it into the monsters on either side. This threw the movements of the line from synchronicity to chaos. Like a pileup on a freeway, a chain reaction erupted, and the giant monsters crashed into each other.

"Now!" he roared. He thrust the bulky creature forward, and I found myself beneath the broken, stumbling monster. I ducked between its legs as it fell forward. And just before the line began to compose itself once more and the gap resealed, I raced into the woods. Inside, I didn't bother looking back. I knew they wouldn't chase us into the forest. The skeletons weren't suited for the environment. They would've tangled themselves among the tall trees and reaching branches.

No, something else waited for us in the woods.

40
COME, LOOK

It felt like being inside a vacuum, as if the air had been sucked from beneath the canopy. It was unnaturally still. Deathly quiet. The tree limbs stood frozen. No sounds of critters scurrying could be heard. After our dramatic entrance, there was no question our arrival had been broadcast to every corner. Still, with the absence of ambient sounds, it felt as though we had a strange obligation to take slow, careful steps so as not to alter the ghostly atmosphere. One snap of a twig beneath our feet would've produced a sound so amplified, it would've been like setting off an alarm. And the last thing we needed was to draw more attention to ourselves than we already had.

Our feet disappeared beneath the umbrellas of a large patch of mayapple. Before committing to a firm step, we attempted to feel for sticks under our shoes. Stepping this way made me think of the Indians who lived in the area hundreds of years before, how they had walked on the same ground, under the same moon, had passed some of the same trees. I had read that skilled Indian hunters knew how to walk through the forest without making a sound. I imagined Phillip and I possessed that skill as I led him toward the spot where I had seen Ginger in my dream.

Low growls began to emanate from the darkest corners, where the moonlight couldn't reach. It was apparent far more skillful hunters lurked in the forest. As we made our way deeper into the trees, the growls came closer and closer, surrounding us until it sounded as if a demon lurked behind every tree. I didn't want to take another step, fearing my movement would trigger an ambush. But Phillip persisted. "C'mon," he ordered in a whisper. He wasn't about to freeze up or turn back. He was almost there. Like the demons sensed us, he sensed her.

But when a low gurgle came from beneath the blanket of mayapple just ahead, I froze again. This time, so did Phillip. Before us, a set of horns rose from the foliage like a pair of shark fins appearing from underwater. Slowly, it sat up, waking from its slumber. Seeing it awake from its bed of soil, covered in dirt and leaves, seeing its green skin next to the green mayapple, I understood how it could've originated from nature like everything else. But as Everett had taught me, monsters were also once removed from nature. Corrupted. Bastardized.

I thought of how each species of demon had found their apt dwelling after escaping from my wall. The reclusive cloaked monsters preferred the cover the cornfields provided, where they could stealthily stalk their prey. The skeleton creatures settled in the open fields between the corn and the woods, where they could lumber freely with their tall frames blending against the backdrop of the trees. And the horned demons dwelled in the tiny forest, where they could burrow underground, staying hidden from sunlight during the day.

The demon before us worked to clear blood and mucus from its throat before slowly twisting its neck to face us. A vast and sinister grin spread across its face. Its oversize teeth glistened in the moonlight. Its wide, circular eyes did not blink. I braced for it to arch its pointy fingers and hold them beside its horns in the creatures' usual position of menace. Yet instead, it extended its arms and slowly turned over its hands so that its palms faced upward. This curious gesture seemed to signal some sort of appeasement. It relished our fear, of course. But it did not approach. Did not attack. Rather, it spoke. "Cooomme," it said in its eerie childlike voice filtered through a lacerated throat. After taking a few steps, it turned to assure we'd follow. "Cooomme," it repeated.

Keeping our distance, we cautiously followed the monster as it led us out of the mayapple. It stepped forward in a trancelike state, keeping its palms upward. As we made our way deeper into the forest, growls and deep groans drifted from behind the trees and from within the shadows. We passed the old beech tree with the deep hole in its trunk. We passed the dozens of unmarked Indian graves. I couldn't help but think of the two graves, somewhere among them, that did *not* belong to Indians.

Ahead, a beam of moonlight illuminated a small patch of barren forest floor. The monster stepped into the light. Its shadow stretched across the clearing and up into the trees, making it appear as a towering devil with sickle-shaped horns. Still displaying its persistent grin, it waited patiently for us to join it in the clearing. When we finally stood beside it, it cocked its head up to us. Slowly, it turned its palms over and used its extra-long index finger to point to the ground. It continued to stare up to us, saliva beginning to drip down its enormous teeth. What I had first interpreted as another attempt to clear its throat of congealed, bloody phlegm, I soon realized was laughter. It cackled in the most perverted way. When it finally finished its fit of evil merriment, it spoke once more. "Looooook," it told us. It turned its gaze to the ground and then cocked its head back to us to capture our reactions. "Looooook," it said again.

We studied the ground as it had asked. But I didn't see anything out of the ordinary. It was just the forest floor covered in sticks and dead leaves. Yet when I looked closer, I began to notice small strips of bark tied into knots. The knots held together sticks that were woven into a matting of compressed leaves, feathers, and small animal bones. I wasn't wholly comprehending what this tapestry was—or why it would be in the middle of the woods. But Phillip, thinking quicker than me, leapt forward and grabbed the edge of the organic tarp. And as he did, the forest erupted in dark laughter. Phillip was overcome with horror as the removal of the camouflaged covering revealed an oval-shaped pit.

The monster eyed me intently. "Looooook," it said, encouraging me to step forward and peer into the pit along with Phillip. At first, all I could see were roots jutting near the surface. It took my eyes a moment to adjust to the darkness below. And when they did, several feet into the pit, I saw her.

She was on her back, encased in a swarm of roots and vines. The thickest roots crisscrossing beneath her suspended her body in midair, while the others acted as restraints. Roots wrapped around her wrists, forcing her hands beside her head. They coiled around her ankles, twisting her legs beneath her torso. One root, reaching from the bottom of the pit, formed a loop across her forehead.

If I hadn't known it was the work of the horned demons, I would've guessed she had fallen into the pit, and upon struggling to climb her way out, the roots had come alive to ensnare her. Her eyes were slightly open, as was her mouth, locked in an eternal scream. Her fingers were clenched, appearing to have been desperately clawing for the surface. Yet even in death by certain torture, she was graceful. Her loose curls extended delicately onto the roots above her head. Her skin, although covered in dirt, cuts, and bruises, had retained its golden hue. She was simply — a frozen beauty.

As I viewed Ginger's contorted body, I was taken back to the first time I had stood in the metal forest. In the dream, it was the same spot. Sure, it was different. But it was the same. The patch of ice was the barren patch of forest floor. The light that lit her from below the ice was the moonlight that illuminated her from above. The same frozen beauty I had seen in my dream all those years ago was the same frozen beauty I looked upon that night with Phillip. *Of course* we hadn't found her body when we dug for the Indians. She was *not* one of the Indians.

I heard Everett's voice in my head say, "Dreams are tricky." I was never in the metal forest to find a lost Indian burial ground.

Nor was I there to find hidden coins. The purpose of that dream—was to find Ginger. Before I had even met her, before she had ever gone missing, I was to see her future. "It was the future," I proclaimed under my breath. The forest of sterile, silver metal meant the future.

Two more horned monsters slunk from behind nearby trees. They stood at the opposite end of the pit, their fingers curled beneath their noses, chuckling deviously at the sight of us at last discovering Ginger. The demon that had led us to her wedged itself between us and the pit. Finally, slowly, it drew its hands into clawing formation and lifted them before its horns. It threatened us with its razor-tipped fingers as the pair of monsters behind it plunged over the edge. They balanced on the roots, positioning themselves just above her body. One sniffed her neck, while the other took in deep breaths up and down her torso. They let out disturbing grunts and snorts as they took their time absorbing her aroma.

Phillip's anguish became only more excruciating at the sight of the monsters desecrating her body. "Get away from her!" he wailed. "Don't touch her!" Yet I knew if the demons were enjoying her smell, if they were still able to sense the aromas of horror and misery emanating from her pores, then Ginger was more than a beautiful corpse.

41
NOT HUMAN

Revived by the sensation of the demons salivating over her, Ginger began to flutter her eyelids. At first, she focused on the foul creatures. Then, her eyes shifted to Phillip and me towering over her in the moonlight. Her hope renewed by his presence, she struggled against the roots. She tried to speak, but her mouth was too dry, her voice too weak.

Discovering Ginger was alive, Phillip was equally renewed. Boldly, he grabbed the demon before us by its horns. But the powerful monster bunted back, knocking him to the ground. With a quick turn of its head, the tip of its horn lacerated Phillip's leg. Phillip rushed to stand in defiance while holding pressure to the gash. The demon held steady with its claws to its horns and delivered a warning in the form of a vigorous hiss.

As if to hammer home how outmatched we truly were, the remainder of the demons began to emerge. They crept from behind the trees and out of the shadows. They crawled from beneath the soil. They came forward slowly, stepping with precision over the forest floor without looking to their feet, their eyes fixed on the exposed pit. They drooled at the sight of it. They had been waiting so long. All that time, they had been keeping her alive, seasoning her with fear and hopelessness, waiting for the moment Phillip and I would find her. They knew, with Phillip near and in his deepest anguish, that she'd be ripe. Her scent the sweetest. Her flesh the most savory.

"My God," cried Phillip as the gathering demons formed surprisingly ordered rows around the edge of the pit. He began to weep. He knew he was no match for the demon in front of him, much less the group of thirty that had come forth for a taste of Ginger. He was truly, completely powerless. And in the midst of his swirling despair, he turned to me. His striking blue eyes glowed in the moonlight. His stare was piercing, as if he were looking *into* me, behind my eyes. It forced my gaze to the forest floor. "Has she not suffered enough?" he sobbed.

I felt a chill run through my body as cold as his stare. "She has," I agreed, my mouth dry, "suffered too much."

"Has she not suffered enough—because of you?" he finished.

The blood drained from my face. I couldn't process what he was suggesting. *"Because of me?* I haven't done anything to Ginger."

"I'm talking about these creatures. *Your* creatures."

I felt nauseous. "But—they're not *my creatures.*"

"You control them," he accused.

"No," I protested. "I gave birth to them," I conceded softly. He forced me to admit it—to him, to myself—for the first time. "But I don't control them. Everett—he came up with the demons. He made me create them. He tricked me! He told me they had escaped from my wall. And once they were loose, I had no control over them. Everett had all the control. It was all him. He controlled me. Manipulated me. You even said yourself you thought he was evil. But not me. I'm not evil."

"You're right. He used you. He used you to fulfill his own demented idea of fun. Because of you, he found hidden money, flew spaceships, dropped both of you in whatever fucked-up situation he helped invent. But it wasn't his power to manipulate. That comes from you. I've seen it. I didn't believe Everett all those years ago. But tonight, after seeing what you're capable of, I do now. Those flying metal things. These wicked monsters. They're you. You never really needed Everett at all. You could've removed him from the equation at any time. You asked me not to bring Everett's myth back to life. I didn't. But tonight, you did. You even invented your own version of him to go along with the demons you both loved so much.

"I searched you out to find Ginger. God knows that was the only reason. The *only* reason. And now I know for certain—you orchestrated it all. I wanted her back, so I played your game. I've played along with your—sickness—all this time, fighting off your monsters, witnessing the slaughter of innocent people—all so you would lead me to Ginger. Now I'm begging you. You've got to give me this one thing. You've got to spare Ginger. For me."

"But, Phillip—" I fell to my knees. "I don't control them."

He grabbed my throat with fury in his eyes. And as if placing his hands around my neck was the signal they had been waiting for, the first row of demons plunged into the pit. "Give her back to me," he begged. "I've done everything you've wanted. I've made it to the end."

I gripped his forearms. "I. Don't. Control. I. Only—"

"I am *not* Everett! I never was! I never wanted to protect you from your own creations. I don't care about you. Just give me Ginger back!"

The first group of monsters crawled out from the pit with blood dripping down their chins. The greedy ones that refused to leave were bashed and clawed at by the second group rushing the pit.

"I. Only. Give. Birth."

While channeling his rage at me, Phillip spared himself the horrific sight of waves of demons piling into the pit. They climbed in and out like swarms of excited ants, each returning to the surface having had a quick taste or stolen a small trophy.

"Have you ever loved someone? Or is this—perversion—all you are?"

"Don't. Control. They. Just. Are."

By the time he relaxed his grip on my throat, Ginger was gone. They had taken her. Every morsel. Her flesh. Her bones. Even her clothes. All that was left were trails of blood leading away from the edge of the pit. Phillip slumped his shoulders forward and trembled. I gasped for air. When my throat opened up again, I managed to whisper, "Phillip, I'm sorry."

But her death wasn't the end of our terrorizing night. Having finished Ginger, the cadre of still-hungry demons gathered to stare at us with their cold, unblinking eyes. Phillip grabbed a stick and climbed the nearby ridge. Curious, excited, the demons gathered at its foot. He raised the stick over his head. "Come for me!" he bellowed. The monsters, happy to grant his request, rushed the hill. I imagined he didn't expect to last long, maybe a moment or two. But it was clear he no longer cared. It was what he wanted after coming so far only to lose. It broke my heart to learn that with Ginger gone, Phillip felt there was nothing left for him.

The demons first to reach Phillip clashed horns in a twisted display of bravado. They circled him, allowing the juices of fear to percolate until his meat was properly tenderized. I watched through my fingers. I couldn't bear the thought of Phillip removed from the world. Even if he hated me, even if he was to never speak to me again, I wanted to know that somewhere on the planet, his heart was still beating. I wanted it possible for him to one day heal, to once again become the Phillip I knew. So when one of the demons had worked itself into a frenzy, when it could stand it no longer and swiped at Phillip with the intent of clawing out the contents of his abdomen, I found myself shouting, "Stop!"

And just as its razor-tipped fingers were to meet Phillip, its form began to change. Its green arm turned a smoky gray and folded into itself. It then unfolded into small sections, each moving independently. And when these individual pieces turned themselves over, the monster's arm was no longer. In its place were tiny undulating wings of the most vibrant shade of yellow. Each wing held a pattern of a black arc over a cluster of black dots. When the wings fully separated from each other, they carried the graceful insects fluttering above Phillip's head. As the frustrated demon continued its attack, the rest of its body was replaced by the births of the yellow, black-speckled butterflies.

This startling occurrence only made the other demons want to rip into Phillip even more ferociously. They slashed at him. Charged him with their horns. Opened their mouths as wide as they could and snapped at his legs. They climbed upon his body to chomp his neck. Yet any demon that dared harm Phillip was instantly transformed into a swell of harmless, fluttering butterflies. The demons, motivated purely by their desires of bloodlust, were slow to realize that attacking Phillip only meant their demise. By the time it was over, more than half of the monsters had been transformed.

Hundreds of butterflies populated the woods. They clung to trees. Rested on logs. Some fluttered along, seeming to enjoy the miracle of flight. Their dazzling wings gave an entirely different feel to the forest. They lit the distant trees, threatening to bring forth the dawn. I couldn't revel in their beauty, however—because I knew what they meant. Like Phillip, I began to tremble. Stunned. Phillip stood with his back to me, a butterfly atop his head and another perched on his shoulder. He knew what they meant too. "Phillip," I pleaded, but he wouldn't face me.

"It might be strange for you to hear that Everett was afraid of you. But he was." Phillip spoke to the woods, to the butterflies that explored the forest, to the remaining demons at the base of the hill. "You're why he left for Texas. He wanted to get away from you after he realized how out of hand things had gotten, after he saw the way you chose to use your creations. Like me, he didn't want to believe it at first—that you had murdered Ian and Todd. I certainly didn't believe a word of it. I was convinced it was his pathetic way to place the blame on you for what he had done. After all, *his* hands were covered in blood—not yours. I wasn't about to believe his story that he was actually trying to *save* Todd as 'child-size green monsters with horns—that Ayden somehow controls—tore him apart.'" He looked over his shoulder to the bloody pit. "'Their deaths, he was willing to cover up, take the blame for if he had to. But I will not let anyone else take the blame for this—but you."

I wanted so badly to grab him by the shoulders, to spin him around and deny his accusations. But I couldn't. The proof fluttered all around us.

"Why?" he asked simply.

I didn't know why. The only thing that came to me was a conversation I had with Dr. Griffin. He asked me how I coped with stressful or hostile situations. I admitted that I often simply fled such situations by allowing my mind to wander through daydreaming. "When your mind wanders, where do you go? What do you daydream about?" he asked.

I replied, "Being chased by demons and barely escaping."

"But when you use daydreaming to escape reality, why not go someplace serene? Why go someplace so dark?"

I finally answered, "Because first you have to go someplace dark in order to feel comforted. To be saved."

It started with Everett. He was the one who first took me to the dark places. He instigated it. Encouraged it. Loved it. Yes, I was the one who created it. Controlled it. But I believed in it so fully that I was able to suppress the fact that it was I who pulled the strings. Immersed in the fantasies we created, all I knew was that Everett would be there to protect me. I was the happiest then, with Everett, during our most terrifying adventures. But when he fled to Texas, I was left only with the evil I produced, the demons I manufactured. Without his strength and protection, the equation was set out of balance. And I craved those missing pieces so badly.

It had to be Phillip. He was the closest thing I had to Everett. After Everett's death, he unwittingly kept my monsters at bay. When he too fled from me to begin his life with Ginger, I was OK for a while, alone, convinced my past was built on hallucinations Everett had forced me to see. But I was empty. Something was missing. And eventually, I sought my addiction once more: that feeling of danger tempered with comfort. Phillip wouldn't have come back to me on his own. No, I had to give him a reason to seek me out. And this time, for the equation to become fully balanced, it needed to be just the two of us, Phillip and me against evil. Just like it had been with Everett, I would provide the darkness, and he would be my protector. It was all I ever wanted.

This would've been my explanation had I offered one to Phillip. But I didn't. I couldn't. My reason wouldn't have been reason enough for what I had done to Ginger.

Then something happened that I could *not* control: tears began streaming down my face. I took off through the woods. I tore my way through the mesh of wild grapevines that hung over the outside of the forest like a thick curtain. Outside, the skeletons no longer guarded the perimeter. I ran free through the field behind my parents' house, weaving mechanically through its uneven terrain filled with hills, holes, and overgrown weeds.

As I ran from Phillip as a coward, the thought that stuck with me most was that if I gave birth to evil and controlled evil, then it meant I *was* evil. I was the entities I created. I was the cloaked demons. The skeleton beasts. The horned monsters. It was I who killed Ian by placing the metal daggers at the bottom of the pit. It was I who devoured Todd while distracting Phillip with the naked tree woman. I *was* the naked tree woman. I was the voice of Thomas Gouldman, conjured to draw attention away from Ginger. I was the metal tornados that killed the officers who dared interrupt my time with Phillip. I was even the spaceship Everett and I flew in over the cornfield. And it was I who abducted Ginger and tortured her in the woods.

I could've argued that I was none of these things—that I did not perform these deeds because, physically, it was not I. But Phillip would know the truth. It was me just the same. I wondered if I even had a soul. When I finally peeled off my mask and looked in the mirror, what was underneath was not human. I was a monster.

42
UNNATURAL NATURE

Compelled to retreat to the place where it all began, I trudged past the garden and yanked open the sliding glass door. The house was dark and empty. Perhaps the police had evacuated the neighborhood on account of the mayhem surrounding the woods. I locked the door behind me before racing up the stairs.

I sat on the end of the bed in my old room. The faces hidden in the wall peered at me in the dim moonlight. They were just as menacing as they had been when I was the frightened child who lined his stuffed animals between himself and the wall. It had been so long since I studied the simplistic faces to which I had gifted perverted flesh and bone and then unleashed upon the world. They were a part of me, controlled by the dark parts of my mind. They came from an evil place I couldn't trust. Even I, the creator, wasn't safe from them. I searched my thoughts. What did my own subconscious will for me?

My question was quickly answered as the darkened corners of the room began to swell. I rushed to the hallway and shut the door behind me in an attempt to keep the mushrooming black portal contained. I gently placed my hand on Everett's door. It creaked open slightly before I pulled away. Of course he wasn't in there. How could he have been?

The tapping that began with a slow persistence could've just been the wind causing the surrounding pines to strike the windows. But I knew better. The night was still. Clearly, it was the horned demons. They had followed me from the woods and were calling me downstairs—just as they had when they were eager to coax Everett and me into battle. As I headed down the stairway, their tapping overlapped with their low growls.

I entered the sunroom and stood before the glass door willingly, though not without tremendous dread. Yes, I had willed them to come. But the revelation that I controlled their actions did little to diminish my fear. In fact, I was more afraid than ever, knowing unequivocally what they had planned for me. With nothing but blackness behind the glass, I looked upon my own trembling reflection. At first, they were polite. Tap! Tap! Tap! Yet as their excitement grew, they pressed with increased vigor. I watched the reflection of my face twist as the glass bowed from the pressure.

My instinct told me to hide. But how could I hide from what was a part of me? My only wish was that Everett could've been there when it happened. Sure, I could've conjured him. But it wouldn't have been Everett. Not really. It would've just been another perversion. Without Everett—or Phillip—there was no one to ease my fear. No one to remind me of the cats. The cats—it seemed so long ago that I had petted their shimmering coats and enjoyed their circle dance at my feet. They too had come from me. How was it then that they were so innocent? So playful as they followed me through the weeds?

So utterly, unbearably alone, I stepped forward and flipped on the floodlights. Incensed by the light burning down upon them, the group of horned monsters that hadn't been transformed into fluttering butterflies crowded the window. Wet from traveling through the dewy field, their green, moldy fingers slipped and squeaked across the glass. Several began butting their heads against the door. It shook and began to splinter. They licked the cracked glass, letting it cut their tongues. Their mouths oozed green blood. Their eyes glowed red. Soon they'd be inside.

In a final infusion of panic and fear, I deliriously rushed to the dining room table. Despite my quaking arms, I managed to topple it over. The vase in the center of the table, which held freshly cut lilac blooms, rolled to the floor. I dragged the table into the sunroom, crushing the blooms. Their powerful fragrance filled the air. As soon as I propped the table in position against the door, the glass shattered. I stumbled back to the dining room as the demons clawed and chewed their way through the oak.

There, I lay on the floor in surrender, with the water that had spilled from the vase soaking into my back. With the moment imminent, a strange peace came over me. I accepted it. It was the perfect solution. Fitting, really. My life had become more manufactured than natural. More metallic forest than organic forest. The monsters that had crept into the house, had crowded around me, and were about to masticate my body were once removed from nature. They didn't create or control their energy; I did. And with the energy I possessed, I chose to create a dark world. But if I was to be devoured by my own creations, be reabsorbed back into nature, I'd create balance. Zero out the equation. Realizing that, I found pleasure in the thought of being consumed by the demons. Pleasure from finally submitting and being released from their torture.

I closed my eyes. I felt their fingers all over my body. Sliding under my shirt and across my chest. Cramming into my mouth. I felt their tongues licking my flesh, my neck, my stomach. They liked my stomach most. They went for it first. It didn't hurt so bad. In fact, when they tore into it, it just felt like being tickled too hard. After a while, I couldn't feel anything at all. Even their hot and vile breath dissolved. The only sense I experienced was the smell of the powerful lilacs. I used it. Focused on it. Allowed it to transfer me to another world.

When it was over, I was afraid to open my eyes. I wasn't sure where I was or what form I had taken. Was I a speck of dirt? Or a seed? Was I a leaf? A tadpole? Or was I a free-flowing spirit about to ride the wind?

Strangely, I didn't feel all that different. Slowly, I opened my eyes and was dumbfounded upon realizing I was still inside my same body. I brought my hands to my stomach and then to my face. I hadn't changed forms at all. Hadn't been devoured. In fact, I hadn't even moved from the dining room floor.

Above me, Phillip stepped into view. The morning light coming through the windows struck his golden hair. He towered over me like some sort of god. Illuminated. Larger than life. I swallowed and asked, "Where are the monsters?" He pointed to the shattered glass. I lifted my head to see a multitude of yellow butterflies escaping into the approaching morning. With his touch, Phillip had transformed the remaining horned demons into harmless butterflies.

He helped me stand. Together in silence, we watched the sunrise through the broken window. The rays made the fields glow. They cleansed the dark shadows in the forest. I did not question Phillip on why he had followed me to the house. At that moment, I didn't understand what compelled him to stop the demons from devouring me. But for me, I knew what it meant. If I was to keep the form I was in, I knew what I must become.

Stephen Stromp is also the author of *In the Graveyard Antemortem* and *Cracking Grace*.

Books primarily rely on word of mouth to find their way to readers. The best way to help spread the word about books like *Where the Cats Will Not Follow* is to leave a brief review on Amazon.

Connect with Stephen Stromp
Join email list: eepurl.com/caHNZT
Website: stephenstromp.com
Facebook: facebook.com/StephenStromp